A WEDDING IN THE SUN

LEONIE MACK

Boldwood

First published in Great Britain in 2024 by Boldwood Books Ltd.

Copyright © Leonie Mack, 2024

Cover Design: Alice Moore Design

Cover Photography: Shutterstock and iStock

The moral right of Leonie Mack to be identified as the author of this work has been asserted in accordance with the Copyright, Designs and Patents Act 1988.

A CIP catalogue record for this book is available from the British Library.

Paperback ISBN 978-1-80415-864-7

Large Print ISBN 978-1-80415-863-0

Hardback ISBN 978-1-80415-861-6

Ebook ISBN 978-1-80415-865-4

Kindle ISBN 978-1-80415-866-1

Audio CD ISBN 978-1-80415-857-9

MP3 CD ISBN 978-1-80415-858-6

Digital audio download ISBN 978-1-80415-859-3

Boldwood Books Ltd
23 Bowerdean Street
London SW6 3TN
www.boldwoodbooks.com

For Lyndon, Calvin and Josie. So glad you're mine.

1

'He punched me in the arm, Mum! He's a little shit.'

Jo paused, grumbling inwardly as the busy airport around her faded at her daughter's words. Ben couldn't take a little responsibility for his kids' emotional stability at a time like this? Another ten days and the 'little shit' would be their stepbrother.

'I'll be there tonight,' she assured Liss, hoping her daughter couldn't hear the tightness in her voice. Tonight, she would turn up for the happy pre-wedding festivities for her ex-husband and the beautiful woman he was marrying. Sarcasm would only protect Jo from the shards of her marriage for so long.

'That's *hours* yet,' Liss complained. 'This whole time Dad's made us look after Oscar.'

Her grip tightening on her suitcase, Jo swallowed some choice words for her ex-husband and wondered what she could say to placate her daughter when she agreed wholeheartedly. Ben should be supporting them through all the changes in their family, not forcing them to babysit, as though that was the only reason they were invited to this wedding that would create his new family. And from what Jo had seen of seven-year-old Oscar, he *was* a little shit.

'I don't even want to be here!' Liss cried. 'I'm seventeen. I'm not a flower girl! I don't want to stand up with *Mónica* like she's my new best friend, and the dress she bought is hideous!'

'I thought you liked it,' Jo responded to the easiest part of that sentence. She pressed the back of her hand to her forehead, as though that would slow down the spinning of her thoughts. 'I just assumed it was what all the kids wear these days.'

'*Mum!* I didn't think I had a choice so I was nice about it. If you thought it looked ugly, you should have said something! I don't even want to go to the ceremony. I'd rather be at *school!*'

Jo didn't appreciate the reminder that the kids were missing school for this farce. The requirements of Mónica's Spanish family seemed to be more important in the schedule than the children's education and apparently the wedding was such an important occasion that it involved more than a week of 'festivities'.

'Maybe we can choose something else when I get there,' Jo said, grinding her teeth. Ben even needed her to sort out the kids while he *married* someone else. God knows there was no other reason she'd attend his wedding. 'Put Declan on?'

There was some rustling and then an inarticulate grunt, which was the usual greeting from her fourteen-year-old son.

'Hey, Dec, hang in there, okay?'

'Yeah, Mum.'

'If Oscar gets too difficult, just let him play with your phone,' Jo suggested, trying to tamp down on her worry.

'I'm not going to let him touch my phone!' Dec exclaimed, as though he'd rather be punched in the arm than let a seven-year-old near his prized possession.

Jo stifled a sigh. For all she knew, Mónica was one of these anti-screen mothers who would be horrified and Jo really shouldn't feel satisfaction at the prospect of riling up Ben's bride. Urgh, the word 'bride' made her gag.

Shaking off the awkwardness, she hitched her rucksack back onto her shoulder and started walking again, peering along the check-in desks for the one marked 'Zaragoza'.

'I'll see you soon anyway, sweetie,' she said to Dec.

She got another mumble in farewell before Liss came on again for a few more gripes that Jo was very willing to indulge. But despite her sympathy for her daughter, there was no point in escalating the already insufferable situation.

She softened her voice and said, 'I'm sure Dad doesn't realise that you feel sidelined and Oscar—'

The name of Ben's future stepson got stuck in her throat as she caught sight of a familiar figure at the check-in desks and whirled around, turning her back. She'd forgotten she'd see *him* at the wedding. If she stayed very still, perhaps he wouldn't see her. Even if he'd heard his son's name, he wouldn't imagine the woman with her hair coming out of its clip and an ancient Fjällräven backpack would have said it.

He wouldn't recognise her. He was just the ex-husband of the soon-to-be wife of *her* ex-husband – which was complicated enough to give her a spontaneous migraine. But he was also her former Parent Teacher Association nemesis and she didn't want to risk having to talk to him right now, on what was shaping up to be one of the worst days of her life. There wasn't even a word for the relationship she had with that man – although awkward was one, certainly, even though she hadn't seen him in three years.

His voice reached her ears: the burr of his Spanish accent, the animated tone, raised in indignation at that moment.

'Mum?' Liss prompted her over the phone.

'I have to go, sweetie. I'm checking in my bag.'

'Dad said we can't come with him to collect you from the airport,' her daughter said glumly.

'What? Why not?'

'Mónica's husband is arriving on the same flight and we won't fit in the car with all your luggage.'

Jo's stomach dipped, wishing she'd had that information before she'd almost run into him. Glancing his way before she could stop herself, she saw him raise his hands in frustration, gesturing to a guitar case. At least Liss couldn't see her eye-roll.

Adrian Rivera Morales – oh, sorry, Adrián, pronounced with an accent – and his blasted guitar.

'I really have to go, but I'll be there soon and we'll work things out. I know it doesn't feel like it right now, but we'll find a way to have a good time together. After the family party is over, we'll be down at the beach for a few days before the wedding.' *The wedding* in a pretentious castle on the coast north of Valencia in Spain.

'Yeah, we're going to the beach in Peñíscola,' Liss said with a snort, 'where you'll drink all the—'

'Liss!' Jo warned her in a low tone. If her daughter said 'cocktails', Jo would dissolve into laughter herself and hysterics might alert Adrián. Even an innocent cola joke would have pushed her too far right now. 'I'll see you soon! Love you. Bye!'

Ending the call with a stifled groan, Jo stowed her phone in her backpack and hesitated. Would Adrián be gone yet? Risking another glance over her shoulder, her frustration rose again to see him still arguing with the man at the check-in desk.

'I'm sorry, sir, but if you wanted special care taken with this item, you should have booked an extra seat,' the man said calmly.

'I talked to someone on the phone a week ago and they assured me the instrument was booked!' His voice was even higher than it had been before.

'The *luggage* is booked, sir. Here, I could put a "fragile" sticker on it for you.'

'¡Ay! You think a little sticker will stop your staff from throwing this around like a rugby ball?' She heard his exaggerated sigh from where she was standing and peeked over her shoulder again, wondering how long she would have to hide before he finished berating the poor man for doing his job. Why was he even bringing a guitar? The flight was in sardine-class with a low-cost carrier.

Adrián shoved his hands through his unnecessarily long, curly hair and grimaced. He had a moustache and a goatee too and that air of self-importance that only an attractive man can get away with, not to mention a thick gold chain that always peeked out of his collar as though he were a hip-hop star.

'How much is an extra seat?' he asked, his voice tight. Jo unfortunately understood the reluctance to shell out more money for an ex's wedding. She was annoyed enough that she had to take time off work to attend a family party in a place with too many z's in the name before the actual wedding the following week.

'The flight is fully booked, I'm sorry.'

Jo clenched and unclenched her fists as Adrián lost it, Spanish curses tumbling out of his mouth and his arms gesticulating wildly. He slapped the counter in frustration.

'Sir, I'm going to have to ask you to—'

'Fine!' Adrián cried in a tortured tone. 'Take it into the hold! Sit on it and toss it to each other and if anyone asks, tell them your airline damaged a palosanto de Rio guitar made by Ricardo Martín Gonzalez himself!'

'If it's damaged, you can download a claim form from our webs—'

'I don't need a claim form! I need my guitar to arrive in one piece!'

'This seems like a good instrument case, sir. If I just put the sticker on it—'

Maybe he would decide not to get on the plane after all, Jo thought with expanding hope. Imagining Ben collecting them both from the airport made her nauseous.

With one last melodramatic choke, Adrián pushed off the counter and stalked away with a dismissive wave, as though he couldn't bear to watch his precious guitar disappearing down the conveyor belt. Jo used her last dregs of human compassion to challenge the unkind thought that there had probably been a good reason Mónica had divorced him.

What fun this wedding was turning out to be!

* * *

Jo was nearly ready to turn around and go home ninety minutes later when she stepped onto the plane and caught sight of that familiar head of dark curls a few rows away, in an aisle seat, just to make her afternoon worse.

It was a small aircraft with a single aisle – even though the flight was booked out, not *that* many people wanted to go to Zaragoza on a Wednesday night. Two of them probably didn't want to go to Zaragoza at all.

She wondered why Adrián was coming. Surely as the father instead of the mother he could have pleaded paternal incompetence and claimed it would be awkward if he turned up. For once, she wouldn't have resented a man for that.

She peered at her boarding pass, holding it up to hide her face.

'Thirteen F – it's on the left just past the emergency exit row,' the smiling flight attendant told her unnecessarily. Jo made her way along the aisle, inspecting the seat numbers intently enough that it was plausible that she hadn't seen Adrián. He was reading the flight safety card with a stormy expression – although perhaps that was just his resting face.

She sensed movement as she walked past and her throat swelled uncomfortably, as she wondered if he'd looked up and opened his mouth to acknowledge her. It might have nipped the awkwardness in the bud, if only she'd had the courage to do that herself.

Oh, hi. Adrián, isn't it? Oh, my, haha, isn't this awkward going to the wedding of our exes? Are you on the PTA this year? Still refusing to play Santa at the Christmas Fayre? How about the choir? Are they skimming PTA money for their excursions this year as well, even though there are only two members?

Nope. There was no way she could have done that. With her instincts for self-preservation raging, she hurried to her row, flinging her suit bag into the locker over the seat and squeezing past a middle-aged woman and a young man with baggy clothes and baggier body language to reach her seat.

What had been Adrián's problem with playing Santa anyway? Only someone a long way up their own arse would refuse to make children happy at Christmas and there was no harm in kids believing Santa had a Spanish accent.

Pulling her phone out to turn it to flight mode, she noticed she had a voice message from Liss and put the device to her ear to listen without Mr Baggy overhearing.

'Mum, I just wanted to say sorry.' Liss paused to take a breath and continued in a contrite tone, 'I know there's nothing you can do and I don't mean to stress you out. But I just... needed to vent for a minute. I don't even want to think about the wedding when I remember how things used to be...' She sucked in a breath that might have been a sniff and Jo's stomach sank. She knew what her daughter felt because she felt it too. 'Anyway, I love you, Mum.'

Jo typed back:

Love you too, sweetie. Taking off now.

Only two hours and she'd be there to smooth things over for her kids – as best she could smooth over the fact that their father was getting married again. Liss was nearly an adult herself, but Jo was worried she'd taken the divorce four years ago harder than Declan had. She'd been old enough that she wanted to understand why the marriage was crumbling – something Jo still couldn't answer with actual words.

Crap, now she was thinking about Ben and the twisting, crunching feeling when she saw him with Mónica that was one part disgust, two parts impotent moral high ground and fourteen parts heavy failure – with a pinch of jealousy that she didn't want to admit to. She swiped at her eyes, gritting her teeth against tears. She was *not* still grieving their fourteen-year marriage, only the fourteen years of her own stupidity for thinking their marriage was worth all the sacrifices.

This was not where she wanted to be at forty-six: divorced, with a job that left her no time for her kids' crises and in a narrow plane seat heading to a party with a bunch of strangers who only knew her as Ben's ex-wife. If the mother of the bride was supposed to wear a nice outfit with a flamboyant hat, perhaps the ex-wife of the groom was supposed to wear a jute sack. That would have saved her bringing her suit bag with the flowing green evening dress that hopefully didn't look as old as it was.

Rummaging in her rucksack, she tugged out her headphones, untangling them with a huff of frustration. Glancing ahead, she saw Adrián had managed to calm down now and she couldn't help thinking he wasn't the only one struggling with emotional outbursts today. She shoved her headphones in and sat back in her seat, closing her eyes.

It would all be over in ten days. She'd never have to see Adrián again – although the same wasn't true for Ben and Mónica.

Listening to Pearl Jam and Radiohead and the bands that had got her through the nineties, the flight passed quickly, despite the seatbelt sign lighting up regularly as the little plane juddered its way southeast. A few times, Jo's stomach dropped as the aircraft lurched, but she'd experienced turbulence before and, with her headphones in, she missed the murmurs of alarm that rippled through the passengers.

It was only when a flash of lightning lit up the dimming sky through her window that she sat up straight and pulled out her headphones. A flight attendant dashed up the aisle, stumbling as the aircraft heaved again and Jo gripped the armrests, trying not to let her brain wander in the direction of orphaned children.

'Erm, this is the captain speaking,' came a mumbled voice over the loudspeaker. 'The predicted storm has hit a little earlier and a little more strongly than expected, so keep those seatbelts on, folks.'

Jo forced herself to breathe out. A storm. Surely planes flew through storms all the time. Another few minutes passed, the air in the cabin still and tense as lights flicked on and the aircraft shuddered and creaked.

Then the loudspeaker clicked on again and the captain cleared his throat. 'I'm sorry to have to tell you,' he said, pausing, 'that weather conditions over the Pyrenees have worsened. We can't fly any further.'

Jo's breath stalled. No, she didn't want to go to Zaragoza, but she didn't *not* want to go to Zaragoza either. Panic burst over her in a thousand questions without answers. Would they return to London? When was the next flight? How quickly could she get to Liss and Dec?

Jo's hand flying to her forehead, her gaze settled on the back of Adrián's head. She couldn't even make this his fault.

The captain continued gravely, 'We are preparing to make an unscheduled landing at the nearest airport.'

As she watched, as though in slow motion, Adrián turned and unerringly met her gaze.

2

Jo Watters didn't like him.

That wasn't a news flash, but the passage of three years should have been enough for her to make peace with the fact that the choir and not the softball team had been awarded the PTA funds. Although he shouldn't underestimate the psychological damage a year on the PTA could inflict and she'd managed six of them.

To be completely fair, their reunion wasn't happening in the best of circumstances either. Hurrying across the tarmac through driving rain and whipping wind to a squat terminal with 'Tarbes Lourdes Pyrenees' on a large sign, their evening well and truly gone to shit, wasn't conducive to making friends. Then there was the fact that they were both on their way to their ex-spouses' wedding – to each other.

Friends was definitely too much to ask.

He held the door open for her and she gave an enormous sigh when the shelter of the airport enveloped them. Her blonde hair was a mess around her face, her clip askew. She was a tall woman, attractive and noticeable, not to mention articulate, intelligent and persuasive. Those were his memories from that year on the PTA.

She had a stud in her nose that suggested an intriguing rebellious streak.

But that evening, as she swallowed and hitched her backpack higher, looking grimly around the terminal, she didn't look so in-charge.

'This way, please!' called a flight attendant and they turned in tandem to follow.

She still hadn't said anything to him. He hadn't greeted her either, but they fell into step as they made their way through the terminal, reluctant allies now disaster had struck. But he didn't need to talk if she didn't. Anything they discussed right now would probably be unpleasant anyway.

'Are you going to call Mónica or shall I call Ben?' she muttered as they trudged on.

Damn, he'd been right. Conversation was unpleasant. She'd been right to ignore him on the plane, even though he'd felt a little stupid trying to say hello while she was pretending she hadn't seen him.

She rolled her eyes when he didn't immediately answer and pulled out her phone, tapping the screen and then holding it to her ear. 'Hi, Ben,' she said in a tight tone when the call connected. 'I'm really sorry, but our flight was diverted and I'm nowhere near Zaragoza.'

'Well, actually, it's just over the other side of the Pyrenees,' Adrián pointed out. She levelled a sharp look at him.

'They have to get the plane back to London so they're putting us in a hotel for a night and chartering a coach in the morning. I'm sorry you left already. My phone was on flight mode.'

Why did she keep saying sorry?

'I'll call you in the morning. Can you—' Her eyes closed briefly. 'Yes, I know the party is the day after tomorrow. It can't take me too long to get across the Pyrenees.' Her gaze flitted warily to him. 'But can you spare a thought for Liss and Dec, please? No, it's not that they don't like Mónica – it's not that simple. I haven't said anything!' Her mouth snapped shut and Adrián shoved a hand in his pocket, looking away as though that could stop him feeling every bit of awkwardness along with her.

They had more in common than being stuck in the wrong airport.

'I'll see you tomorrow,' she said firmly, disconnecting the call and stuffing her phone roughly into her backpack. 'You could have at least moved a discreet distance away,' she grumbled at him.

'Because I don't know anything about difficult relationships with exes and the complications of sharing custody of children,' he responded casually, keeping his gaze fixed on the flight attendant who was leading them through the chaotic labyrinth of travel delays.

'Maybe it's better if we don't talk,' she mumbled.

'That's the conclusion I'd come to.'

They continued in silence, past advertising for perfumes and mountain sports that made him shudder at the thought and shops selling religious trinkets that looked as though they'd been imported from the blessed factories of China.

The only association he had with the French town of Lourdes was Catholicism, the religion his parents had all but abandoned, although the rosaries and crucifixes still made him think of his childhood, of respect and good behaviour. The last time he'd been in a church had been the one with the golden dome near Mónica's parents' place for Oscar's baptism. And the next time he would find himself in a church...

The fun just never stopped today.

'They're using my kids as babysitters,' Jo snapped at him suddenly.

'And that's my fault because...? They're not *both* my exes.'

'But he is your kid that nobody can manage!'

Even sarcasm couldn't protect him from that shot. The bleed of hurt trickled down his spine. 'We can't all be model parents like you.'

Her gaze whipped to his. 'What do you mean by that?'

'I said you were a good parent.'

'But you *implied* otherwise. I have an ex-husband and a well-developed bullshit detector, Adrián.'

At least she remembered his name. He'd wondered for a moment. She'd even pronounced it with the accent. 'Good for you,' he muttered, meaning it genuinely but not prepared to give up his sarcastic tone yet.

'Yes, I work full time, but *everything* I do is for those kids. Why else do you think I'm tearing my hair out because we're stuck *here* instead of in Zaragoza!'

'Zaragoza,' he muttered, correcting her pronunciation for lack of anything else to say.

'The place is seriously pronounced Tharagotha? It sounds like something out of *Game of Thrones*.'

He winced at her terrible accent. 'No, Zaragoza,' he repeated more firmly.

'Oh, fuck off,' she muttered under her breath, swiping a hand through her hair. He felt the strangest urge to smile.

Adrián tried not to stare, but his gaze was drawn continually back to her as they followed the slow crowd to goodness-knows-where. Although she'd made it clear that being stuck with him wasn't her idea of a good time, she didn't storm off. She just walked silently beside him, thrumming with emotion.

Ben must have been a real idiot, a first-class cojón, and not only because he was marrying Mónica. What a mess – and that was just his own feelings.

After the marathon through the terminal came the hell of

queuing. As a British airline, they expected the passengers to form a tortuous queue in a patient, orderly fashion. But due to a misunderstanding between the strict British passengers and the Spaniards who would wait longer to be saved the agony of standing in line, the queue became a disordered clump of people, pushing to the front for their hotel vouchers. Jo looked as though she'd like to break out the 'f' word again.

'Boarding passes, please!' called out the poor flight attendant, overwhelmed by the flood of disgruntled passengers. She had to squint at the mobile boarding passes to read the names and wrote each hotel voucher by hand.

'¡Madre de Dios! This is going take forever!' Adrián exclaimed, slapping his thigh in aggravation.

A middle-aged woman in front of them turned and made the sign of the cross at him rather aggressively. 'Nuestra Señora give you patience!'

'Oh, that's why I've heard of Lourdes,' Jo mumbled as she rummaged in her backpack. 'A virgin in a cave was just what today was missing. And why can't I find my phone? I just had it!' She opened the zip all the way, still searching as Adrián's lips twitched with a smile. 'What?' she asked.

'I— nothing,' he said. 'Here, let me hold the bag.'

She looked up with a furrowed brow, but handed over the backpack so she could use two hands to search for the device. By the time she found it, the clump of people had thinned as the passengers received their hotel assignments and headed for the coach to the city centre.

'Will you hold this?' she asked, thrusting her phone at him. He took it and tucked it on top of his own as she took a swig from her water bottle, wiping her hair off her neck. Stowing the bottle, she hastily whipped her hair back up into its clip, but the effect was still dishevelled. He couldn't help thinking it was a good look on her: a strong woman with wisps of wavy blonde hair and a penchant for wry jokes.

He was still holding both phones when their turn came, so he handed his to the flight attendant, who scribbled something hastily onto a list and handed him a pair of hotel vouchers. Jo pulled up her boarding pass in the app and the woman nodded dismissively.

'The second coach, please. We'll depart for Zaragoza at nine o'clock tomorrow morning from outside the hotel. Please don't be late. Your luggage will be forwarded ready to collect when you arrive.'

'But—'

Jo grasped the cuff of his shirt and pulled. Giving her a sharp look, he tugged his arm back.

'My guitar—'

'She's answered the question,' Jo said through gritted teeth. 'You're not going to achieve anything by waving your arms around.'

He drew himself up. 'You saw me at the airport,' he accused.

'I saw you lose your shit over a guitar, yes.'

There was no way Jo would understand and he wasn't about to explain the full story in the terminal, but he tried anyway. 'Not just any—'

'Yes, a Rancho Valdez something-santo gold-plated twenty-carat guitar and that makes zero difference to this poor woman who just wants to go home.' She shared a sympathetic look with the flight attendant.

'Ricardo Martín Gonzalez,' he mumbled. He sighed deeply. If anything happened to that guitar... Damn Mónica and her wedding – and her pre-wedding party and the coming ten days that were sure to be the worst of his life. 'Fine. Let's go.' Juggling the paperwork, his phone and his trolley bag, he set off for the coach in a hurry.

'It's not going to leave without us!' Jo grumbled, catching up with him and snatching the vouchers, stowing them in her backpack.

'It might!' he contradicted her with a shrug. 'Besides, we've been standing in that queue for years and I'm starving,' he said snappishly.

'Wow, exaggerating just a little,' she quipped.

'And you're not sarcastic at all.'

She stopped up short with a snort that he was fairly certain was supposed to be laughter. 'What is wrong with us?' she murmured.

He turned back to her, his hands on his hips, and said with a straight face, 'We were on our way to the wedding of our ex-partners when our flight was diverted and we found ourselves stranded in the place where the mother of God reveals herself to the faithful in a cave. And I haven't had dinner.'

Jo gave him a withering look that only made her look more attractive – a sign his thoughts were even more off-course than he'd realised. Searching in her bag again, she produced a wonky muesli bar and handed it to him. He snatched it eagerly, his stomach clenching in both anticipation of the snack and the faint hope that she'd meant it as a peace offering.

'Thank you!'

'My kids play a lot of sport. I usually have something in my bag.' She watched him with a curious expression as he ripped off the wrapping and dug in. 'But you should probably stop talking about the mother of God that way. It sounded like you meant she gave a strip show.'

The joke caught him at the wrong moment and he inhaled a few oats, choking and spluttering. But he was surprisingly glad they'd given up ignoring each other, even if she was the ex-wife of the soon-to-be-husband of his ex-wife and had said 'mother of God' and 'strip show' in the same breath.

3

'I'm sorry, there's been some mistake,' Jo said, peering at the hotel keycards in her hand.

The harried receptionist at the cheap and soulless chain hotel glanced from the vouchers to the keycards. 'What mistake? You have room 209, on the first floor. If you have any problems after you arrive in the room, you can call.'

Jo shook her head, blinking back her own confusion. 'But... it's one room.' She couldn't bring herself to glance behind her at Adrián, especially since both of them were so strung out that they could only manage to insult each other and make bad jokes.

The receptionist frowned. 'Yes? Two people, one double room – for you and your husband.'

The word made her almost throw up a little in her mouth. She was done with husbands and ex-husbands and weddings for all time. 'He's not my husband.'

'Your... boyfriend?' the poor receptionist tried, which was cute given Jo had a few streaks of grey in her hair these days and two teenage kids. Hysterical laughter rose in her chest as she contemplated the next twist on the worst day of her life.

Imagining Adrián as her boyfriend was a sick joke. He was attractive, with that curly hair and expressive mouth, not to mention dark eyes with an intensity that made her knees wobbly. But he knew he was attractive and he slapped things when he was frustrated and steamrolled poor parent-teacher associations with his big ideas.

Not to mention he'd been married to her ex-husband's new bride-to-be. Urgh, it was definitely weird that they'd somehow connected after the flight and she'd laughed at his jokes and fed him a muesli bar – just when she'd been enjoying having no ravenous mouths to feed.

She also felt bad for her comment about Oscar. Even if he truly was a little shit, Jo knew as well as anyone that kids were kids and it wasn't his fault. The way Adrián's face had fallen when she'd said it...

He seemed to finally comprehend their predicament. 'There's only one room? But we're not— we're just—' As he met her gaze, she could feel the whole ex-wife of ex-husband spiel flashing between them again.

'We're essentially strangers,' Jo explained. 'We just happened to be talking to each other and the flight attendant must have got the wrong idea.'

The receptionist gulped audibly. 'Oh, I'm very sorry. We booked up all of the rooms we had left with your airline. We already have a large group of bikers staying and... Can I call another hotel for you? Or I might ask a colleague to help because it could take a while. The motorcycle pilgrimage is one of the busiest weeks of the year.'

Jo blinked, trying not to imagine a bunch of tattooed bikers kneeling while the virgin revealed herself to them. She shook off the image. It was a real pilgrimage, not a porn film. And why did Mary always look like 1980s Madonna in Jo's imagination? Although it was honestly better to imagine a Catholic biker club than to picture sharing a room with Adrián, watching him walk out of the tiny bathroom in a towel, water droplets sluicing down his—his *hair*. That's what she'd been thinking.

'Is it a twin room at least?' he asked. 'Or can it be made into a twin room?'

The receptionist nodded eagerly. 'Yes, of course! In fact, I can change a room with another guest and give you a triple. Will that be okay?'

Jo's breath whooshed out in relief. They could keep a bed between them at all times. She might even forget he was there, across the wide expanse of the room, snoring peacefully. Actually, he'd better not snore.

But her relief was short-lived after they trudged up to their room. Swiping the keycard with a grim expression, Adrián grasped the handle and opened the door with a flourish – that the room definitely didn't deserve. It was little more than a box with cream textured plastering, a red feature wall and a flat-screen TV that would have looked inviting if it hadn't been so close to the beds that they'd get eye strain if they watched something.

Rather than three individual singles, two beds were pushed together and made up as a double and the extra bed was more like a small sofa under the window, designed for a child.

Adrián made a rumbling noise in disapproval. He gulped and said, 'At least we don't have our suitcases. They would never fit in this room.'

'Always look on the bright side, hmm?' she responded faintly.

'I'll take that one,' he said, striding into the room and heading for the extra bed as though staking his claim. But the room was so small that his trolley bag got stuck between the bed and the wall and he had to stop to manoeuvre it sideways.

Jo grasped the bag to stop him. 'Don't be ridiculous. I'll take it.'

'Because it's so ridiculous to want to help you.'

She pulled a face at him. 'Do I look like I need help?'

He made another of his rumbling noises as though he was fresh out of sympathy for the entire world. 'No, but I'm sick of hearing you apologise for everything.'

Jo paused, blinking. Did he expect her to thank him, even though he was behaving like a grumpy arse? 'I could apologise for making you take the small bed,' she pointed out.

'God, I need a drink,' he muttered, rubbing a hand over his eyes.

'I thought you needed food! I don't have an emergency stash of alcohol in my bag.' Although she liked the sound of that.

'Good,' he snapped in return. 'Because *I'm* buying *you* a drink – whether you like it or not, even though we are "essentially strangers".'

* * *

Bellies full of quiche and misgiving, they dragged their feet in the corridor on their way back to their room later that evening. Jo wished she'd drunk another glass of wine, but given her weird mood, if she'd drunk enough to knock herself out, she might have said something stupid beforehand and she couldn't risk that.

Although they'd sat for a long time at the hotel restaurant over their meals, Jo had mainly talked on the phone to Liss, who had had a lot to say about the delay, which Jo suspected was more her daughter's need to process her emotions about the wedding.

She'd glanced up at one stage to see Adrián smiling into his phone screen as he video-called his son and she'd been so distracted that Liss had accused her of not listening. The sigh when he'd hung up had come from deep in his chest.

'We'll... see them tomorrow,' Jo said as they approached the door.

He gave her a faint smile. 'And then your daughter won't have to babysit my son any more.'

Shame rippled up her chest, but he pushed the door open before she could say anything and then the claustrophobia of the tiny room made talking about anything serious impossible. He had to duck out of her way so she could reach the tiny bed by the window and she squeezed past, close enough to smell the last hint of his cologne after the long day.

It wasn't an offensive scent, but the fact that she was near enough to identify it triggered all her frustrations. She still recognised Ben's cologne whenever she smelled it – four years after the divorce. Although she'd dated a little – okay, she'd been on a total of five disastrous dates – being attracted to someone was not something she could deal with right now.

Pulling the same clothes back on after her shower was an unpleasant experience, but the hotel had placed toothbrush packages in the bathroom, to her relief. She finger-combed her hair, went to the toilet again for good measure and then dived into bed, pulling the covers up high. The waistband of her capris dug into her hip, so she wriggled out of them as quietly as she could, her efforts wasted when she whacked her head on the windowsill, the stupid tiny bed.

Adrián eyed her but switched the main light off as he headed for the bathroom and Jo breathed an enormous sigh of relief. No bare-chested towel walk to endure. She could close her eyes and overthink the next ten days in peace – the next ten days where she'd have to avoid Adrián and try to forget he'd seen her in this state.

He was finished in the shower quickly and Jo pretended she'd already fallen asleep – not that either of them wanted to talk anyway. The bed was so small her feet hung off the end. She curled up on her side facing into the room and squeezed her eyes shut, trying to let her thoughts drift.

She unfortunately succeeded, which was why, a moment later, her eyes blinked open automatically at the sound of him unzipping his trolley bag and then they grew round and refused to close again. The curtains in the room were drawn, but the fading light from the long June day still crept around the hem, casting him into shadows – and what a set of shadows that man had on his back.

He wasn't overly muscular, just defined – and fine. Her gaze snagged on the spot where his shoulder merged into his arm, a hint of bone protruding. Ouch, how long had it been since she'd found herself in the same room as so much exposed skin?

The lucky bastard obviously had fresh clothes in his trolley bag and he slipped on a white T-shirt with a sigh, running his hand through all those curls. Then he dropped his towel and it took every ounce of self-control for Jo to swallow her yelp of surprise and then she promptly fell off the bed.

His head whipped around as he hurriedly tugged on a pair of boxer shorts, hopping as he overbalanced. Climbing over the bed, he held a hand out to help her up and she was too messed up to refuse it. 'Are you okay?'

Nodding feverishly, she hurried back into the cot, but hit her head again as she lay down. 'Ow,' she whined. 'Why can't this day just end?'

'Take the big bed,' Adrián said gruffly.

Letting her eyes slam closed for a moment, she took a deep breath and said what needed to be said. 'Let's just share it.'

'Are you sure? I'll see if there's an extra blanket to put a divider down the middle—'

'I don't need a divider, Adrián.'

'I promise I won't—'

Jo's thoughts ranged off to all of the things he might promise not to do to her, which was disconcerting to say the least.

'...even know you're there,' he finished. 'I sleep heavily.'

She was *not* disappointed. 'Good for you,' she mumbled as she swung her legs out of the bed again and hopped into the near side of the double, Adrián looking pointedly away. Aside from the relentless awareness of his presence, the bed was heavenly after the cramped confines of the cot and she managed to convince herself it wasn't unusual at all to share a bed with her nemesis and she could drift off comfortably now.

Then he spoke. 'Were you awake, when you fell out of the bed?'

'If you're trying to work out if I saw your naked bum, then the answer is yes. Now can I go to sleep?'

'Sorry, I thought you were asleep.'

'I didn't imagine you... revealed yourself on purpose.'

'Illuminating, was it?' She heard the smile in his voice.

'Not a religious experience, but I could hardly ignore the light of the enormous moon in our tiny hotel room,' she grumbled, tugging the blanket more firmly around herself and hoping he'd get the message that she didn't want to chat like a pair of kids at a sleepover.

'Hey!' he protested. 'I need some of the blanket too!' He pulled it roughly and she rolled with it, her thigh falling against his.

She wrenched her leg back to her side, but not before her imagination headed off into the wilderness again – a rather pleasant wilderness that featured warm skin and crisp hair and closeness she hadn't experienced in too long. She had to stop thinking about him like that.

'You're worse than my son,' she complained. 'I had to sleep in his bed a lot when he was little, because he— Anyway, we should go to sleep.'

As he mumbled in agreement, she thought about Dec again,

about the affectionate and rowdy little boy he'd been before he was swallowed by his smelly bedroom and his computer. He could finally wash his own hair these days – although not very well – but how was he feeling about all the changes in the family?

'You miss them a lot,' Adrián commented, making her realise she'd been moving restlessly in the bed.

'Of course I miss them,' she retorted. 'They're like my own body.' Except young and not-yet battle worn.

'How are they dealing with the wedding?' he asked.

Jo grimaced, flopping onto her back and abandoning thoughts of sleep for the moment. 'I wish I knew. It's all so drawn out. Why are they having this pre-wedding party anyway? Is that a Spanish thing?'

'No,' he answered defensively. 'But Mónica's family is... big. Not all of them can travel for the actual wedding next week, but they can't be excluded either – that's a Spanish thing.'

'What about exes? Are they usually included?'

When he didn't answer, she risked a glance at him to find his face alarmingly close, his gaze dark with dismay.

'Forget it,' she grumbled, rolling over again. 'I don't want to talk about this right now. It'll land on us soon enough tomorrow.' She wasn't sure she liked the way 'us' had crept into that sentence, but it was better to think about the unpleasant wedding than his naked body right now.

'You're right. Good night, Jo.'

'Good night, Adrián,' she mumbled in reply. 'Um,' she began before she could hold it in. 'I'm sorry for what I said about Oscar. I was upset and took it out on you. If there's one thing I shouldn't have forgotten, it's that seven-year-olds are jerks and that's not your fault.'

She peered over her shoulder and caught his quick smile between that musketeer facial hair.

'Is that what you learned from parenting two? Kids are jerks?'

'Yep,' she said with a firm sigh.

'Thanks for the pep talk. I hope teenagers are better.'

'Nope. Teenagers are arseholes.' She should have left it at that, but he caught her with the intensity in those eyes and she rolled over to face him warily. It must be tiring for him to be so passionate all the time. She was exhausted just looking at him – which must have been why she had to suck in a heavy breath.

But his expression grew sad and distant. 'I know Oscar is difficult. I've heard it from every nursery nurse, every teacher. You can't imagine I didn't know what you meant.'

'But he's your son,' she filled in, which only made him fix her with another unsettling gaze.

'Yes, and I'm worried about how he'll cope with the chaos of the wedding preparations – without me. I— We—' He cut himself off to consider his words.

'We had a bad day,' Jo filled in for him.

'The worst,' he agreed roughly. 'Maybe we should try to be friends – just until we arrive in Zaragoza tomorrow?'

'What's not friendly?' she asked in a peeved tone.

'I can see it in your eyes every time you think about the softball team missing out on the PTA money,' he commented.

'If you think I'm forgiving you for *that*, then you're dreaming.'

'A truce then,' he suggested, tucking his hand up under his chin. 'A verbal ceasefire.'

'I didn't think we were at war, but okay – a truce.' She met his gaze and it was worse than catching a whiff of his cologne. Too long looking into that handsome face and she'd start to think of their relationship as more of an *alliance* and that was going too far, considering they were about to be tortured by the nuptials of their exes.

'Unless you steal the blanket in the night. If you do that, all bets are off,' he said sternly.

'Are you looking for a pillow in the face? If *you* steal the blanket, I'll come over there and get it back!' His silence made her mistake quickly evident. 'Um, I mean, I'm staying on my side of the bed. No matter what. And now I'm going to sleep.'

At least she hoped she was.

4

Jo had always liked to be the big spoon – well, not always, but since those days when Dec had awoken often with sleep terrors and she'd flung a tired arm and a leg over him and crooned for him to go back to sleep, she'd got used to sleeping that way.

If her little spoon seemed larger that morning, she was woozy enough to ignore it. There was a soft cotton shirt under her fingers. The temperature had dropped overnight and the mix of cool air on the back of her neck and warm human plastered to her front was heavenly.

It had been so long since either of the kids had let her snuggle like this. She tightened her arms as the daylight streaming through the crappy curtains roused her reluctantly awake. She refused to open her eyes as everything about the moment – the scent of clean sheets and sleepy person, the subconscious knowledge that she wasn't at home and someone else was taking responsibility, the residual tiredness from the day before – worked to lull her back to sleep.

Until the little spoon gave a rasping sigh and groggily said, 'Mónica?'

Jo scrambled out of the bed in a panic, wishing she could bury her head under the blankets the way Liss did. Instead, she plonked down onto the cot and rubbed her palms briskly over her face and through her hair. Phew, maybe he was still asleep.

'Were you hugging me?'

She blinked her eyes open to find him peering at her over his shoulder.

'Moment of weakness,' she muttered. 'I thought you were one of my kids.' His brows shot up. 'You thought I was your ex-wife, so let's just forget it ever happened.' If only that worked for her tactile memory. That shirt was incredibly soft.

That was when she realised she'd slipped off her tailored capris last night and she was sitting on the bed in her undies. Inwardly panicking, she inched her hand towards her trousers as casually as she could as Adrián yawned and stretched, only half awake.

After she'd slid into them surreptitiously, she snatched her phone from the windowsill and frowned when she couldn't wake up the screen.

'Shit, my phone didn't charge,' she said as she checked the cable and charger with the adapter. 'What time is it?'

He checked his watch, an old-school number that actually ticked. 'Eight forty-five,' he said, his voice still scratchy.

'Eight forty-five!' she repeated in alarm. 'Get up! We only have fifteen minutes to get the bus!'

'That's plenty of time,' he insisted, giving himself one more stretch that showed off his tanned arms. 'You don't even need to change,' he added, glancing at her in a way that made her wonder if he'd noticed she'd only been half-dressed five minutes ago.

'You do!'

'Fine!' he said, hauling himself upright. 'I'm not a morning person.'

'Nobody is a morning person,' she said, a little too forcefully, 'but most of us adapt in adulthood.'

'I see the truce didn't survive the night. I'd just like to point out that the hugging wasn't my fault.'

'You could stop talking about it, though,' she said through gritted teeth. 'I just want to get out of here.'

With another long groan, he got to his feet. 'I know. We won't be late. I'll be ready in a minute. What was it you said yesterday? "The coach won't leave without us?"' He hobbled to the bathroom like an old man and Jo thought he really could tone down the dramatics for both their sakes.

He was ready in more like seven minutes, meaning they didn't have time for the buffet, but that didn't stop Adrián from heading into the breakfast room to pour an espresso, holding up a hand when Jo opened her mouth to protest.

'You don't want to sit with me on the coach if I haven't had a coffee,' he said in his gravelly morning voice. 'What's the hurry? We have six minutes.'

'I'm not sure I want to sit with you at all,' Jo grouched, but she softened a little when he gave her the first mini cup of espresso. As she paused to appreciate the sharp aroma and creamy texture, she wondered whether Adrián really wanted to sit with her either. Why would he, when she'd been as friendly to him as a bear with a sore tooth? To make things worse, her prickly behaviour had been an oddly satisfying way to deal with her roiling emotions. As much as she wanted to see Liss and Dec, the kids unfortunately came with a dose of Ben today. She couldn't blame Ben for the flight redirection and the awkward night with Adrián, but she wanted to.

'Are you nearly finished?'

Shaking off the spiral of unhelpful thoughts, she remembered the time with a spike of panic. If Adrián was suggesting they needed to go, then they *really* needed to go. She remembered the number of times he'd turned up fifteen minutes late to a PTA meeting, missed some vital piece of context and made her or Annie Winters repeat everything they'd discussed.

'What time is it?'

'Relax, it's three minutes to nine. I've been paying attention.'

'Three minutes!'

'It doesn't take three minutes to walk twenty metres, Jo!' he called after her as she rushed for the foyer.

'If we miss the coach because you thought *three minutes* was early enough, the truce goes right out the window!' she said when he caught up at the sliding doors to the street. Outside, the sun was already radiating hot over the city, even though the mountains that rose into view in the distance were still speckled with snow. The only sign of yesterday's storm was the lingering heaviness in the air with a prickle of electricity.

'Does no truce mean no more hugging?'

'It was an accident! The hugging was not part of the—'

His lips were twitching, despite his grave expression.

'Oh, look, the coach is here,' he said cheerfully.

Jo was too relieved to even process the fact that he'd been teasing her and approached the vehicle with a sigh. It was a posh-looking coach with air-conditioning and a wheelchair-friendly section in the middle and she was pleasantly surprised she wasn't going to spend the four-hour drive suffocating in the stinky, carpeted relic of the 1990s she'd expected. The driver greeted her with a brilliant smile that didn't seem appropriate to the situation, but she appreciated it.

He first spoke in another language that sounded like Italian rather than French and Jo had to ask him to repeat himself in English. 'Perhaps you and your husband could take seats in the back? It's difficult for some of the others to reach those seats,' he suggested.

'Oh, he's not my—'

Adrián grasped her elbow and propelled her forward, giving the friendly driver a curt 'thank you'. 'What were you going to say to him? That we're strangers again? That's just confusing. And I assume you don't want to explain that we're the ex-partners of a couple who are about to get married?'

'Urgh, that's so weird,' she grumbled as she tugged her arm out of his grip and headed for the back of the coach. As she took her seat with her rucksack on her lap, she tried not to think of Ben and Mónica, of the flowery invitation with a quote about true love, how everything about this wedding felt like a personal affront, but the only other thing she had to think about was that she was wearing dirty underwear and yesterday's clothes and had snuggled a stranger in her sleep.

Except Adrián didn't feel like a stranger. That must have been what happened when you ran your mouth at someone on the worst day of your life.

'Are you okay?' he asked after he'd squeezed his trolley bag between his legs.

She wanted to snap that of course she wasn't and she was allowed to not be okay today of all days, but she'd just decided she shouldn't rail at him the way she had yesterday.

'Yes,' she insisted, busying herself searching for her phone cable to plug into the USB slot on the seat in front of her. 'Damn it,' she muttered when the blasted thing still wouldn't charge.

'Do you want to try my cable? Maybe it will work when the bus is running.'

'I hope so.'

It took fifteen minutes for everyone to board, fraying Jo's nerves further.

'Do you think...?' Adrián began, studying the other passengers.

'Don't say it,' Jo warned him. 'I'm sure people with disabilities travel just as much as everyone else.'

He tilted his head as though he wanted to agree, but couldn't. 'But on the plane, I didn't see...'

'This won't be everyone. Remember most of the passengers ended up at another hotel.'

'You're right. I just wish we'd eaten breakfast, if we'd known it would take this long. By the time we get to Zaragoza, I'm going to be—' He cut himself off, glancing warily at her. 'Quite hungry. And I'm not begging for a muesli bar. Given our terrible luck, we should save them for when we get stranded in the Pyrenees and it takes the mountain rescue team three days to reach us.'

'Even I don't have that many,' Jo said with a faint smile.

The engine started and she breathed a sigh of relief, especially when the charging symbol appeared on her phone. The driver said something in Italian, which seemed to please the other passengers. Then they set off through the low-rise stone apartment buildings of the city centre, past green spaces planted with begonias and blooming pink roses, dotted with palms that were the only reminder of how far south they were.

Jo glimpsed the hills that ringed the city, a glowing green with fresh spring grass. Low clouds hid the more distant mountains, a hint of the crushing humidity that awaited them that afternoon in the unseasonably warm June weather. An imposing fortress on a hill looked down over the city and Jo was just beginning to think Lourdes was a cute sort of place and she was glad to have glimpsed it when the coach pulled into a car park, only five minutes from the hotel.

Those passengers who could stand independently did so, grasping for their walking sticks or the arm of a loved one. The doors of the coach opened with a hiss and Jo shared an anxious look with Adrián. Only after all the other passengers had disembarked did they stand and trudge to the doors in dismay.

The car park was right by a shallow river, gurgling peacefully. On the other side, gleaming white in a sunbeam sparkling with moisture, stood an ornate church. Even as Jo's mind raced with the many possible explanations for what had gone wrong, the view struck her with a deep sense of mystery – the church nestled in the green hills, the mist of clouds behind, swirling and changing, the flowing turquoise water.

The peace was only interrupted by the intermittent rumble of an engine from one of the numerous motorbikes parked densely along the river. Among the leather-clad people milling in the car park there were almost as many beards as vehicles and Jo remembered what the hotel receptionist had said about motorbike pilgrims. One strode past in a creased jacket featuring an embellished image of Mary, her halo emitting beams of light and embroidered tears dotting her cheeks. Another had 'God Squad' emblazoned across his shoulders.

'Excuse me, I believe there's been a mistake,' she heard Adrián saying to the coach driver behind her as she grappled for focus.

'Don't worry,' the man continued in a soothing tone that could have convinced a lion to retract its claws. 'I'll find an English-speaking guide for you. There are always many English-speaking pilgrims and the next Mass will take place soon. You could always walk the stations of the cross while you wait.'

'No, you don't understand. We're not—'

'It's not a problem if you didn't pay for the bus. Please, go on to the sanctuary. The hospitaliers are here to help everyone, even the able-bodied.' With a twinkle in his eye, he continued on a whisper, 'And most of us don't mind if you're not married either. God sees into your heart.' He made an upward gesture with his hand. 'Trust me. You will find what you are looking for at the sanctuary.'

The fake smile Adrián gave him almost made Jo laugh.

'Would you mind?' the coach driver said, indicating the handles of a wheelchair where an older man sat, his legs wrapped in pressure bandages.

'Would we mind what?' Jo asked in confusion, distracted by the flicker of emotions on Adrián's face, from dismay to dread to defeat.

'Pushing him, obviously!' Adrián said, grasping the handles and taking off in the direction of the other passengers. They had gathered around a woman in a white linen dress with a blue apron and a conspicuous lanyard that identified her as someone who knew what she was doing. She greeted the group in Italian, gesturing for them to follow her, and the passengers walked and limped and rolled in the direction of a narrow bridge.

Adrián and his new charge followed along, leaving Jo staring after him in disbelief.

'What are you doing? We're not supposed to be here. We have to get back to the hotel!' she called, grasping the handle of his trolley bag and hurrying after him.

'And which one of the other passengers will push him? The one with the walker? The youngest person here is that lady and she's using crutches! Or do you think we should ask one of these biker gangs?'

'Are you crazy? You can't just join a pilgrimage!'

'Actually,' said the bus driver, who was pushing another wheelchair, 'you can.' Both Jo and Adrián just blinked at him.

'What about the kids?' Jo pointed out urgently. 'The family party?'

Adrián stopped suddenly, giving the poor man in the wheelchair a jerk. 'Do you really think the coach will still be there?' he cried, holding her gaze.

'Maybe we can catch it up if we know which way it went. They could wait for us.' Even as she said it, Jo realised how unlikely that solution was. It must be past nine-thirty now. Resentment rose in her throat. If Adrián hadn't been so relaxed about the time—

His jaw was moving, his eyes even more fiery than usual and Jo realised with a start that he was holding himself together by the slightest thread. His Adam's apple bobbed as she swallowed.

'Give me your phone,' she instructed.

After carefully setting the brake, he rummaged in his shoulder bag for his phone and handed it over, rattling off the code which she guessed was Oscar's birthday. The wallpaper showed a grinning toddler wearing a princess dress and a cape and holding up a toy pizza. The photo was a few years old, but it had been an age since Jo's kids were that small.

'I'll call the airline. You look after Mr...'

'Bonetti,' the man in the wheelchair said in a raspy voice, gazing straight ahead.

Adrián clapped him on the shoulder. 'Well, Signor Bonetti, would you like slow and sedate or warp speed?'

She faintly heard Mr Bonetti's chuckle as she searched for the phone number of the airline.

After the initial inquiry, waiting for the customer service agent to call her back was nerve-racking. She fell into step beside Adrián, dragging his bag behind her, as they navigated the long ramp up to the bridge. All eyes were on the sanctuary church, built on a rock above the riverbank.

'You are English?' the man in the wheelchair asked quietly.

'Yes,' she replied.

'My wife was English.'

'I'm sorry for your loss,' Jo said automatically.

'She should have come on this pilgrimage,' the man added, which caught Jo unexpectedly in the chest. 'We were married for sixty-four years. She looked after me when I couldn't use my legs any more. When she died six months ago, I wanted to cancel this trip. I didn't have anyone to help. But something stopped me.'

He gazed at the church, still in sunshine despite the clouds gathering behind. 'Now I see the Santuario, I can already taste the water on my lips and I know I was supposed to come.'

Despite her worries about Liss and Dec, the heartache about the wedding she was putting off, a moment of reprieve stole over Jo courtesy of the frail Signor Bonetti and she dragged in a few much-needed breaths.

'I'm glad you made it,' she said earnestly. She was strangely glad Adrián was there to push him.

She felt her reluctant travelling companion's gaze and found him studying her doubtfully. 'I thought you didn't believe in the virgin who reveals herself in a cave,' he said out of the side of his mouth.

'Shh,' she hissed in reply, giving him a sharp look.

His phone rang, rending the stillness, and Jo's anxiety ramped up again. But the phone call contained no good news. 'It's already on the motorway?' she parroted. 'You can't ask the other passengers to wait.'

Adrián threw his head back and stared up at the sky with an agitated moan, as though divine intervention hadn't already happened – to drag them here in the first place.

'We're... on our own?' she asked the customer service agent, although she already knew the answer. For this calamity they had no one to blame but themselves. After a polite farewell, she let the phone drop from her ear in slow motion. 'We're stuck here. We have to make our own way to Zaragoza.'

Adrián's eyelids crashed closed and he muttered something she suspected wasn't appropriate for one of the holiest places in European Catholicism. 'What are we supposed to do?' he spluttered.

Signor Bonetti piped up. 'Perhaps you should be pilgrims for the day.'

5

If Adrián hadn't been present in his own life over the last twenty-four hours, he never would have believed how he'd ended up in the Grotto of the Apparitions, the words of the Rosary on his lips as he listened to a Spanish pilgrim recite them fervently from her place in the pew.

'Are you religious?' Jo asked, giving him a sidelong glance. There was another thing he could barely believe, even though he'd seen it: Jo Watters had been nice to him for most of the day.

'I feel I can't say no or my grandmother would have lived in vain,' he explained thoughtfully.

After the disaster with the wrong coach that morning, they'd spent over an hour on the phone and in internet searches looking at hire cars then public transport, only to discover that the latter didn't exist without circumnavigating the Pyrenees and the former cost the equivalent of a kidney on the black market because of the country border crossing and one-way trip.

Just when he was about to jokingly suggest resorting to prayer, a solution had presented itself in an unexpected manner. Perhaps it wasn't an ideal solution, but it was all they had.

'Are you two going in?' asked Georg, the bearded biker who'd adopted them when he'd found them strung out and desperate by the stations of the cross. He clapped Adrián on the shoulder hard enough that he stumbled.

'Oh, we can just... stay out here.'

'I'm not Catholic,' Jo volunteered apologetically.

Georg roared with laughter. 'Neither am I! We are members of the Free Protestant Church. We might not believe exactly what Catholics do about Mary and the holy water, but do you think bikers are worried about those details? It's the spirit that counts. Go and drink the water, touch the stone. If you don't want to pray, just make a wish and see what happens.'

Jo gave a weak laugh. She'd looked decidedly green when they'd finally accepted Georg and his friends' offer of transport to Zaragoza the next day by motorbike. Georg and his wife Claudia were members of a 'gang' of middle-aged bikers who called themselves 'Godspeed' and were making their way slowly from Cologne to Santiago de Compostela, seemingly via every religious monument they could find. They'd tried to reassure Jo that their bikes were top-of-the-range luxury BMWs with plenty of space for a passenger – and that they couldn't do better than a group with 'I Ride with Jesus' on their number plates – but she obviously wasn't looking forward to their journey across the Pyrenees with a hunk of hot metal between her thighs.

'A wish and a prayer aren't the same thing, though, are they?' Jo asked, her expression perplexed. Her hair was limp with sweat and her blue eyes were glazed with tiredness, but there was definitely something endearing about her wry acceptance of the chaos in her life. Chaos was a heading he was certain she included *him* under – quite rightfully.

'Not really,' Georg agreed. 'With prayer, we strive to find the heart of God and not our own desires, although the Lord always has a listening ear for whatever we pray, however flawed.'

'The church sure has a nice husband,' she mumbled, too quietly for Georg to hear.

'Go in and see what you find.'

'At least we'll be out of the sun for a few minutes. I didn't think June in the Pyrenees was supposed to be so hot,' Adrián said casually, pushing off from the fence where he'd been perching to head for the queue making its way slowly through the cave.

He kept his hands shoved in his pockets, his expression carefully neutral, but his thoughts swirled as he glanced between the pyramid of candles, the white statue of Mary in a small hollow above the cave and the dark recess in the rock. Husbands... mothers... prayer and wishes and the strange path to this moment, where he lifted a hand carefully out of his pocket to skim the grey stone, a path that had been worn by a century of fingertips.

Oscar was over a country border he couldn't seem to cross – while the old guitar had crossed before him by now. Mónica was marrying someone else and he had nothing to do with his fingers except graze them across the stone. The moment was an exercise in futility.

'What are you going to wish for?' Jo's voice startled him, curbing his spiralling thoughts.

'I have no idea. Have you got over your aversion to revealing virgins to make a wish?'

'You haven't got over *your* cynicism,' she observed softly.

He nearly stumbled. For a moment, it sounded like she cared about what he felt. Of course she did. She'd been vice-chair of the PTA for six years. You didn't do that without a strong sense of compassion – and perhaps a touch of masochism.

'I know cynicism is the easy way,' he said, almost reluctantly.

They'd reached the middle of the cave, where bouquets of flowers and wreaths with ribbons and bows had been left as offerings to the Lady. 'We should wish for something outside of ourselves like Georg said.'

'Like our children?'

They paused in front of the water rushing beneath a hole in the flagstones – the spring Saint Bernadette had discovered when Mary had appeared to her. 'That works.' They'd phoned the kids with the last 10 per cent of Adrián's phone battery and he'd gathered Jo's daughter hadn't taken the news of their further delay well.

'I wish we could get to our children quickly,' Jo said, turning her gaze awkwardly upwards.

He made the sign of the cross out of habit and she watched as though the gesture was something exotic. 'The heart of God...' He sighed deeply, the mixed feelings rising again, but within his control this time. 'If we prayed with the heart of God, it would be for blessing on Ben and Mónica's marriage,' he managed to finish, although his voice nearly gave out at the end.

The violence of emotion that flitted over Jo's face took him by surprise and he grasped her wrist instinctively. She shook him off. 'I know this place specialises in miracles, but I will never be able to wish that.'

The message was clear: back off. They were bantering adversaries, not friends. She didn't want to share her feelings with him. What surprised him was that he wished she would.

* * *

It wasn't difficult to keep things light for the rest of the afternoon. They checked into Georg's hotel in the maze of streets by the sanctuary, taking a twin room when the only other option was for one of them to stay in the honeymoon suite.

'I think the damage was done last night,' Adrián murmured,

earning a scowl from Jo.

She bought underwear and a shirt from the first store they found, complaining that her daughter would be horrified to see her in something designed for a teenager, with a knot sewn at the front to show a hint of midriff.

'But it's not enough for me to go into another shop,' she said with a shudder. 'I don't know what I did before online clothes shopping.'

'I quite enjoy it,' he insisted. 'Trying different styles, "Is this me?" Maybe I could be a professor or Indiana Jones.'

'Indiana Jones *was* a professor,' she insisted.

'By God, you're right,' he'd responded in mock amazement. 'But the shirt looks fine,' he slipped in casually afterwards.

Jo was endlessly amused by the little shops selling incense and candles and rosary beads – along with cheap knock-offs of the statue of the Virgin Mary in the grotto.

'Do you think they've all been properly blessed?' she asked, holding one up next to her face.

'Would you rather buy the real thing, carved by monks under the supervision of the Holy Spirit itself?'

'I'm not sure how it would look on the shelf at home,' she mused, studying the little white statue with its blue sash. 'Is there really a sweatshop of monks somewhere manufacturing these?'

'I have no idea,' he admitted. She raised a hand and for a moment he thought she was about to give him a friendly slap with the backs of her fingers, but she seemed to reconsider at the last moment and dropped her hand again.

They found an ice cream parlour that sculpted the scoops into the shape of roses and Jo was like a kid in... an ice cream parlour, struggling to contain her excitement. He snapped his fingers, gesturing for her to hand over her phone, which she'd charged for twenty minutes in the hotel room. Smiling faintly as he lined up the photo, he captured her staring at her peach-flavoured rose-shaped ice cream with bright eyes.

Leaning on the bar table under an awning outside, she said thoughtfully, 'I can never show anyone that picture.'

'Because I took it?' he asked.

She laughed at him. 'I'm not mad at you. I know it's weird that we're stuck here together, but I know it wasn't by choice.'

'Choosing to spend time together would definitely be strange,' he responded with a nod. She obviously hadn't started doubting the veracity of that statement the way he had.

'But we probably shouldn't be *enjoying* it. That's what I meant about the photo.'

He hoped the flush that rose up his neck wasn't visible. 'After what we've been through and what we've got ahead of us, I think it's your duty to enjoy that ice cream,' he pointed out. She hadn't meant enjoying his company – at least he was pretty sure she hadn't.

'You're right.'

'Careful,' he said, dropping his voice. 'You agreed with me.'

'Did you ever agree to play Santa at the school Christmas Fayre?' she asked.

'No.'

'Are you still in the PTA?'

'God, no. I only lasted that one year.'

'I get it,' she said, taking another slow lick of her ice cream, leaving a smear of pale orange on her top lip. It was definitely bizarre that he was enjoying *that*. 'You join the PTA full of ideals and you leave full of...'

'Trauma,' he finished for her.

She laughed again. 'Do you know how hard it was to find a Santa? In my memory, I asked about fifty people and the one we ended up with was from Kerala – although that was fine in the end.'

'You could have asked me to find a Santa. I just didn't want to *be* one. That would have meant leaving Mónica alone with Oscar at the Fayre and she was already angry at me because I didn't take equal responsibility. I stupidly thought joining the PTA would send her a message – or maybe just prove a point,' he admitted.

'Maybe we shouldn't talk about this while enjoying our ice cream,' she mumbled and he indicated his agreement with a lift of his eyebrows.

Georg and Claudia invited them to dinner that evening at a low-key café full of beards, leather jackets and helmet hair.

'What do you two do for work?' Claudia asked conversationally. 'Or are you at home with the kids, Jo?'

She nearly choked on her omelette. 'No, I'm a software developer,' she explained, taking a sip of wine – actually it was more like a slug. 'My kids are older now.'

'But they only seem to need us more and more!' Claudia exclaimed with a broad smile. 'Our kids are twenty-one and twenty-three and they just bounce in and out of the house. I'm still cleaning up after them. But you said you two aren't married, so—'

'We're both divorced,' Adrián supplied, feeling the frustration vibrate out of Jo. 'And just friends,' he added with a wince.

He should have guessed what was coming next. 'And what do you do?'

'I work in a care home for the elderly,' he replied. That was the simple answer anyway.

'And you're from Spain?' Claudia asked.

He glanced at Jo, realising she probably didn't know any of this stuff either. He hadn't realised she was a software developer. 'I'm from Madrid, but I moved to London twelve years ago.'

'So it's one of your friends or family who's getting married?'

'Not exactly,' he answered. 'Mutual... eh... friends of ours.' He hoped that didn't sound too suspicious.

After dinner, the entire town was drawn to the sanctuary like iron filings to a magnet. The sun cast long shadows and the still river reflected the balconies of the buildings built along it. The shops selling the Virgin Mary knock-offs had closed their shutters for the night. Only the shop promising to cure your ills with gourmet sweets and chocolates was still tempting passersby.

They arrived back at the posh hotel with its Belle Époque stonework and wrought-iron balconies and Jo turned for the doors into the foyer.

'You're not going to miss the procession, are you?' Georg asked in horror that appeared genuine.

Adrián started to make their excuses. 'I thought we should get some rest before—'

'The candlelight procession is the most restful experience. You'll see,' Georg assured them.

There was a faint furrow between Jo's brows. 'I suppose when the other option is sitting around in the hotel room...'

'Good! We went last night as well. It will be something you won't forget,' Georg said with a grin.

As they followed the 'Godspeed' crew towards the sanctuary, he couldn't help saying in a low voice, 'Going to Mass is more interesting than hanging out with me?'

She eyed him, then drew close to speak quietly into his ear. 'I don't exist to address your insecurities, but that's not what I meant.' With a look that brooked no nonsense and gave him tingles all the way to the tips of his fingers, she said, 'You're all right, Adrián. I'm kind of glad you're here.'

'I think I just fell a little bit in love with you,' he said with a huff, before he'd properly thought it through. He was joking. She knew he was joking.

Her sigh was long and deep. 'You'll get over it.'

6

Jo silently added 'flirting' to the list of the infuriating habits of Adrián Rivera Morales. They passed the statue of the crowned virgin on a plinth near the entrance to the sanctuary grounds with their lit candles, moving as part of the crowd.

She felt frustratingly unbalanced. She tried to give herself a break, tell herself she was facing a lot of crap and only time – and wine – would help, and focused instead on her slow progress across the enormous forecourt.

Up ahead were the two basilicas: the upper church with its imposing white spires, the sun setting in the background in a jumble of puffy clouds, and the lower church with its gold embell-ishments and marble detailing. It all seemed so strange and earnest to Jo, who understood little of the theology, but underneath the images of robed virgins and the dying Christ, the commitment of such a large group of people to hope and blessings – for them-selves, but mostly for others – spoke a deeply human message into her scattered thoughts.

Even if all she could do was hold her candle in its cardboard protector, there was something striking about being one of hundreds – possibly even thousands – of little flames. She wished Liss and Dec could have been there.

The candles didn't glow as strongly when it was still light, but only God could make night fall before nine on a June evening. He'd apparently chosen not to, meaning the procession began in full evening light, with the tolling of the bells. Flanked by priests, nuns and monks and accompanied by the strains of a men's choir, an illuminated statue of Mary was carried on a litter past the gold-leaf representations of biblical stories and down the steps.

As they shuffled along, Adrián warbled the 'Ave Maria' quietly with the crowd. He was pretty much in tune, but that was all she could say about his voice. He might play the guitar, but he was no singer.

They passed the grotto and the singing grew more enthusiastic. Adrián stopped suddenly and then darted between a pair of nuns.

'Signor Bonetti!' she heard him say as he shook hands with their acquaintance from that morning as though they were long-lost friends. The old man was sitting in a different chair, an old-fashioned one with a wheel and a pole at the front for pulling. 'Here, shall I push you?'

Adrián waved to Jo with an urgent flick of his hand and gave her his candle before grasping the handles on the back of the wheel-chair, helping the tiny nun who was pulling from the front. Signor Bonetti was singing in his unsteady voice and Adrián joined in with more enthusiasm – or at least more volume.

'You have to lift up the candles when they sing "Ave Maria",' he told Jo with a sharp look.

'Okay, keep your shirt on,' she muttered in reply, obediently raising both candles the next time the heavy voices sang that part.

'Singing along wouldn't hurt you either,' he murmured during the next verse.

'Why would I know the song?'

'Because we've repeated it about a thousand times since the start of this procession,' he replied in a stage whisper. 'And the words are on the candle!'

Exaggeration, sarcasm, flirting, speaking uncomfortable truths – she had so many reasons to detest Adrián right now. But in a place where the souvenir shops were called Pax Mundi – 'World Peace' in Latin – she could show him a little charity. With a final gulp, she opened her mouth to sing for the first time in... years, maybe?

It turned out she hadn't forgotten how to do it. Sound came out, smooth and in tune. With a sense of detachment, she modulated her voice out of habit until the resonance swelled. Wow, she'd been good at this.

Her voice dropped away again when she noticed Adrián staring at her with his jaw around his collarbone. 'Don't stop!' he rasped urgently.

'*You* stopped,' she accused.

He pulled himself together and started singing again when the next 'Ave Maria' sounded and she joined him, amused at his attempts not to look at her.

'I had singing lessons as a teenager,' she explained as an aside during the next verse.

'I can tell,' he said, still wide-eyed. There was something in his expression that reminded her of him saying he'd fallen a little bit in love with her and she wrenched her gaze away, staring instead at the basilicas as the crowd returned to the forecourt behind the brightly lit Mary.

She noticed with a start that the sky had dimmed and soft lights now illuminated the gold on the façade and bathed the square in a warm glow. The little flames of a thousand candles created a luminous carpet, holding back the shadows.

Jo clutched her two candles tightly, feeling both a part of something and desperately alone. She couldn't wait to get back to Liss and Dec, but if it weren't for the kids, she would have been quite happy to be waylaid in Lourdes, to spend a few days exploring the rocks in the hills above the sanctuary and the narrow streets of the town. Even having Adrián in the picture wasn't the misfortune she'd feared – when she managed to forget he was Mónica's ex-husband.

But the day in Lourdes hadn't been a pilgrimage, it had been a complication. Tomorrow she had to straighten her spine and deal with Ben and the upcoming celebration of how terrible his first marriage had been – or at least she had to try to stop making it all about her.

The blessing she needed was *not* these little tingles of something with Adrián. But maybe some peace about Ben's marriage. Was that too much to hope for?

* * *

She regretted not getting the honeymoon suite later that evening when they returned to the grand stone hotel, now lit by streetlamps. The room was larger than the cheap chain hotel the airline had paid for, but there was barely a foot between the two single beds. She couldn't help remembering the night before, the way he'd watched her from across the pillow. It would also be the third night in a row when she'd gone to sleep thinking about seeing Ben the next day, of the unpleasantness of being the ex-wife at the wedding.

'Are you okay?' Adrián asked after he'd emerged from the bathroom – thankfully a comfortably large one so he'd had plenty of space to get dressed after his shower instead of coming out in a towel.

Jo's novel sat unopened in her lap and she realised she must have been staring into space – probably with a fierce frown. 'Yes,' she insisted.

'I'm sorry we have to put up with each other for another night, but at least there won't be any accidental hugging – not that I minded at all.' He cut himself off with a choke. He swiped a hand across his mouth that left his slightly unkempt beard askew. 'Just forget I said anything,' he muttered, turning back the covers of his bed. He climbed in and clicked off the main light in the room, leaving only the weak glow of the bedside lamp on Jo's side.

The window was open, but it was still uncomfortably warm and he kicked off the blanket as he rolled around, eventually settling on his side, facing away from her. His dark brown hair curled even more, slightly damp from the shower, and she wondered how often he cut it – and for a weak second, what it would feel like to bury her fingers in there. It was probably oily and coarse, but it didn't look that way.

The jut of his shoulder was an unexpectedly intimate view and all their conversations and shared glances from the day replayed in her mind. It should have been unbearable to be stuck with him, this overconfident distant acquaintance who, on top of everything, had a child with the woman Ben was marrying.

But as she slid down the pillow and stretched out, her legs pleasantly sore from all the walking and her mind chasing after new horizons, she admitted to herself that she was glad he was there.

'Did you seriously wish for happiness for Ben and Mónica at the grotto today?' she asked because she couldn't hold it in.

He stilled, obviously deciding whether to turn around and make this a real heart-to-heart. Jo should have taken the time to do the same.

'Yes,' he said with a sigh. 'But my heart wasn't really in it.'

Jo's breath whooshed out as his answer curled around her. 'Are *you* okay? With all the wedding stuff starting tomorrow?' she asked. 'How long have you two been divorced?'

'It's two years since we separated,' he answered. 'You know how long divorces take. What about you and Ben? You were already divorced that year in the PTA, right?'

'Yeah,' she said softly. 'We've been separated nearly five years.' But five years seemed to pass in the blink of an eye these days. 'Wonderful small talk, huh? It's not, "When's your birthday? What's your favourite colour?" Instead we have to talk about what went wrong in our marriages.'

'I think we're over small talk now that we've got stuck on the wrong side of the Pyrenees together, have shared a hotel room for two nights and accidentally went on a pilgrimage to the Grotto of the Apparitions.' He rolled over and she was almost scared to look at him, in case he was giving her one of those bottomless looks. But he wasn't. His gaze was on his hand, where a small indentation on the ring finger was still visible in the slanting shadows cast by Jo's bedside lamp.

Glancing at her own hand, she noticed dispassionately that all evidence of the wedding and engagement rings she'd worn for thirteen years had disappeared. Taking off a ring was all too easy.

'Do you know all of Mónica's family who'll be at this party?' she asked.

He nodded, his mouth twisting and making a caricature face with his beard. 'I tried to convince her I shouldn't come. I'm not expecting her family to treat me well. They didn't exactly bless our marriage and the divorce confirmed all their suspicions about me.'

'What's supposed to be wrong with you?' she asked.

'Oh, I'm from the big city, my work situation is unstable, I would put my own musical career before hers. "Adrián will cheat on you, querida,"' he parroted, his thick brow deeply furrowed. 'Plus we got a quick registry office marriage because we were moving to London.'

Jo knew she shouldn't ask, but she couldn't help it. 'Did you cheat?'

His gaze snapped to hers with that intensity she'd feared. 'No!' he insisted immediately. 'Because between trying to hold down a job while repeatedly collecting my kid from daycare because he kicked the nursery teacher and fitting in the occasional concert, I was really motivated to go out and find someone to have sex with! "Extra-marital" always sounded incredibly inconvenient to me when "marital" was already a big enough challenge!'

The hurt in his voice was audible, hidden as usual in sarcasm, but saying an affair would be inconvenient was different to denying that he'd thought about doing it.

That was Jo's own insecurities talking in a knee-jerk reaction to her biggest trigger, but it took her several long moments to convince herself to stand down. Adrián hadn't cheated, it wasn't fair to judge him for what Ben had done and she was trying not to make everything about her anyway.

'But isn't Mónica a performer too? A dancer?'

He nodded. 'With two performance careers, we were doomed from the start. She's an excellent dancer – and dance teacher, these days. She toured a lot with various flamenco groups when we were first married and is one of the most well-known bailaoras – flamenco dancers – in London. We moved because there was an opening at a dance school and she made a big success of it.'

'Did you play guitar for her?' The idea would have sounded romantic, except that the end of that story had already been written.

'That was how we met. We both toured Spain with different groups and ended up sharing the stage on several occasions. But

I'm not a flamenco guitarist. I can play a little, but I am classically trained.'

'You say that like I should understand the difference,' she commented.

'Surely you've heard of the great works for classical guitar? *Recuerdos de la Alhambra*? Vivaldi's concerto for guitar? *Concierto de Aranjuez*?'

She blinked, hearing only the rasp of his voice when he spoke Spanish.

'You are musical, though,' he insisted.

'I learned to sing pop songs and Broadway numbers when I was a teenager,' she answered wryly.

'Yes, exactly. You're musical. You'd like classical guitar music if you heard it.'

There was that overconfidence again. 'Even though it means you can't serenade me from the twin bed, I think it was a good thing you had to check your guitar as luggage. You wouldn't have been able to take it with us on the motorbikes,' she mused.

But before she'd even finished speaking, he shot upright in bed, his hair flying in his face. 'The guitar!' he murmured.

'Ben collected the luggage today. I told you that.'

'But did you double check that the guitar was among the items?'

'No, but—'

'I have to call Mónica!' Leaping out of bed, he grabbed his phone off the charger by the desk and frantically tapped in the code.

'Adrián, it's nearly eleven!'

'She'll be awake.'

'Yeah, but she might be—'

His gaze whipped to hers and Jo hadn't known it was possible to mutually gag until that moment. He put down his phone slowly, then snapped it up again. 'I'll send a message.'

Jo tried not to watch him, tried not to think about what Ben and Mónica might or might not be doing, but every direction her thoughts went was off-limits and she felt vaguely dizzy. It must have been the heat – or possibly the result of Adrián swanning around the hotel room in tight boxer briefs and a threadbare T-shirt that she knew was as soft as skin.

Off-limits. She'd hoped talking about their divorces would at least have banished the butterflies from her stomach. He flung himself restlessly back onto the bed, one arm above his head.

'Are you going to be able to sleep? I'm exhausted just watching you breathe.'

He glanced at her with an amused half-smile and the man had no right to be so attractive, the T-shirt riding up and his lips looking soft and lush beneath his moustache. 'I'm hoping she'll reply.'

'Why is that guitar so special to you?'

'It's a very expensive instrument,' he replied, 'made by a famous luthier from Seville.' Jo wasn't sure if she was imagining something he was leaving out, but she remained silent for a moment to prompt him. When a grimace crossed his face, she knew her hunch had been correct. 'Mónica's father gave it to me when we got married. He was a flamenco guitarist, but he damaged his wrist years ago and he can't play any more. He wants me to play that guitar at the wedding reception.'

'Ouch,' Jo responded after her initial gulp of sympathetic discomfort. 'I thought you said they didn't like you.'

'The less they like you, the more expensive the gift,' he explained with a shrug. 'I suppose they wanted to bind me to them – to Mónica. And they succeeded,' he said, his voice trailing off. 'It's a beautiful guitar – the sound is like no other I've ever played. I offered to give it back numerous times during the divorce, but they refused. I can't sell it because it's been in the family for years. Maybe Ben will want it,' he said with a laugh that was a little broken. 'A wedding present.'

'This is really screwed up,' Jo murmured and his eyes rose to hers again, that bubble of understanding growing familiar. 'But Ben doesn't know anything about music. He's just a corporate Human Resources guy.'

'The perfect husband for Mónica, then,' he said drily. 'Stable job to balance out her unpredictable commitments and lots of... resources.'

'I earn more than he does,' Jo said casually. 'It used to bug him, but he doesn't complain about the child support payments now. How lucky for him we got divorced. He'll have everything he wants after the wedding.'

She hoped he was too distracted to dwell on the bitterness in her voice. He was silent for a long moment and she looked up, wondering if he'd been distracted by something else. But he was giving her another of his looks.

'Jo...' His voice was low and rough.

'If you ask me if I'm still in love with him, I'll push you into the Peñíscola surf with your own guitar!' It was more complicated than that. 'Stop looking at me like that. I'm not going to run to the front of the church and stop the ceremony at that part where the priest asks if there is any impediment.'

Oh dear, she was a little too worked up about this, but at least she wasn't admiring the smooth lines of muscle in Adrián's arms any more.

Before she could announce that she was turning off the light, Adrián's phone beeped and he hopped up to grab it. When he grasped his hair in a fist and spat a string of harsh Spanish curses, she suspected his evening had just taken another turn for the worse.

'It's not there?' she asked carefully, with the unexpected urge to stroke her hand down his back to soothe him.

'No,' he said, his voice high with disbelief. 'They thought the guitar was with me! I told them... at least I thought I did. Joder,' he said fiercely, the foulness of the curse clear from his tone, even if she didn't understand the word. 'I've fucked up.'

Unable to stop herself, Jo got out of bed and haltingly grasped his arm, giving it an awkward squeeze. The action only seemed to shock him, so she snatched her fingers back. He buried his face in his hands, shaking his head.

'What am I going to do?'

7

'Did you sleep at all?'

Jo's pity was something else he couldn't take that morning. He'd been up since six phoning the airports in Lourdes and Zaragoza and Gatwick and the central customer service number for the airline. None of them had been able to tell him anything, although the man from the airline had promised to do some more searching and call him back.

One thing was certain: the guitar *wasn't* in Zaragoza. It was nine o'clock and they were outside the hotel with the Godspeed bikers, who were packing their saddle bags for the journey over the Pyrenees to a soundtrack of distant thunder and a backdrop of billowing clouds.

'I slept,' he lied. He'd probably had a few hours, but he'd rolled around a lot, his mind turning over with thoughts of the wedding, the guitar and Jo in the little shorts she'd bought to sleep in.

When that lock of blonde hair fell over her forehead, he wanted to smooth it away – and then cup her cheek and brush his thumb over the ring in her nose and maybe kiss her until her eyes glazed over. He should have been more surprised by how much he liked Joanna Watters, but he wasn't.

Although perhaps it wouldn't have been so clear to him how much he liked her if it wasn't also self-evident that nothing was going to happen between them. On the way to the nuptials of their exes, where their thoughts were consumed with the wellbeing of their children or the impending wedding from hell, it was enough of a miracle they'd developed such camaraderie – perhaps thanks to Our Lady of Lourdes. He didn't think the saints were concerned with whether he would get to kiss her or not.

The miracle they should be praying for was to stay dry as far as Zaragoza – and hopefully find his guitar when they arrived.

'I'm not quite sure how we will fit your bag, but I have some of these.' Georg held up a few bungee cords that didn't fill Adrián with confidence. At least Georg and Claudia and their gang had located some extra helmets. It had been no trouble, apparently, with so many biker-pilgrims in town. They'd also produced spare jackets with protective panels and Adrián was sweltering in his already.

Adrián had ridden a motorbike throughout music school in Madrid and Seville, although the engine of his had puttered rather than roared and he'd rarely been a passenger, but he swallowed his own nervousness for Jo's sake. Her frown grew deeper and deeper as she stowed her crumpled suit bag in one of Claudia's storage boxes. Her small rucksack seemed the more sensible option today, even though it had meant buying emergency clothes.

'This will be one of the most beautiful rides of my life,' Georg said cheerfully as Adrián climbed on between the German motor-cyclist and the trolley bag strapped to the back.

That part was definitely true, as they followed the river out of Lourdes, rumbling through a valley with views of wooded hills and the occasional glimpse of the taller mountains. After several towns that were little more than a cluster of houses with pitched roofs and pale blue shutters, plus a small grocer and a grand town hall, the road opened out before them and straight ahead rose the snowy peaks of the Pyrenees.

Buildings were sparse along the road; a handful of camping grounds, a chapel or two and a café and souvenir shop by a dark turquoise lake. It was a route full of soothing scenery – until the road narrowed and started to climb. The small group of motorbikes zoomed along the winding trail through a narrow valley, sometimes with a dramatic rock face on one side and a drop-off on the other. Stony crags ranged overhead, ominous under the grey sky.

The first set of hairpin curves made Adrián's stomach lurch and he hated to think how Jo was feeling. A drop of rain landed on his thigh. Due to late spring snow, there was still a dusting on the summits up ahead and he fought against a sense of doom that probably had more to do with their imminent arrival in Zaragoza than their slow progress into the mountains.

Did he even want to arrive? He needed to get to Oscar, but the day stuck in Lourdes had been a blessing. Perhaps this journey through the mountains would turn out to be too.

He almost believed his own reassurances when the sun briefly broke through the swelling clouds as they passed another lake, this one alpine aqua with forested slopes rising behind and a bright green meadow above. Soon after, they pulled into a little restaurant in a rustic chalet-style cabin for an early lunch. There was an inviting trail head nearby and the sound of the river rushing over the rocks. The temperature at that altitude was several degrees cooler than in the sweltering Lourdes and Adrián was glad of the motorcycle jacket.

Jo stumbled as she dismounted and she let him take her arm for a moment while she shook feeling back into her wobbly legs. She struggled with the fastening of her helmet and consented with a grunt when he offered to help. As he fumbled with the strap, she swallowed and he remembered how vulnerable she'd sounded the night before talking about Ben. Her ex-husband had obviously hurt her badly and there was another feeling he'd have to hide when they arrived: protectiveness, maybe a hint of jealousy.

When he tugged her helmet off and her hair fell around her face in limp waves, her eyes wide, he wondered for a moment whether she'd let him gather her into his arms. But she drew away with a deep sigh, glancing around the valley, her eyes fixing on the snowy slabs of rock up in the mountains ahead.

'Please tell me we're halfway there,' she said, her voice quavering.

'Not quite, but we'll be in Spain soon. Welcome home, hmm?' Georg said with a smile for Adrián. 'But first, our last French meal.'

The interior of the chalet restaurant was even more charming than the log-cabin exterior. One wall was packed full of local products for sale: jam and pickles, honey, wild tea and little tins of pâté. Untreated logs formed the internal walls while curtains in rich fabrics, embroidered with patterns, provided accents in red and blue and white. Add in the scent of coffee and Adrián thought he'd gone to heaven.

'Do you think they'll let me live here?' he murmured to Jo.

'You'd play the guitar for the cows every night to earn your board?' she joked in reply. He shared her grin, glad she seemed to be recovering.

As they lingered over enormous omelettes, a charcuterie board, fresh salad and then blueberry tartes and coffee, Adrián pushed away the sense of impending misfortune that intruded continually. It was a lovely meal in a beautiful location, with excellent company. In a little over two hours, he'd be reunited with Oscar. The sun was—

Actually, the sun had completely disappeared. When they returned to the bikes, the clouds felt close enough to touch and looked heavy with gloom. Georg assured them there wasn't much rain forecast and Adrián tuned out his thoughts about the unpredictability of the weather in the high mountains.

They pulled away from the restaurant as the first fat drops fell. Georg brought up the rear, trailing the rest of the group through little half-tunnels that protected the road from rockfalls, alongside a babbling stream, ever closer to the snow-caps and the mountain pass that would take them into Spain.

The landscape was wild and open, the peaks foreboding, especially when the cloud filled the valley with mist. The spatter of rain on his trousers grew stronger. A flash of lightning ripped through the sky without warning and Adrián flinched, wobbling the bike. A storm in the mountains was something to be taken seriously, but what could they do aside from keep going to reach the next town?

Slowing down, the motorcycles wound through the mist and the rain, their headlamps sending glowing rays ahead, illuminating the rocks and trees and one lone pony taking shelter in a thicket by a waterfall. Time slowed down for Adrián, his focus limited to the light and dark of the dim afternoon, the tipping motorcycle and the patter of rain on his helmet. It would have been better to stay in Lourdes or take the ten-hour train connection via Toulouse and Barcelona, even if it cost a week's salary.

Whatever happened to that blessing from Our Lady?

He'd barely finished that sour thought when a sudden bang and a lurch of the bike ripped him out of his complacency. Georg swerved with a shout and shock sliced through Adrián. Too fast for him to have any idea what was happening, he sensed only movement – whooshing in his ears, falling, a distant crunch, panic rising in his throat. And then only pain – so much pain.

'What?' he mumbled, but his own voice sounded distant. 'Oscar... guitar... Jo?' His mind was listing, his thoughts slippery, but he held onto that last word. Jo... She was somewhere in the present. He needed to stay in the present, not in the past with Mónica or the future with Oscar – the *present*.

Stay... conscious. Jo is here.

'Yes, I'm here,' he heard distantly. He felt as though a bubble had swallowed him and struggled against the fastening pulling tight under his chin. He could only move one arm, but the other managed to wrench the bubble away, to be replaced by cool hands on his head. 'Shhhh. Stay still. I've got you.'

The world began to come back into focus: the rain on his face, the dark sky above him, something hard and scratchy under him. He groaned, even the feel of gentle fingers in his hair not enough to banish the hazy black at the edge of his vision. 'It hurts!'

8

It took all of Jo's seventeen years of experience in parenting to stay calm and grapple with the situation rationally. Rain sluiced down her face, but she wasn't cold because her heart was pumping in double time. The contortions of Adrián's face struck panic through her. She didn't know what had happened, only that nothing *could* happen to Adrián right now. His son was waiting for him. He might never find that guitar. She might never find out – actually, she was currently discovering what it felt like to tangle her fingers in his hair, but it wasn't the context she'd pictured.

His beard was smooth under her thumb, his face familiar now after the past forty-eight hours.

'Shhh, it's all right,' she lied spectacularly, brushing his hair back from his face.

He groaned, squeezing his eyes shut, and Jo's heart forgot its usual rhythm. She gripped his jacket harder, too panicked to think of anything else to do, but he yelped in response, his hand flying to his shoulder, which only made him jerk and yelp again and spit a string of foul-sounding Spanish curse words.

'Fuuuuck,' he finished, his voice high. But the swearing cut through Jo's unfocused haze as she figured that he wouldn't be biting out curse words if he was about to die. He'd managed to tug off his own helmet and he was definitely fully conscious and lucid. She also couldn't see any blood.

After hearing a shout from behind them, Claudia had braked sharply, pulling to the side of the road just in time to see Adrián's trolley bag flying off the back of Georg's bike and skidding down the slope towards the stream, ripping open and haemorrhaging fabric. It had taken a moment too long to realise that Adrián himself lay at the side of the road, sprawled on his back, but when she'd noticed him, she'd thrown her leg over the back of Claudia's bike and sprinted over, scraping her knees as she dropped down beside him.

'Someone call the emergency services!' she hissed at Georg and Claudia, who seemed dazed themselves. Supporting Adrián's head, she tucked her backpack underneath and smoothed her hand down his chest in a silent instruction for him to stay still. 'Do you remember what happened?'

'No,' he said, ratcheting Jo's alarm up another level. 'I mean, I was conscious, but it was too quick. I just remember feeling like I was on a rollercoaster,' he said with a whimper.

His voice seemed to be returning to normal, although his breath was short. She settled her hand more firmly on his chest, glad to feel the rise and fall under her palm. 'Where does it hurt the most?'

'Shoulder,' he said with a grunt. 'Hurts like fuck.' He took a sharp breath against the pain, his brow low and twisted.

She looked up at Georg, relieved to see him on his phone. The other bikers drew around solemnly. 'Hang in there,' she murmured gently to Adrián. 'We're getting help.'

The moans escaping his lips were alarming and he clutched her wrist painfully. She calmed him as best she could, struck by the memories of soothing children with hugs when there was nothing else she could do. He turned towards her and settled his face into her side.

'No, there is no puncture that I can see,' she heard Georg say as he crouched down, the phone still at his ear. 'No blood. He is breathing, but he seems to be in pain.'

'Fucking understatement,' Adrián said through a groan.

'Uh, a lot of pain,' Georg corrected himself. 'Fifteen minutes? Okay, we're waiting. No, he's definitely breathing.' He turned to Jo. 'Pulse?' he asked.

She lifted her fingertips under his chin and immediately found the wild beat of Adrián's pulse. 'Racing,' she confirmed. She shared a look with Georg after he'd finished the call. 'Fifteen minutes seems quick.' For the middle of nowhere. The only other living thing she could see in this valley was a large, circling— eek, it was a vulture. She gulped and drew her arms more firmly around Adrián.

'This is terrible,' Georg said. 'That stone fell right in front of us and I had to stop suddenly.'

'It's... all right, Georg,' Adrián murmured. 'I'm glad you and the others aren't hurt.'

Those fifteen minutes were some of the longest of her life. The bikers moved the stone that had caused the accident, but all Jo could do was try to stop her legs going to sleep while she held Adrián still as he mumbled and grunted and yelped in turn. His face was red and she didn't want to think about internal bleeding or what she'd tell little Oscar if— It wasn't going to come to that.

She'd been watching out for an ambulance to come swerving up the road through the drizzle, but instead the thwack-thwack of helicopter rotor blades reached her ears. Then time sped up again as a team of rescuers jumped out and the doctor dropped down beside Adrián.

'A dislocated shoulder,' the doctor diagnosed after a quick assessment. Jo's lungs deflated like a bouncy castle at the end of the day. That didn't sound too bad. 'It hurts a lot?' the paramedic asked.

'Are you joking?' Adrián snapped. 'It's burning like the fires of hell!'

A hysterical laugh rose in her chest. He was going to be fine. A dislocated shoulder was a relatively minor injury. The shock was wearing off and he was already sounding more like himself, while she was a sluggish mess of post-adrenaline shock and relief.

Helping him shrug out of one sleeve of the jacket, the paramedic administered a painkiller. As Adrián calmed down, Jo melted even further in relief until she felt as though she were made of jelly. She was beginning to believe everything would be all right when the doctor said, 'I will try to put it back in, okay?'

'Sure!' Adrián said, too enthusiastically to be in his right mind.

'Madame, you hold his hand?'

Her heart rate wound right back up again as she gripped his hand, squeezing his forearm with her other one. The rescuers took up well-practised positions holding Adrián in place and with a move that looked more like a karate master vanquishing his enemy, the doctor pulled and twisted and manipulated Adrián's arm until he was wailing again despite the painkiller.

The paramedic murmured to the team in French, before rolling Adrián slightly and giving it one more shot until he was gasping in pain. Judging by the head-shaking and mutterings in French, it wasn't working.

'Jo?' he said pitifully, making her turn to him in dismay. 'Your fingernails are digging in,' he said between clenched teeth.

'Oh, sorry!'

The doctor stopped his torture and Jo sighed deeply, brushing the hair out of Adrián's sweaty face.

'This is a fun day out,' he said, meeting her gaze, his eyes not quite clear.

'He needs stronger anaesthesia, so we will immobilise him and try again at the hospital,' the doctor explained. 'Will you travel with your husband? Or do you need to return with the motorcycle?'

'I'll travel with him,' she answered immediately, without enough energy to explain that he wasn't her husband.

Claudia approached her, giving her arm a squeeze as they loaded Adrián onto a stretcher. 'Will you be all right? Should we meet you back in Lourdes? Are they taking you to Lourdes?'

'We will bring him to the hospital in Tarbes,' the doctor explained, but Jo had no idea where that was anyway and she was still recovering from the floods of adrenaline.

'You continue on, Claudia,' Jo said once she'd finally realised why they'd asked. 'Is the bike okay?'

Georg gave her a thumbs up from where he had righted the motorcycle and was inspecting a scratch on the saddle bags. Pressing the throttle, he nodded when the engine roared to life. The only victim had been Adrián and his poor trolley bag.

It might have been littering, but Jo didn't have the presence of mind to wander along the hill and collect his underwear while the helicopter waited. When she was ushered into the aircraft, she had no choice but to climb up and leave the case. Adrián still had his little shoulder bag of valuables – and Claudia would have to keep Jo's dress for the wedding. It was ugly anyway.

Claudia and Georg and the rest of the Godspeed bikers waved earnestly goodbye as the rotor blades started to spin and one of the rescuers slid the helicopter door closed.

'Ooh, that morphine's good stuff,' Adrián muttered emphatically.

* * *

She had no idea how she was supposed to explain to Liss and Dec that, rather than being en route to Zaragoza to support them at the strange family party tonight where no one spoke English, she was in a hospital in a place called Tarbes with the delirious ex-husband of their dad's bride beside her, shirtless, with his arm in a sling. She had at least ten messages on her phone, but she needed to call them to have any hope of them understanding.

She hated disturbing the quiet of the hospital room where Adrián was dozing after the trauma of having his shoulder popped back in, but she needed to call – everyone. Unfortunately, she knew who she needed to call first.

Adrián's phone had facial recognition, so she held the camera in front of his woozy face and told him to open his eyes – he was rather agreeable with his system pumped full of painkillers. She found Mónica's contact – with a profile picture of her holding her arms above her head in a flamenco pose, wearing a striking, frilly red dress that draped off one shoulder – and pressed the call button with a sigh.

'Adrián? ¡Por fin! ¿Dónde estás?' She said a lot more than that, but Jo only caught the agitation in her voice.

'Um, sorry, Mónica, it's Jo.'

'Who?'

That hurt. 'It's Jo. Joanna.' *Joanna Watters* – Watters, *like your fiancé!*

'Joanna?'

'I've not come back from the dead,' she snapped, but kept her voice to a mumble so Mónica wouldn't catch it.

'Why are you calling from Adrián's phone?'

'That's the thing,' she began, glancing at his resting face, his muscles occasionally twitching with discomfort. 'We're in hospital. There was an accident on the road.'

'Hospital where? The party is starting in two hours and I can't send someone to collect you.'

'We're not going to make it to the party,' Jo said clearly.

'But... you came all this— *Oscar!* Stop poking the dog!' She continued in muffled Spanish and Jo guessed she'd pulled the phone from her ear. 'Look, if Adrián doesn't want to see my family, then he doesn't have to come. He can just collect Oscar later. You too. I understand it might be a bit difficult for you both.'

Heat rushed up Jo's neck and out her ears until she felt like the head-exploding emoji. Ben had told her the party was important – almost more important than the wedding, because all of the family and friends from the close-knit neighbourhood where Mónica had grown up were invited. He'd said it would be strange if Jo wasn't there with the kids. Now Mónica was letting them off the hook – several weeks too late to change that fateful flight that had led to the worst two days of Jo's life where everything she'd tried to do had gone wrong.

'Mónica,' Jo cut her off. 'We're still in France. We're further away from Zaragoza than we were this morning.' She couldn't stifle a laugh at that realisation – and at the memory of Adrián pronouncing 'Zaragoza' with that Spanish lisp. 'Adrián hasn't been discharged yet and might have to stay overnight so we can't even arrive in time to *not* come to the party!'

'Adrián is hurt?' At least she seemed somewhat upset – finally.

'He dislocated his shoulder.'

There was a long silence where Jo imagined Mónica feeling sympathetic, but then she asked, 'Can he still play the guitar?'

'I think that's the least of his worries right now,' Jo grumbled. 'He's in a lot of pain.'

'But Adrián is only half a man without a guitar!'

'Considering his guitar has gone missing, you might have only half a man attending your wedding, then,' she snapped. 'Maybe you should look for another half a guitarist, since you seem to be perfectly able to quickly find other men!' Jo cringed, wishing she could reel those words back in. She wasn't sure what bothered her more: that she'd shown weakness to Mónica or that she was still so emotional about Ben's wedding. 'I just mean if you understood how awkward this situation is for us, perhaps you shouldn't have asked him to play.'

'I *do* know how awkward this is – when you meet my family, you might understand. But you and Adrián are part of this. I can't erase the past so I wanted to... integrate it.'

'Well, I'm sorry you can't integrate us tonight. We're in hospital in Tarbes and I don't know how or when we'll make it to Zaragoza.'

'But we're heading to the coast on Monday to prepare for the wedding. Weren't you going to travel with my brother?'

'I have no idea.' Jo had blocked out all plans except the most immediate. 'But the wedding's not for a week. I'm sure there aren't enough mishaps in the world to delay us that long.' More's the pity. 'I have to call my kids,' she said curtly.

'All right. I hope he feels better soon.'

'I'll pass that on.'

Jo had just buried her face in her hands when she heard Adrián's weak voice from beside her. 'Mónica?'

'She says she hopes you feel better soon.'

'You...' He lifted his good arm and groped clumsily for her. She reluctantly held her hand out to him and he took it, slipping his fingers between hers. She stared, her stomach churning with shame and regret and a protectiveness she'd rather not feel. It was his right hand, the one that still had the little indentation on the ring finger, and there was a brush of black hair on the back. But holding his fingers knotted with hers didn't feel wrong or strange. 'I'm so glad you're here,' he murmured.

He meant Mónica, right? He was delirious and he'd just said his ex-wife's name.

But then he continued, making all her hair stand on end. 'Joooooo-annnna,' he said on a sigh. 'You feel really good.'

9

'I'm sorry, Jo.' His muttered words were nowhere near enough to make up for the current situation, but there was nothing else he could do.

'"Thank you" will do better,' she said gently, her brow furrowed as she concentrated on the task at hand, which was unfortunately dressing him. Pulling an enormous black T-shirt bearing the words 'I'm not perfect, but I am French' out of a shopping bag, she snapped off the tag with her bare hands and held it up critically.

'Is that what size you think I am?' he asked mildly. '*And* I'm not French.'

'No, I didn't think you were size XL, but I didn't like the idea of squeezing you into size M with your arm in a sling.'

'Ah. You're right.'

'Sometimes that does happen.' She helped him undo the Velcro of the sling and take it off so she could slide the sleeve of the T-shirt up his arm. With one sleeve in place, she tugged the rest of the shirt gently over his head and he could slip his other arm in – all without moving his shoulder.

'Did the nurses teach you how to do that?' he asked.

'The nurses at King's College Hospital in London,' she said with a nod. 'Liss broke her arm when she was ten.'

'Well, I thank them, then. And you.'

She gave a shrug in response. 'I also didn't miss the fact that you're not French,' she said drily as she carefully closed the Velcro on the sling. The nurses in Tarbes had given them both instructions on that. 'But I didn't have much time and you needed underwear, too.'

'I hope you didn't choose extra-large for those as well.' He choked when he picked up the unintended implication of that. 'I mean... not tiny either.'

Her gaze flitted to the ceiling. 'Yes, I bought you tiny-penis-sized underwear. Mini-aubergine was the brand name. For goodness' sake, I guessed probably medium, but I didn't want them to be too small so I went with large. The size of your penis is probably the only thing I *don't* know about you now.'

'Hmm?'

She gestured to his shoulder bag. 'There were a lot of forms to fill in. It's nice to meet you, Juan Adrián Rivera Morales, birthday 15 February, forty-two years old, birthplace Madrid, Spain, resident of 21 Acreage Road, London, SE27 2HP. I can't believe your name is actually Juan.'

'The first part of my name. And you're all ready to steal my identity.'

Instead of laughing at his stupid joke, she gave a withering sigh. 'I liked you better when you were high on painkillers.'

Something in her tone triggered a distant memory. 'Did I... was I an idiot? I remember screaming a lot. Did I say something?'

She shook her head lightly, patting his chest with a faint smile. There were hollows under her eyes, her hair was limp and messy, but she was somehow more beautiful every time he looked at her.

'What's the matter?' she asked. 'Does it hurt? The hard stuff they gave you might be wearing off already.' She settled a hand on his good shoulder and peered at him. Her eyes were so lovely – shades of blue, with pale lashes and— Perhaps he was still feeling the effects of the drugs.

'The pain is okay,' he assured her.

It was disorienting to step out of the hospital into the evening light of a place he'd never seen in his life. After crossing a busy road, Jo led him up a suburban street, checking the directions on her phone.

'Let me know if you need a rest. The hotel is quite far, but there was nothing around here.'

'Jo, you've bought me clothes and dressed me, called my ex-wife, dealt with all the French bureaucracy and now you're leading me to a hotel. You can't do anything wrong right now. I will play Santa this year, if that's what you want. I owe you – probably more than I'll ever have the chance to repay.'

'I'll have to think of something,' she said, but there was a tightness around her mouth that made him think he'd touched a nerve. She seemed tense.

The walk to the hotel took over twenty minutes and when they passed a little fast-food van on a green with tables set out under two bushy horse chestnuts, a shared look was enough to confirm that they both wanted frites for dinner and they made a beeline for it.

'I know fine French restaurants are supposed to be the ultimate dining experience,' Jo said, licking a spot of burger sauce off her thumb, 'but these snack places are heaven.'

He had to agree, especially when he could almost see the stresses of the day falling from her shoulders. 'I don't want to eat a burger again if it's not a goat's cheese and honey burger,' he joked, laboriously lifting the bun one-handed and dipping his head to grab a bite before something fell out. 'Although I can't seem to eat it without embarrassing myself.'

She nabbed a morsel of goat's cheese from his paper plate and brought it to her lips. Ouch. Strange things happened to him when a woman had held his head in her lap while he was delirious with pain. His heart had migrated to his eyes.

'Adrián, you're looking at me weirdly again.'

He cleared his throat and tried to snap out of it. 'Sorry, I must be tired.'

'I've never seen you eat so slowly. The painkillers haven't upset your stomach?'

'No, it's just difficult with one hand,' he said dismissively, noticing that she'd finished her burger. His stomach *was* upset, but not from the painkillers. He was a bit green from the embarrassment of mooning over Jo on the night that his ex-wife was celebrating her upcoming marriage to someone else, while also making a mess at the table like a toddler.

'You've never heard of asking for help?'

'You've done so much already—' When she held his burger up, his words petered out and he had no choice but to take a careful bite. Jo snorted a laugh that almost made the tension bearable. He ended up with honey in his beard and a smear of goat's cheese on his nose, but he got through the burger much more quickly, finally batting her hand away and taking the last chunk when it was small enough to manage.

When he mopped up his face with a serviette and ran his fingers over his beard, he felt her eyes on him, but she looked away before he could begin to guess why.

The rest of the walk to the hotel was quiet. The suburban houses gave way to low-rise historic terraces with slate roofs and mansard windows, the streets lined with palms that gave him a stab of nostalgia.

But all he could think about was holding Jo's hand.

Arriving at the hotel, he said pointedly, 'I'll fill in the form,' when they walked up to the reception desk in the drab foyer. 'I'm right-handed and you've filled in enough forms today.' But he quickly realised he didn't know any of her personal information, whereas she knew all of his.

She picked up the pen to fill in her section and he peered over her shoulder to note her birthdate: 18 April. She was four years older than him. He hadn't thought it was quite so much, but that was because it obviously didn't matter whether she was older or younger.

'If I steal your identity, you'll at least have mine to fall back on?' she asked casually when she caught him looking.

'Just checking when I need to send you a singing card next year,' he joked, heading off in the direction of the rooms.

She eyed him. 'Are you trying to remind me about the PTA thing with the choir? I've been very good about the truce, you might have noticed, but I am still angry on behalf of the softball team. The choir had, what, five members? The softball team was the best in the county!'

'The choir would have had even fewer members if it was up to you and the PTA mafia. If they hadn't done well at that competition – that we paid for – the school might have cancelled them!'

'Like you cancelled Santa?'

Adrián couldn't tell if they were fighting or flirting, but his skin prickled. It was a nice prickle, a pleasant ripple of life over his nerve endings. 'I can't believe *you* didn't support the choir! You're a singer!' he said, suddenly making the connection.

'I *was* a singer.'

'Maybe because there wasn't a decent choir on offer at your primary school.'

'Are you breaking the truce? After I nursed you back to health?'

His lips twitched. They'd stopped walking. The number of their hotel room glinted silver behind her in the light of the kitschy wall sconces.

'Thank you for nursing me back to health,' he murmured, feeling lightheaded from the combination of banter, earnestness and the uncertainty in her eyes.

'You've already thanked me too many times,' she said in reply. 'I'm not a nurse. I'm not good at that stuff.'

'Which is exactly why I keep wanting to kiss you— I mean, *thank* you.' Phew, close call. Maybe she wouldn't notice.

Of course she'd noticed. Her eyes widened and her mouth dropped open, just enough for his thoughts to run away with themselves. 'You what?' She shook her head to clear it, which only swung her hair onto her cheek. He wanted his hand there.

'Eh, forget—'

Whoosh, his stomach dropped and then soared. Jo's lips. That was everything. Jo's lips – on his. *Wow*. She kissed him softly, gently, pulling away again quickly, but it was too fleeting. He lifted his good hand to her head and swept his mouth against hers. That was much better.

Sparks went off inside his brain. He couldn't have said how it happened, but her tongue nudged his and he was a second away from some kind of meltdown. Stepping closer – a move that pressed her into the door of their cheap hotel room – he tilted his head with a groan and came back for more – and more.

She fumbled for the key without tearing her mouth from his, contorting her arm to stick it into the reader, and then they tumbled into the room. He caught a glimpse of her closed eyes, felt her hand fist in his oversized shirt and marvelled that he felt rather drunk with all of these feelings roaring to life in him.

Then the heavy door fell shut with a click and threw the

cramped entryway into complete darkness. The sound of their lips breaking apart was audible in the empty silence, as were the shared gasps of breath.

He couldn't see her, but he could feel that she was there, only a foot away. 'What are we going to do about what just happened?' she asked in a whisper.

His thoughts flashed with a thousand terrible answers: forget everything else and tumble onto the bed; find out what the skin of your waist looks like; me on top; you on top; something wild and creative with nobody on top.

'Adrián? Are you still there or have you buggered off?'

'I'm still here,' he choked out. 'I'm just struggling to find an answer that's not "Let's just do it again".'

'Because it was probably a fluke, right, an amazing kiss? We don't really know each other. We were just teasing each other and emotional about... God, so much to be emotional about.'

At least she admitted it had been amazing. The rest he didn't like so much. 'I'm pretty sure it wasn't a fluke,' he said drily. 'But we can always test that theory.'

She gave him a playful shove, but it caught him on the shoulder and he yelped, whacking into a hard, poky object to his left and then jumping backwards into the door with a bang when he tried to extricate himself.

'Argh!' The throbbing in his shoulder flared up like a distress signal. She grabbed his shirt and for a second he wondered if she was trying to give him a hug and his hopeful other arm came around her.

But with a little click the lights in the room came on, glaring white to suit the generic hotel room. Adrián froze, realising his hand had landed on the little concave spot above her bottom and was rather happy there.

She'd just lifted her face to his, her eyes clouded – unfortunately not with unfettered desire – when the shrill sound of her ringtone sliced through the silence.

10

Sound normal – normal!

Jo swiped her hair up over her forehead, leaving her hand there to cool her skin, as she connected the call. 'Hey, sweetie.' *What are you up to? I just made out with a guy I didn't think I even liked and now I'm quietly freaking out.*

'Mum, I don't know what's going on! One of Mónica's cousins translated a dinner speech for us and apparently this is Dad and Mónica's first marriage? I thought it was hard for you to get a divorce, but now they're saying you guys weren't properly married? What does that even mean for Dec and me?'

Jo's stomach sank and the kiss was forgotten – an indication of how much her daughter's words cut right to her scars, that she could immediately stop ruminating about that kiss. The sounds of the party were raucous in the background: delighted voices and clinking cutlery – Spanish mealtimes. Ben's new family – Ben's *first* real in-laws? Although he hadn't told her about this specifically, a few little details now made more sense to her.

'We were legally married, Liss,' she assured her daughter. 'And legally divorced. I assume what they're talking about is a Catholic wedding. Your dad and I weren't married in a church. We had a civil ceremony. In the eyes of the Catholic church, that doesn't necessarily count. You know how Dad was baptised recently? He converted to Catholicism so he and Mónica could have a church wedding and it will be their first *Catholic* wedding, I suppose.'

Her gaze flew to Adrián, who stood white-faced, still in the cramped entryway of the hotel room. She wasn't sure if the pain in his shoulder was bad or if he was as incensed as she was about this loophole that could erase her from Ben's history.

That she sometimes wished she could erase Ben from her own history was beside the point.

'How are you so calm about this?' Liss continued. 'We were only invited as babysitters and to do the washing up and shell the *peas*! We're like the reject children. Mum, what if Dad and Mónica have another *child*? Can we move to Aruba or something because I'll never want to see him again in my entire life!'

Jo felt as though her own stomach acids were eating her insides. She hated being an adult in this situation, but it was clear she had to be. 'I'm not calm on the inside, sweetheart. But we'll get through it together. I wish I could give you a hug right now.' She glanced at Adrián again.

'I wish I was wherever you are and not at this stupid party,' Liss whined, as though she were five years younger. 'I just... need to talk. Dad always said that *you* left, but then why is he able to move on, pretend we don't exist, while you—'

Jo's involuntary choking sound might have tipped off her daughter to the implication of her words. 'It's never that simple. When I get there, we'll take a long walk and find an ice cream bar and talk for hours – not only about this, about everything. I love you so much, sweetheart, and I miss you.'

'Are you seriously still in France? Dad seemed to think you just decided you didn't want to come, like you planned this with Oscar's dad.'

Jo's anger flared afresh – completely impotent anger because imagining scenes of violence wasn't her style. 'I didn't plan a thing. I know it's difficult to believe, but all of this stuff happened and now we're stuck in a hotel room and—'

'We?' Shit, of course Liss wouldn't miss that little hint.

'We're stuck in a hotel,' she corrected, hating that she was hiding something from Liss but incapable of explaining that she had to monitor him for complications following the anaesthetic without somehow letting slip that this was their third night in a row sharing a room and she was getting used to it. 'The place is so Ikea. I could be anywhere in the world right now, except I just ate a raclette burger that changed my life.'

And fed a goat's cheese burger to a sinfully hot man with a smooth beard and a pair of lips she would be dreaming about tonight.

Liss sighed deeply. 'Do you think you'll make it here tomorrow?'

'Even if it costs two thousand euros, I'll hire a car and head for Spain. Assuming Adrián doesn't dislocate his other shoulder, we should be there.'

'Psst! Jo!'

She turned to find Adrián beckoning wildly with his good arm and mused that strapping one arm was like giving him half a muzzle. 'What?' she mouthed silently.

'Oscar! Can she put Oscar on? He'll still be at the party. We don't bother putting the children to bed in Spain. He'll just pass out on the floor later.'

'Um,' she began rather stupidly. 'Liss, I just remembered that Adrián really wanted to talk to Oscar, but Mónica was busy. Do you think you could put him on a video call? I'll just go knock on the door of his room,' she said with a wince.

Tiptoeing to the door, she tugged it open and slipped through, discovering the forgotten shopping bag full of clothes outside, where she'd dropped it to grab handfuls of Adrián's T-shirt and tug his mouth closer to hers.

'Yeah, okay. I've found him. Hey, your dad wants to speak to you.' Her daughter's words were a little gruff, but at least she hadn't made up an insulting nickname for the boy.

'Papá?'

Jo truly was a mess because that little voice set off a string of emotional fireworks inside her. Oscar was still so small – and Adrián so desperate to check on his son's wellbeing. Her reluctant comrade opened the door to continue this farce, his gaze hollow and agitated. But when he accepted the phone and peered into the camera, his eyes lit up and a smile stretched on his lips.

She had no idea what he was saying to his son in Spanish as he strode back into the room and flopped onto the bed, but his tone was that soft, rumbly one. He showed off his sling proudly and Oscar's oohs and aahs tugged a laugh up through Jo's chest.

'Does it hurt?' the little boy asked in English.

'Nohhhh,' Adrián insisted, but Jo could tell from the indentation in his forehead that he was putting on a brave face.

He continued to speak in animated Spanish, propping his good arm behind his head and looking so inviting that Jo had to force her gaze away. She came around the beds – carefully, because there wasn't much room – and stretched out on her own. When they began to run out of words – Jo remembered seven-year-olds were not accomplished conversationalists – she gathered Adrián was instructing Oscar to give the phone back to Liss and she realised she'd never heard him say her daughter's name. It struck her again how awkward their situation was with the new family about to be created after trampling on their old ones.

'Te quiero mucho, cariño,' he said, his voice rough. Jo ignored the goosebumps that crept up her arms listening to him tell his son he loved him. 'Uh, hi, Liss. Thank you for that. Do you need to talk some more to your mum?'

'Is that her behind you, lying on the bed? In your room?'

Jo jerked upright, an agitated hand flying to her hair.

'We, eh... She's very tired. She had to hold me down while the paramedics tried to shove my shoulder back in.'

'Ew.' Liss was thankfully easily distracted and Jo opened her mouth to ask for the phone back.

But then Adrián continued, 'Yep, that's your mum. She's like superwoman.'

Jo choked before she could get a word out and he chose that moment to plonk the phone back in her hand. Clearing her throat with a hacking cough, she forced a smile and waved at Liss. 'Love you! See you soon.'

For a moment, she wondered if Liss's bewildered expression would lead to more awkward questions, but her daughter just shrugged and returned the wave with a grumbled, 'I love you too.'

After Jo had ended the call, she turned to Adrián. 'Superwoman? What is wrong with you?'

'I was just trying to distract her,' he snapped. 'And as to what's wrong with me? My bone separated from my body today and had to be levered back into place while I was on drugs! I've lost my most valuable possession and I currently can't even dress myself without the help of someone who is basically a stranger. Meanwhile my son needs my emotional support, but I can't seem to get over the fucking border and my wife has decided we were never married!'

He flopped back into the pillows again and slung his good arm over his eyes.

'I'm sorry, Jo,' he said after a few breaths. 'It's not fair to take it out on you.'

'Because I'm basically a stranger?' She couldn't resist the jibe.

He peered out from under his arm. 'You said we don't know each other.'

Heat crept up her chest as she acknowledged his point. 'I just meant that this feeling that we know each other is artificial. We're... friends, maybe. Getting stranded together and joining forces – it's like they say at the end of *Speed* about tense situations and we're in the same boat with the wedding. But in everyday life?' *What would we be?* She couldn't bring herself to ask the question out loud. They couldn't be anything.

'Are you saying the kiss was so good because it was some kind of revenge against Mónica and Ben?'

'No!' she insisted immediately, but then frowned. 'At least I hope not. But how can anything *not* be about the wedding right now? You just called Mónica your wife and not your ex.'

His grimace was eloquent. 'I was just shocked about the Catholic wedding. Dios, her family must be so happy.' He eyed her. 'Did you have a big wedding?'

'It was a long time ago,' she deflected at first. 'But yes. I had an enormous frock that was suspiciously like Avril Lavigne's wedding dress, but she was sensible and got divorced three years later, whereas I faked it for ten years longer than that.'

'Faked it?'

Her hair stood on end and she hopped off the bed to rummage in the shopping bag for her new underwear. 'I need to go to sleep. Superwoman needs her rest.'

'Jo, I know this is none of my business, but... did Ben cheat on you?'

She collapsed back onto the bed, the knickers hanging from her limp hands. 'Do you really want me to go into this right now? It won't be pretty.'

'You don't have to,' he backtracked. 'But I wouldn't worry about not being pretty. You dressed me like a toddler today and held me while I screamed. I don't know if you even own any make-up because if you did it's in your luggage but—'

'Great, thanks for that.'

'I was going to say,' he paused for emphasis, 'that you're pretty anyway, without it. You were pretty with burger sauce on your chin. You were pretty when you scowled at the poor statue of Mary in the grotto and held your scepticism in a death grip.'

'Aren't you a bit sceptical now too?' she asked defensively, ignoring the ripples still flowing under her skin from his words. She wasn't *pretty*. She had a few wrinkles and a little grey hair that would be more noticeable if she weren't blonde. Young women who starred in romcoms were pretty, but she'd starred in *life*. 'After the blessing we received from Our Lady, we had bad weather and crashed and ended up even further away from our kids than we started.'

He cocked his head in agreement. 'I'm toying with the idea that everything happens for a reason.'

'I suppose missing the party is a positive,' she said faintly, her brain zeroing in on his nosy question again.

'I'm glad I... dislocated my shoulder then – for that.'

She eyed him. 'Don't say that. Maybe we should have just found a way out of this. They're not trying to hurt us on purpose. What Mónica told me about trying to integrate the past... she had a point. But it still *hurts*.'

'I hope not as badly as a dislocated shoulder,' he joked gently.

She glanced at him, appreciating that he was giving her an 'out', but she also remembered the night before, what he'd told her about the guitar in a defeated tone. He'd asked her a question. She didn't want to answer it, but she also didn't want him to wonder.

So she bit her lip and stared at the ceiling as she gathered her thoughts – and what remained of her pride. When she spoke, she was quite satisfied with the lack of emotion in her voice as she said, 'Yes, Ben cheated on me.'

11

Jo continued before Adrián had time to understand the heat of emotion that burned up his spine. 'I don't want to make it sound like he was a philanderer. It was only once – completely unpremeditated.'

'He just *accidentally* fell into bed with a woman who wasn't his wife?'

She gave him an irritated look, as though he wasn't allowed to defend her – or stop her defending Ben.

'You can't simplify these things,' she insisted. 'He even admitted everything to me in tears. He'd been away for work. We'd been busy – you know how family life gets. He begged me to forgive him and promised he'd never do it again – and he didn't.'

Adrián waited for the 'but'. He'd heard Liss say that Jo had been the one to leave, but it didn't feel anything like Mónica leaving him in exasperation, telling him their relationship wasn't worth the effort.

'I promised to try to move past it. In fact, if we'd just decided to pretend nothing had happened, we might still be married,' she mused. 'But he was too conscientious. He suggested we get counselling and it sounded like a sensible idea.'

'It wasn't?'

'No, it wasn't,' she said flatly. 'I mean counselling is an important action to take, but it... exposed a little more than we bargained for. We talked and talked and talked and achieved nothing except upsetting each other.'

'You hated it?'

That got her attention. The look she gave him was wary and injured and caught him in the guts. 'Loathed it,' she confirmed. 'Which was maybe what changed my thinking.' She dropped her chin into her hand, leaning her elbow on her knee. 'When Ben talked about what he valued in our relationship, I started to realise that I'd been playing a role all those years. Maybe it was my fault for being too scared to show him who I really was. As the mask slipped with the stresses of kids and life, I needed to drop the act, but he wanted me to keep the mask on. We did an exercise where we had to list the things we valued about each other and all of his were... wrong. He loved how much effort I put into things, how I smoothed over problems with the kids and how I could talk about politics and current affairs and how well I dealt with his *mother*. I'm proud of all that stuff, but it was all just *work*, things I did right because I had to do them right. He valued me because I made his life easier, not for... me.'

Adrián felt even more powerless than he had in hospital, letting her pull his shirt on because he couldn't do it himself. He and Mónica had argued and distrusted and resented each other, but Ben had ripped Jo's heart out – all the more violently because he hadn't intended to and she hadn't realised in time to protect herself.

'What did you want him to value?' he couldn't stop himself asking. Superwoman. She'd hated that description and now he understood why. He wasn't impressed by her because of everything she did, but because of the way she approached life. Her sense of humour. Her fierce sarcasm and fiercer protective streak.

'I suppose I wanted him to love me because of some of the things I do *wrong*. I wanted him to say he loved that I'm really bad at craft and I get frustrated when I have to do something with my hands. I wanted him to like me drunk and on the nights when I couldn't be bothered to shower.' She laughed, but he suspected she was crying inside – not that she would show him. He knew her well enough now to know that. 'I had an individual session with the counsellor and she encouraged me to consciously stop hiding my inadequacies, to let Ben see me and at first I really hoped *I* was the problem and all I had to do was be myself and let him love me.'

'Shit,' Adrián muttered, upset before she'd even finished talking.

'Yeah, it didn't work like that. He kept asking me what the matter with me was and when he brought it up in counselling he said I was manipulating his feelings on purpose. And I had to accept that I'd spent years of my life trying to please someone I wasn't capable of pleasing. The fact that he'd slept with someone else was a hint that I hadn't been enough for him for a while. When I stopped trying to please him, the marriage went downhill *very* quickly, but there was an element of relief. I have too much else to do to trick people into liking me.'

He thought back to when he'd first met Jo, the veteran vice-chair of the PTA. She'd stood up for what she believed and kept the meetings on track. He hoped she realised that her new attitude to pleasing others had been a boon for the people who knew her – who had the opportunity to truly get to know her now.

'You don't have to trick people into liking you,' he insisted. *I like you – a lot – even though we've been through enough to bring out the worst in each other.*

She smiled wistfully. 'I'm old enough to know that now – one of the best things about my forties. Not that I was ever so particular about this, but some women wax and laser and shave all the time, but...'

'You needed Ben to love you hairy,' he finished for her solemnly when she didn't seem capable of it.

She blinked at him. 'Is that supposed to be a joke?'

'I don't know,' he admitted. 'But he should have loved you hairy.'

'For better or worse, in sickness and in hair?' she said with a huff.

'As long as we both shall not shave?'

'Oh, shut up.'

'At least you are starting to understand Mónica's grounds for divorce,' he joked. 'And I'm the one who needs a shaver right now.' He stroked the annoying bristles on his neck. He hadn't tidied up his beard in nearly three days. But instead of smiling and sharing the joke, Jo frowned.

'If Mónica picked Ben, she obviously doesn't have very good taste.'

He was going to make a quip about Mónica choosing *him* first until the complexities of her statement caught up with him. 'Huh,' was all he said instead.

'I don't mean *you*. I mean *leaving*,' she qualified her statement. 'I mean if she left *you* then she can't know—' She swallowed. 'I'm going to get in the shower,' she said suddenly, shooting to her feet.

'I'm sorry I made you talk about all this,' he called after her.

She paused in the doorway of the tiny bathroom. 'No, I think I needed to. We can't escape the wedding much longer and my feelings are better out than in.' Leaning against the doorframe, she turned more fully back to him. 'I know I'm not supposed to care what other people think, but give me the damage: are you going to look with pity at this scorned wife or are you thinking of the pushy softball mum from the PTA who left her husband even though they were getting counselling?'

'To be honest, a bit of both,' he answered immediately, but rushed on before the fold between her eyebrows could deepen. 'But mainly when I look at you, I think of everything we've done over the past few days, how much we've laughed despite everything.' He paused and when he spoke again, his voice didn't quite sound like his own. 'Your hands holding me together when everything hurt and I was afraid, the sound of your singing voice. I hope we're friends, Jo. I'll be sad if we're not.'

'You're a smooth talker,' she accused quietly.

'Maybe, but I'm telling the truth,' he insisted.

'Well then, you're a smooth talker, my friend.'

His smile stretched as she disappeared into the bathroom and closed the door. *Friends.* He was glad to earn the title. He was glad she cared what he thought. He just had to convince her that his friendship was offered freely – hairy or not – but the kissing probably hadn't helped that cause.

With Mónica and Ben waiting for them in Zaragoza, kissing definitely wasn't a constructive activity.

* * *

'I'm sorry, it's not possible to return the car in Zaragoza.'

'What do you mean, "not possible"? I'm prepared to pay the one-way fee *and* the fee to drive the car outside of the country. I realise it will be very expensive. I checked online and it quoted me €1,200.'

Adrián gulped and then choked on his own breath, pressing his good hand to his chest and coughing to clear it. *How much?* Jo sent him a distracted glance, but she was too busy dealing with the hire car company at the airport – the Tarbes Lourdes Pyrenees airport, where this cursed journey had begun three nights ago.

'That might be the case, but I can't offer you a car today for that journey. Our bookings won't allow it, I'm sorry. Perhaps a larger location? I could phone Toulouse for you.'

'Toulouse?' Jo's voice rose up at the end. 'By the time we get there and collect a car, we may as well circumnavigate the entire Pyrenees!'

'That could be another option,' the saleswoman said kindly, not realising Jo was being sarcastic.

'Where are all the minibus pilgrims when you need them?' she muttered to herself. 'We'll try somewhere else, thank you.'

'Do you think we could try somewhere for coffee first?' he dared to ask after she'd taken a couple of fuming steps away from the desk and breathed out once, sharply.

'Our kids are waiting for us and all you can think about is coffee?'

'Not *all*. But I can drink it fast. And my shoulder hurts.'

'Is the caffeine supposed to help with that or are you just using your injury as leverage?'

'I need liquid to take my ibuprofen,' he explained, heading for the only café in the tiny terminal and hoping he'd softened her into following him.

When they reached the drab seating area under the institutional airport lighting, she pushed him into a chair and thrust her water bottle into his hands. 'Take your tablets. I'll get the coffee.'

'But this is your—'

'You're worried about my germs *now*?'

His gaze swerved to her mouth and his memory fired rather pleasantly. 'I'll share germs if you will,' he muttered.

She turned away quickly, fluffing her hair in an agitated manner. Her clothes were rumpled from wearing them for too many days and her hair unkempt from their quick departure that morning, but Adrián watched her progress towards the bar with a smile. Waking up barely able to move his arm, with a dull ache throbbing despite the dose of ibuprofen he'd taken through the night, had been much more pleasant when her concerned face had appeared above him and she'd asked if he was all right.

'Jo!' he called after her. 'Milk and lots of sugar!' She replied with a dismissive nod as though she would have guessed correctly. 'And maybe a croissant!'

She returned with two coffees, a croissant and a pain au chocolat and two ham and cheese baguettes. Collapsing into the chair opposite him, she took a slug of her coffee.

'I'm sorry I made us leave so early this morning. We could have taken the time to get some breakfast and you have to tell me if you need a rest.'

'Wow, the caffeine kicked in quickly,' he joked.

'If you're trying to stop me being grumpy, that is not the way to go about it,' she replied through gritted teeth. 'Pick a pastry. I don't care which one I have.'

'Jo,' he began, waiting until she glanced at him. 'You're allowed to be grumpy. I'm grumpy! We're back at this stupid airport we never wanted to arrive at in the first place! I want to see my son too, but I also wanted coffee. Twenty minutes won't hurt.'

She stared at him for a moment, holding her cup between both hands. Then she snorted a laugh. 'You're right. And if we turn up this grumpy, they might revoke our wedding invitations.'

'Really?' he asked with mock enthusiasm.

'You definitely can't play guitar any more, anyway.'

As if on cue, his shoulder spasmed and his chest tightened and he thought of the lost guitar – and his strapped shoulder. *You can't play guitar any more.* She hadn't meant forever, but for a second, the panic had struck him. His fingers were suddenly restless.

'Shit, I'm sorry, Adrián,' she muttered. 'I know you're upset about the guitar.'

'It's okay. I'll call the airline again after breakfast. Are you sure you don't have a pastry preference?'

'Pick one!'

He couldn't argue with that tone, so he dragged the pain au chocolat sheepishly in his direction. He was about to take a bite when his phone rang. Assuming it was Mónica, he tugged it out in a hurry, only to see a UK number flash up.

As he answered, Jo's phone rang too and they shared a glance, food and coffee waiting between them. When he realised his call was from the airline, he ignored everything else, hoping for good news.

It wasn't what he'd expected. 'Mr Rivera, the item of luggage you registered as missing has been located, but unfortunately it didn't make it onto your flight.'

'That might be a blessing at this stage,' he grumbled.

'It's our policy that when an item misses loading onto a flight that isn't scheduled daily, it is sent on the next flight within courier distance. That's what happened here, but it wasn't recorded correctly in the system so it took me a few days to track it down.'

'Okay. I appreciate it. But where is the item now?'

'It's waiting to be couriered to Zaragoza and should arrive on Monday.'

'Monday!' he repeated stupidly. 'That's too late! I'm leaving Zaragoza on Monday.' If he ever arrived there in the first place.

'Perhaps they could courier the item to an alternative address?'

'An alternative address?' he parroted again, his vision tunnelling as he pictured the valuable guitar being thrown into a courier's van and then delivered to a clueless receptionist at the hotel at the beach town where the wedding would take place – if it even arrived safely. 'But... where is it *now*?'

'It's at the Girona-Costa Brava airport.'

12

'We are *not* going to Girona!'

'Hear me out, Jo. It's the perfect solution.'

Gargh, just when she'd started tolerating his company! 'There is nothing *perfect* about this situation, especially not your hare-brained idea to go in the opposite direction from where our kids are!'

'I know, that's the only slightly inconvenient part of this.'

'Going around one of the major mountain ranges in Europe instead of over it is "slightly inconvenient"?'

'Firstly, we wouldn't have to hire a car, because there's a connection—'

'We still have to hire a car,' she grumbled. 'That's what Ben was calling me about.'

'What's happened now?'

'Mónica's aunt María has broken her toe and she can't drive at the moment. That means one less car is driving to the coast.'

'Aunt María Rosa or Aunt María Dolores?'

'It could have been Aunt Mary Magdalen for all I know! Apparently Liss told him we were hiring a car and he thought that meant we could drive all the way to Peniscola. Another man with a *perfect* solution who hasn't thought things through.'

'It's... Peñíscola,' he corrected her with a frown. 'It has nothing to do with penises. But this makes *my* solution even more perfect.'

'"Perfect" is an absolute adjective. "More perfect" doesn't exist,' she snapped.

'It's Saturday – ten o'clock,' he said, glancing at his watch. 'If we hire a car from Toulouse – for over *one thousand* euros – we would arrive late this evening at best and my guitar maybe never. As you've realised, I can't drive with my arm in a sling. It's 400 kilometres from Toulouse to Zaragoza – over the Pyrenees.'

'I promised Liss,' she protested, but she suspected Adrián saw how daunted she was at the prospect of the long, mountainous drive in a hire car.

'Your daughter is what? Fifteen? She'll understand.'

'She's seventeen, but that's old enough to value a promise!'

'Well, maybe that's another detail that is less than perfect, but the headline is, arriving in Zaragoza today will be a huge – dare I say *superhuman* – effort. The other option is we arrive tomorrow – Sunday.'

'I know what tomorrow is.'

'And only one day later we have to go to the coast anyway. Why don't we go to Girona today – on the nice, relaxing TGV train – pick up my guitar and then travel directly to Peñíscola on Sunday. Save money. Save hours of driving. I get my guitar back. We see the kids only one day later.'

She crossed her arms with an inarticulate grumble, hoping he didn't realise she was running out of complications to throw in his face. 'What about Oscar?'

Adrián's face fell and she almost regretted bursting his bubble. 'Fine. Nothing about this situation is perfect, but if we have to pick a set of problems, I'd pick Girona. I can't drive anyway. If you weren't here…'

Asking herself what she'd do if he weren't here made Jo's thoughts spin. She liked travelling alone and had a book in her bag she'd barely opened. She could have sat in peaceful silence – and continued on to Zaragoza with Godspeed. What concerned her was that the prospect didn't sound as appealing as it should have.

'You're not seriously going to play the guitar at the wedding, are you?' she deflected.

He shrugged, which resulted in a grimace of pain. 'By the time the wedding comes around, it will be a week since the crash. The doctor said I should move it when the pain has lessened and the exercises she showed me even look a little like holding the neck of the guitar.'

'Adrián!' she groaned. 'You have the perfect excuse not to play – even if we go and collect the guitar.'

His gaze rose to hers with a sheen of eagerness that suggested he'd worked out she was about to agree to his crazy plan. She wasn't ready to accept that fact herself yet, although his puppy-dog eyes helped.

'I know the situation is uncomfortable, but I'd rather be at the wedding with a guitar to play than just… at the wedding. I mean, for you I'm sure it'll be fine—'

'It's *not* going to be fine – and it's not perfect. But we do what we have to do, I suppose. I only hope we actually make it to Spain this time.'

* * *

Jo didn't recognise France – or her life – that afternoon when every train ran on time, the air-conditioning worked, there were no accidents or strikes and Adrián managed to reserve seats facing forwards. She even used the free WiFi between Toulouse and Narbonne to talk to the kids.

Liss had been surprisingly understanding about the next delay. Ben had agreed that she and Dec needn't come on the family outing to a restaurant in the wilderness somewhere on Sunday and she was in a good mood at the prospect of a day on the sofa with her phone.

The only slight hiccough was the next phone call from the airline in the missing guitar saga. The office where they could collect it wasn't open on Sundays, meaning they would have to spend two nights in Girona. Jo was struggling to resent that.

Adrián appeared to have an uncanny ability to fall asleep within minutes of nestling down in a train seat and the hours flew by with pages read, blank gazes out of the window at the passing towns and a couple of passable coffees.

They had an hour in Narbonne to wander the warm stone streets – baking in the evening sun – and find something to eat. It was noticeably hotter now they'd almost reached the Mediterranean – still over thirty degrees at seven o'clock. Jo couldn't face steak or noodles or a kebab in the heat and when they found a little brasserie that offered takeaway in a hurry, she was delighted with her salade niçoise, although Adrián made a joke about the name of the brasserie: La Bonne Excuse.

'Don't show anyone from the wedding or they'll think we came here on purpose.'

It was completely irrational, but her nerves multiplied as they waited on the platform for the train that would take them over the border.

'Do you think Spain has erected a kind of forcefield to keep us out for our own good?' she asked, scrunching up her nose.

'We're about to find out,' was all Adrián said in response.

But the train pulled out on time, slipped into a tunnel after

Perpignan and emerged without incident on the other side. Her phone beeped with the 'Welcome to Spain' message and Jo's stomach swooped. She'd been so focused on Zaragoza and the kids, but now they were getting closer to the *wedding* venue.

Surely something would go wrong before they got there. She'd been thinking along the lines of a train failure or a riotous demonstration closing the line, but she'd never expected her next surprise to come from Adrián himself.

As the conductor announced their approach to Figueres, the stop before Girona, he stood and slipped his shoulder bag over his head one-handed. She didn't think she was imagining the spots of colour on his cheeks. Instead of giving him the satisfaction of asking, she just prompted him with a look.

'We have to get off,' he said curtly.

She raised her eyebrows.

'I only booked us tickets as far as Figueres.'

Swallowing an outburst of frustration, the emotion vibrated out through her clenched jaw and stiff arms crossed over her chest. She mustn't have been in her right mind last night when they'd kissed. She must have imagined the heat of it, the *rightness*. She dropped her chin and eyed him darkly.

'Someone is picking us up from the station,' he mumbled.

'I don't want to know who, do I?' she finally asked.

'Probably not,' Adrián said, his voice high.

'If it's your mum, I think I've come down with a horrible illness and you won't want to expose her.'

'I think it's a little late to worry about exposure,' he said with an infuriatingly straight face, a quick bite of his lip the only hint of what he was talking about. But that little nip was enough to send a flush up Jo's neck. Could he tell she'd just been thinking about the kiss too?

The train stopped, leaving Jo off balance – both physically and figuratively – and she rushed to shove her book into her backpack and grab the shopping bag that contained the rest of their things to scramble after Adrián.

'*Is* it your mum?' she confronted him as soon as they were on the platform. She tugged at her trendy T-shirt, which seemed to stick to her skin immediately in the sudden heat.

'It's not my mum,' he mumbled in reply.

That's when she heard the booming shout from along the platform: 'Adrián! Gordito!' An older man with a broad smile, deep, crescent-shaped dimples and a comb-over continued speaking in Spanish and held up his arms as though Adrián would run into them.

'Your *dad*?' Jo asked between clenched teeth.

'No,' Adrián assured her, 'although perhaps a father figure. I don't even know if he speaks English.'

'Not speak English?' the man cried. 'I, who played concerts in New York and Chicago and Milwaukee.' He pronounced the city 'Tchicago', rather ruining the effect of his mock-offence. '*Adrián!*' he said again, with feeling, as he folded the younger man in a hug that appeared to cut off his air supply.

The hug also caught Adrián's shoulder, making him gasp in pain and extricate himself apologetically. 'Thanks for collecting us,' he said. 'Where's Esther?'

The older man's face transformed, the smile dropping away. 'She... passed on. Is it really so long since we've been in contact? She's been gone nearly two years.'

'Dios, I'm sorry, Carles.' Adrián's expression was stricken. 'Oh, God, if I'd known—'

'London is further away than you think, hmm? Come, introduce me to your girlfriend.'

Adrián looked genuinely upset, so Jo stepped forward to make one of the most awkward introductions of her life. 'I'm Joanna – Jo. I'm not Adrián's girlfriend, though. We're just...'

Adrián said, 'Travelling together,' at the same moment that Jo said, 'Friends,' and they eyed each other. With a sigh, he explained, 'Jo is the ex-wife of Mónica's fiancé,' and Jo realised there was no end to the potential awkwardness of this conversation. She was going to kill him.

'Dios mío,' the older man muttered. 'I need a drink just hearing that. I'm Adrián's maestro de música. I taught him everything he knows! Except for what he learned at the conservatorio in Seville.' He slapped Adrián on the shoulder, which made him wince again, even though it had been his right shoulder. Jo suspected if it had been his left, the shoulder would have popped out again. 'Let's go home.'

Leaning heavily on a cane, the man Adrián had called Carles led them to a little Volkswagen parked in a spot for people with disabilities. Jo noticed Adrián's brow creasing with concern. She wondered where 'home' was and what they would find there, glancing longingly at the run-down hotel near the isolated train station.

'Carles *was* my music teacher for many years in Madrid,' Adrián explained after they'd got in, the car boot unnecessary as they had so little with them. 'And after I graduated, he invited me on tour with him several times – although not as far as New York or Chicago. After about ten years, I was allowed to call him Carles instead of profe.'

They skirted Figueres in the evening sun, the air-conditioning in the little car struggling to make a dent in the humidity, and Jo had a sudden pang for the Pyrenees as she mopped her brow with the heel of her hand. When they left the city behind, the landscape was dry and scrubby and terracotta, with palm trees and white-washed houses, baking in the June heatwave.

The contrast with the little chalet restaurant in the Pyrenees – had that really only been yesterday? – was stark. In other circumstances, Jo would have soaked up the views of the hills and half-grown cornfields and the endless sky. She had no idea where she was, only that she was looking forward to being a rude guest and going to bed early, but that would be Adrián's fault anyway, so she tried not to feel guilty about it.

Turning off the main road, the houses and factories and greenhouses grew scarcer, the wilderness of the landscape broken only by the occasional silver olive grove. The hairpin curves brought back memories of the accident, but the warm colours and heavy heat chased them away again.

The road followed a high ridge and, at a break in the hills, a long, wide view opened out on the right, making Jo gasp and press her nose to the window. Framed by green hills and the sky was a town of orange and glinting white, rambling down to the sea, dusky mountains in the distance. The flash of the town disappeared again just as quickly as it had appeared, leaving Jo with the impression of a dark blue sea, so vivid the colour still shone behind her eyes.

Feeling Adrián's gaze, she looked up to find him turned in his seat, watching her with half a smile. 'Welcome to the Costa Brava,' he said softly.

13

'Share a brandy with me! No? Anis? Herbero? Tomorrow we'll have sangria together, but tonight I am alone and not as mobile as I used to be.'

Adrián turned sharply to his old mentor at that admission. He shouldn't look so old, should he? It was too early for him to lose mobility. He was only... seventy-something. Adrián grimaced as he appreciated how much older everyone had grown when, in his mind, no time passed in Spain while he was in London.

But he was torn, stealing glances in the direction of the corridor where the two guest rooms were located. Jo had disappeared through hers twenty minutes ago, emerging only to pad barefoot to the guest bathroom. She was angry with him and he appreciated why. He'd tricked her into coming along to this reunion. He only hoped she would forgive him.

'A cigar? Share a cigar with me, gordito. I'm not supposed to have them any more.'

'I don't think you were ever supposed to have them,' he pointed out. 'And you definitely weren't supposed to give me a taste for them.'

A door creaked open and the sound of Jo's muted footsteps reached them before the door to her room clapped firmly shut. Adrián peered down the hall again, wondering if she was comfortable.

'I was sorry to hear about Mónica. She didn't know what she wanted after all, hmm?'

'Something like that,' Adrián mumbled, clenching his good hand into a fist. 'It turned out we didn't have what you and Esther had.'

'Ah,' Carles said with a pained smile that made Adrián regret saying anything. 'She was a saint to put up with me for so many years.'

'She was a saint,' he agreed.

'I only hope she's found someone to gossip with in heaven. She could blabber like a marathon runner,' he murmured with a smile. 'Drove me crazy.'

Adrián frowned, distracted by the fact that marathon runners weren't usually the most talkative sportspeople, but also wondering whether he'd ever heard Carles say anything less-than-glowing about his late wife. He managed a nod and a mumbled platitude that Carles flapped away with his hand.

'How are you... getting on then, here all on your own?'

He gave a shrug. 'My family is close. My niece comes to prepare food and clean for me – the angel. You remember my niece, Mercedes? She never married, so now she's a blessing to me.'

'I just remember you telling me not to talk to her in case her father got worried about a single man from outside the community showing interest in her.'

'Ah, well, nothing to worry about this time, eh?' Carles said with a meaningful glance in the direction of the guest rooms.

'Oh, noooo,' Adrián rasped, but snapped his mouth shut when

he wasn't sure how to respond. 'I mean, I'm just a run-down, stressed-out father. No time for thinking about romance.'

'You can't fool me, Adrián. There's something going on with you and Jo.'

Adrián couldn't resist a twitch of a smile. If he couldn't fool Carles, then he had to admit it. 'Something,' he confirmed quietly. 'But not much. She doesn't like me.' Especially now he'd dragged her to his mentor's house instead of letting her relax on her own in a hotel.

'Go,' Carles said gently. 'I've invited my family tomorrow after siesta. You should rest tonight – unless you want to get a glimpse of the beach before you go to bed.'

Adrián blinked for a moment, wondering if Carles was giving him a hint or if it was his own desires producing the romantic image of him and Jo staring out over the water, her head on his shoulder – not that that would happen, given the scowls she had justifiably been sending his way since they got off the train. But Adrián rose and patted Carles on the arm in a fond goodnight.

'I always sleep late these days,' his former teacher called after him. 'Merce will be here to make breakfast for you and Jo in the morning.'

'Thank you, profe,' he said with a smile.

'I'm just glad you still know you're not allowed to come to this part of the world without staying in my guest room. You remember the path?'

The old man was definitely giving him a hint and Adrián was keen enough to take it without question. 'I remember,' he assured Carles.

When he stood outside Jo's door, he hesitated. What could she possibly want from him? Mónica had only found him satisfactory when he had a guitar in his hands, but Jo didn't even appreciate that – to say nothing of the fact that his guitar was still one hundred kilometres away and his arm was in a sling anyway.

But she'd gasped at their first glimpse of the ocean from the car. She might not want him, but the sky was still light at this time of year. He knocked.

After several moments of rustling and more quiet footsteps, the door opened to reveal Jo in her reading glasses, wearing the same shirt, but the little shorts from Lourdes instead of her cropped trousers. He bit his lip to stop a smile. Her expression wasn't exactly annoyed, but clearly expectant. It wasn't the time to appreciate how inviting she looked.

'Oh, you need help with your shirt!' she exclaimed, tugging off her glasses and setting them on the dresser. 'Here.' She lifted her hands.

'Actually,' he forced himself to begin. 'I wanted to apologise – and show you something. Will you come with me?'

Her expression clouded and he wondered if he'd done the wrong thing, opening this topic again when she'd seemed keen to bury her annoyance. 'More surprises?'

'Not a surprise,' he said with a wince. 'Now you're here, I want to show you the beach. It's ten minutes' walk.'

'So close?' she responded. With a sigh, she nodded and retrieved a pair of socks and her sneakers. 'What I wouldn't give for my sandals right now. It almost makes me look forward to arriving in Penis-town.'

As she followed him onto the walled terrace and out of the gate to the dusty road, he could barely believe she'd agreed to come, but her smile at the view of the ocean suggested it had been the attraction of the sea rather than his company that had tempted her out of her room.

Carles's house was run-down and not large, but the location

made it magic: up in the hills amongst the scrub, with coastline in three directions. Above the orange rooftiles of the neighbour's house stretched the dark blue sea, shimmering in the low rays of the evening sun.

'We can go into Cadaqués tomorrow morning, but there's a little bay not far from here. You can get there by road, but the footpath has nicer views. It has to be somewhere... there!'

'Have you come here many times?' she asked.

'Not many – a few. Carles only bought this house fifteen years ago. His family lives in the area and nothing is more important to him than his family.'

'His kids?' she clarified.

Adrián shook his head. 'Carles and Esther never had kids – but brothers and sisters and cousins and all of their families.' He realised guiltily that she would meet them all – unless he gave her a way out. 'To make everything worse before I apologise, I should warn you that Carles has invited everyone over tomorrow. I will help you find an excuse if you don't want to come to a giant family party. Carles is from the Roma community, so it will be... a real party.'

Her brow knit. 'I suppose I should be thankful that you're telling me in advance this time,' she grumbled. Tripping over a stone, she shook herself. 'There's no point in being annoyed, I realise. And I don't know what kind of grand apology you had planned, but you can probably save it. I'm a bit mad, but I'll get over it.'

He studied her. 'You're allowed to be mad. I should have asked Carles to take you to a hotel. You don't have the same duty to stay with him that I do. I just—' He paused, not sure how to continue.

'Wow,' she muttered under her breath, stopping abruptly. The path took a sharp turn here, but straight ahead was the rocky coast-line, the sea breaking against jagged stone, shining in innumerable shades of blue: pale in the shallows, with gradients out to the deep Mediterranean.

'Watch your step,' he warned her, throwing out his good arm.

'Gosh, this is... wow.' A starling swooped over the bay and Jo's eyes followed its progress. Her gaze moved slowly over the coastline, over the space of several breaths. Her hair lifted in the light breeze and the sun glinted off her array of earrings.

'Come down to the water,' he suggested, holding out his hand before remembering she was mad at him and they weren't supposed to be holding hands anyway. He dropped it again when all she did was glance at it warily.

She trailed him silently down to the inlet with a small rocky beach at the apex. 'Don't you fall either,' she called. 'I don't want to have to take you to hospital again.'

'My dad used to say, "I'm not taking you to la Princesa," when we were doing something dangerous,' he told her with a faint smile. 'That's a hospital in Madrid.'

'I hope he was joking – and that you knew he was joking,' she commented. 'Empty threats like that are such a parenting pitfall.'

'Oh, God, you're right,' he replied, thinking of Oscar and his outbursts and stubborn idiosyncrasies. 'Threats rarely work with Oscar anyway. The number of times I tried to send him to his room as punishment, but he just refused to go and I couldn't carry him there and throw him in.'

He only heard her hesitant footsteps behind him and the warble of a nightingale overhead. Then she asked, 'Did you find anything that does work?'

'Not "work" exactly,' he explained with a shrug. 'But I know I have to take a lot of time – I have to give him time, wait for him, and stay with him, remind myself a thousand times that he's not doing it on purpose. That *helps* – it doesn't work.'

The pang that struck him was unexpectedly strong. He should

have held Oscar in a hug several days ago. He should be there to show Mónica's family how to treasure him.

'We'll reach them on Monday,' Jo said from surprisingly close behind him.

He turned to give her some sort of smile in thanks, because he was feeling too much to say anything: guilt, love, homesickness for those little arms, another dose of guilt. She must have seen something in his expression because she reached out and took his hand before urging him towards the beach.

Staring dumbly at the rather sweaty clutch of their hands, he wondered what was going on here. Was she still mad? Had he even properly apologised? '*You* wouldn't threaten not to take your children to hospital,' he mused aloud. 'You even said you didn't want to have to take me – but you would, if you had to.'

'Of course I would, Adrián.'

'Even though I repaid you for looking after me by tricking you into coming here?'

She dropped his hand, her steps crunching over the shingle to the water's edge. Tugging off her sneakers and socks, she sank her feet into the water and sighed. 'Why didn't you just tell me there was a beautiful beach here? That's why you wanted me to come, right? To show me this? It's hard to stay mad when the water is lapping at my feet and we have all day tomorrow to explore. You have no idea how long it's been since I've had a holiday.'

He watched the starling playing in the evening updrafts and considered his words carefully. It might be helpful for her to assume those had been his motives, but he'd learned his lesson that day about being honest with Jo.

'Actually, it's not the reason,' he said under his breath.

'Hmm?'

'I didn't want you to go to a hotel. I wanted you to stay with me –

to introduce you to Carles, walk to the beach with you, eat breakfast tomorrow morning. I thought if I told you where we were going, you'd refuse to come and that would be it: no more travelling companions. You know you could have continued on.' He paused as the full consequences of his manipulation became clear to him. 'You could go to Peñíscola tomorrow, Jo. *You* don't have to wait for the guitar. Dios, I was such a jerk. I didn't even think this through – I just panicked. But you can go tomorrow. You don't have to stay for some stranger's party. You don't have to stay for some stranger's old music teacher's party and a lost old guitar!'

How many times had Mónica accused him of passive-aggressively manipulating her? He'd just done it again, a knee-jerk reaction he had to stop.

'Adrián.' Her firm voice cut through the fog of guilt that had him thrusting a hand through his hair in agitation. He looked up to see her studying him with concern. 'Do you want me to stay here?'

'Of course! That's the whole point! But I should have realised you wouldn't— It's not fair to you—'

'Adrián, if you want me to stay, I'll stay. The others don't arrive until Monday anyway. But maybe you should have asked me straight up?'

It took him a moment to process what she was saying. 'What do you mean, you'll stay? You were horrified on the train platform. You don't even like me.'

'I only dislike you as much as you dislike me,' she said, dropping her chin and giving him a look that shivered over his skin.

He opened his mouth, distracted by the brightness in her eyes. 'But I *like* you, Jo,' he pointed out in confusion.

With a huff of a laugh, she glanced away and swallowed. 'That means I like you, too, Adrián.'

'But...' Wow, this was not where he'd seen this conversation heading. He'd made a mistake and instead of railing at him for it and storming off, she'd pointed out how he could do better next time and then turned everything he'd thought about their relationship on its head.

'You're going to protest about that?' she asked quietly.

'No,' he answered immediately. He took a halting step closer to where she was standing in an inch or two of water. 'I know "like" doesn't mean— Well, I know you weren't admitting anything, but—'

She turned to him, lifting her hands to his face and he forgot whatever he'd wanted to say, meeting her in the middle instead for a reckless kiss.

* * *

This was why she'd kissed him last time: the firm sweep of his mouth against hers; his hand creeping up her back to hold her tightly despite his sling; the little hitch of breath that told her how much he was enjoying the kiss, too.

His hair was thick in her hands, his beard brushing her mouth just slightly at the edges. He felt so good under her fingers, she remembered what it had been like to enjoy intimacy without second-guessing her partner's feelings. Because Adrián left no room for second-guessing. He groaned against her lips and kissed her again, tilting his head for more contact. She didn't even know which of them deepened the kiss first. She only knew she was clinging to his shoulders, her bones turning to jelly.

His breath was harsh – or was that her breath? Hard, open-mouthed kisses built an ache that felt as though it were between them and not inside her. In the mess of motives and hurts, duties and responsibilities, the kiss was something new – untarnished. She clung to it, reached for it. Perhaps everything she felt when he was around should not have shone so brightly, but on that beach, in the last rays of the evening sun on one of the longest days of the year, she glowed.

Shifting her away from his bad arm, he stepped closer on the shingles and then broke the kiss with a start, wrenching away so quickly Jo stumbled.

'Argh, my shoe!' he cried, his voice high. 'I stepped in the water. It's soaked!'

Jo took a second to mourn the greatest kiss of her forties, before letting the moment go with a sigh. They shouldn't have done it anyway. 'Why didn't you take them off?'

'I can't get them back on without taking off the sling.'

'I would have helped you,' she pointed out.

'It just...'

He sighed and Jo wondered if they'd lost the ability to snipe at each other or if he enjoyed it as much as she did and might engage in it again just for fun.

'It didn't feel right to beg for forgiveness one moment and ask you to tie my shoelaces the next. It's not very... sexy, is it?'

Her attempt to stifle a laugh came out as an unflattering snort that also wasn't attractive. 'Sorry, but honesty *is* actually pretty sexy.'

As his grin stretched and he nodded, his too-long hair picked up by the breeze, Jo had the disturbing thought that lots of little things Adrián did were sexy – even though she generally disliked the word and attraction was very low on her list of priorities right now.

He leaned down to untie his shoelaces and peel off the wet sneaker and sock, repeating the action with the other shoe. Then he stepped into the water next to her with a rough sigh, his shoulder brushing hers.

Jo had been away from the sea too long. She'd forgotten the

calming power of the lapping waves, the endlessness of the horizon – the pleasant ache of one shoulder pressed to another as two sets of eyes soaked up the view.

'So,' he began, 'are we going to kiss again?'

14

She nudged his shoulder with hers. 'Don't you think the moment has gone?'

'The moment for kissing is never gone.'

She gave him a withering smile. 'Does that work with all the ladies?'

'I don't know,' he said. 'I've only tried it on one.'

'Seriously?'

'Why? Did it sound practised? I thought it was a bit corny,' he said, brushing a finger over his chin. He plonked down onto the shingle and glanced expectantly up at Jo until she joined him, wiggling her toes as the surf burst bubbles over her skin.

The question flew out of her mouth before she could stop it. 'Have you dated much? Since the divorce?'

'Dated much? I haven't dated at all,' he said, glancing at her as though she'd lost her mind. 'Did you think I was taking women out in my short lunch break? Or on the rare evenings when I don't have Oscar and I'm not performing and the apartment is halfway clean and I'm not dozing off in the dark at seven o'clock?' He eyed her.

'Did you think I'd be in a rush to put myself on whatever app it is these days?'

'I just thought...' Oops, she probably shouldn't go there.

'Hmm?' he seemed genuinely confused – an expression that was rather adorable.

She cleared her throat. 'You give off these "handsome man" vibes and I just thought you used it to your advantage.'

'Huh,' was all he said to that at first.

'Maybe I misjudged you,' she admitted.

'Did you think I was looking for someone else while I was still with Mónica?' he asked softly.

'No,' she countered immediately, but paused. 'Not specifically, although I might have projected some things about my divorce onto yours.'

'That's natural,' he said – too evenly. 'But Mónica left. I didn't. And I wasn't unfaithful, even in my thoughts.'

Jo wasn't sure if that made things better or worse. 'You wanted to stay together?'

'Probably not the way things were,' he began. 'But I thought we might have been able to work it out. We were both so busy and bad at the practical things – you know the hell of filling in forms, school dates, fixing the dishwasher and all that stuff – but then you need a family planner and a handyman, not a divorce. We just needed to spend time together again, remember why we got married in the first place.'

'She wouldn't get a planner?' Jo prompted, trying to keep things light so he'd keep talking.

'No, she... didn't remember why we got married in the first place,' he mumbled. 'And maybe she had a point. We got together because she's a beautiful dancer and I was a great guitar player, but... well, you know what happened to my career when we moved to London.'

She'd gathered a little, but she hadn't realised how much it bothered him. She also didn't miss that he'd used the past tense when describing himself as a great guitar player.

'Sometimes I wonder how Ben and Mónica function,' Jo said, going still when she realised the can of worms she'd just opened. 'Not that— I didn't want to upset—'

'They're getting married. If I get upset at the mention of their relationship, I'm going to have trouble on Friday when they say "I do",' he pointed out. She detected enough false bravado in his tone to make her uneasy. 'If you ask me if I'm still in love with her, I'll toss you into the sea,' he said, mimicking her words from two nights ago with a dry smile.

'This is a bit of a mess, isn't it – us, them, the wedding... the kiss,' Jo said, but covered her uncertainty with a chuckle.

'Kisses,' he pointed out without looking at her. 'You think it was a mistake to kiss, right? That we're just muddying the water?'

'The water is already muddy,' she pointed out, although the kiss hadn't felt that way at all. Locking lips with Adrián had felt like the clear water in this isolated bay lapping into the chaos of her life. It was the times when they *weren't* kissing that she got confused about what she wanted, what she could and couldn't have. 'The wedding isn't going to be easy. I'm glad we've become friends. I'm actually looking forward to something at the wedding now: downing a glass of wine with you in a quiet corner,' she said with a smile.

'But we should only be friends,' he completed for her. 'Anything else right now would never end well, would it?' he mused with a hint of disappointment that Jo felt in her toes. 'And I've had enough doom.'

'The ultimate doom is still to come on Friday,' Jo pointed out, 'or maybe on Monday when we arrive in Peñíscola.'

'If we ever arrive,' Adrián joked. 'There could be a strike, or an accident, or the roads could melt. We haven't had any flooding yet. Or a lightning strike!'

'Shut up, Adrián! We're not that doomed!'

'Just a little doomed,' he added under his breath and she elbowed him hard enough to make him add, 'oof.'

'Come on, the sun's gone down. Let me tie your shoes and we should head back before it gets dark.'

She was well aware that friends didn't hold hands, but she figured they needed each other for balance as they negotiated the rocky path in the fading light. Instead of obsessing about Ben, the wedding, the stresses of life, she only thought about the feel of his rough fingers over the back of her hand and let him tug her up the steep parts while she grumbled loudly about her tiredness.

'I'm the injured one. Why are you complaining?' he said, but his lips were curled at the corners.

'I don't have your magical ability to sleep like a rock on a train,' she shot back.

They dropped hands when they reached the gate in the white-washed wall around Carles's house. The quiet lilt of a guitar sounded from one end of the house, gently plucked strings in smooth, flowing arpeggios.

Jo followed Adrián wordlessly to the hallway at the other end – the guest bedrooms – and her mind raced with things to say, each more terrible than the last: *Thanks for... um... making out on the beach; good night,* friend; *I hope you sleep better than I will; maybe we should just kiss one more time for luck.*

But it was Adrián who spoke first, with an awkward, 'Um.' His gaze flew to hers. 'Could you... help me with my shirt?'

'Of course,' Jo said, shaking off the effects of moonlight on the rocks and holding hands with someone she liked. It was only when she approached and lifted her arms that she realised undressing Adrián right now might pose a slight problem.

Now the air had cooled, she felt the residual warmth of his skin as she came close to undo the sling, pulling the strap through the loop.

'Does it hurt?' she asked.

'When I move it,' he said with a nod. 'But it's already so much better than it was.'

Keeping his left arm limp at his side, he lifted the hem of his T-shirt with his good hand. 'Now you've shown me the technique, maybe I can do this mys—' He paused, his last words muffled with a mouthful of T-shirt. He'd managed to lift the shirt over his face, his good arm up in the air, but now he was stuck, his bare chest all Jo could see of him. She couldn't decide if that was a good thing or not. He had a lovely chest – not model muscular, as he didn't have time for that, but strong and healthy, with just enough dark hair to look cosy.

It was a much nicer torso than Ben's and that thought was exactly why she shouldn't be standing there thinking about touching him.

'Eh, Jo? I might need help after all.'

With a chuckle, she grasped the T-shirt and helped him pull his good arm free, before working the material gently over his head and down his bad arm, trying not to ghost her fingers over his skin and failing occasionally.

His breath tickled her forehead as his chest rose and fell. Her mouth was dry, but licking her lips only made her think about that kiss and she couldn't go there right now if she was going to resist another. He gave her a lingering look, a gaze so clear and aching that she knew he was thinking about the same thing. She wanted to. She didn't want to leave the clear water of the Costa Brava. They had tomorrow, they could—

She stepped away from him, swallowing regret. If the whole trip was a little doomed, then *this*, whatever it was between them, was doubly doomed. She had to focus on getting through the wedding and that was all.

* * *

At least one of the many mishaps of the past few days had definitely worked out for the best, Jo thought the following morning as she wandered uphill in the direction of the next town. She could never suggest to Adrián that it was a good thing his guitar had missed the flight, but she couldn't imagine missing this place, these views.

Taking the coast roads on foot from Carles's house tucked in the hills, she'd passed the little beach at Port Lligat with its fishing boats moored on the still bay. Gazing up at the white mansion on the hillside that Salvador Dalí had embellished with two enormous eggs on the roof, she marvelled that they didn't look as out of place as she would have expected among the silver olive trees and brown earth.

She glimpsed water ahead of her; there was water behind her – and the sky overhead was endless, without a single cloud. Yes, she missed Liss and Dec like a part of herself, but she'd spoken to them just that morning and Ben was capable of looking after them just as well as she was. Tomorrow was soon enough to arrive back in the real world.

For today, she was in an alternate reality where ancient stone walls lined the narrow roads and prickly pears dotted the dry hillside. She wanted to walk all day, soaking up the sun and exploring the stony headlands and secret coves – like the one Adrián had shown her the night before.

Goosebumps tingled over her skin when she thought about last night, wondering if she'd made the right decision to keep her distance, whether this alternate reality might have made it okay to be intimate with someone so wrong for her in the usual reality – whether part of her reluctance was just nerves, knowing her body wasn't as cooperative as it had been twenty years ago.

In this alternate universe, perhaps Adrián wouldn't care if she needed to pee at the wrong moment. He'd seen her without make-up, with puffy morning eyes, in her reading glasses – in her comfy undies! That he'd still wanted to kiss her was definitely down to this alternate reality thing because she was supposed to be the jaded ex-PTA mum, not a desirable sexual partner.

Yes, her decision last night had definitely been sensible, as well as her decision that morning to leave him to his coffee – and Carles's friendly niece – while she rambled to the next town to hopefully find some more clothes and perhaps a pair of sandals.

Continuing past a chapel with textured whitewash and a little bell in an arch on the roof, the more frequent houses, shops and restaurants suggested she'd reached the outskirts of Cadaqués, the only settlement of any size on this lonely peninsula.

The town was a maze of narrow streets, tiny, walled gardens with washing strung up between the white buildings and continual glimpses of the bay. She mentally added a sangria on the beach to her schedule for later – or perhaps a coffee if it was still morning.

She found a small boutique and left with a frivolous summer dress patterned in green and blue – very much not her usual style – as well as a straw hat that made her feel like an actress in a film and a pair of shoes that Liss would probably have called 'Jesus sandals'. The saleswoman hadn't blinked an eye when Jo had asked to keep the dress on and pack away her (rather whiffy) shirt and shorts in the shopping bag.

After another half-hour of meandering – along the busy water-front and out towards the headland – she caught herself wondering what Adrián was doing and couldn't shake off the thought that he could have come with her after all.

Then her phone rang with an unknown British number, providing a welcome distraction. 'Hello, this is Jo Watters,' she answered.

'I didn't have your number!'

She paused, perching on a low wall by the water and swallowing a smile. 'How did you manage to call me, then?'

'I texted Mónica,' Adrián answered grimly. 'Where are you? Mercedes dropped me off in Cadaqués on her way to church. Did you find some more clothes?' She secretly loved the way he'd taken it for granted that they would meet up now.

'Yep,' was all she said in reply, fingering the soft crepe of her dress and wondering what he'd say when he saw it. She expected something trite like: 'Beautiful dress, beautiful woman,' that he would mean earnestly but would only make Jo self-conscious about the times he'd seen her at her worst.

'Good, me too. I'll text you a place where we can meet for lunch. I'll be there in about ten minutes, but don't worry if it takes you longer.' He hung up without saying goodbye or waiting for her to say anything else.

She blinked at the phone, uncertain whether to be annoyed or flattered, and the message dropped in as she watched, listing a beachside café not far from where she stood. Taking a chance that he would be coming from the centre of Cadaqués, she waited a few minutes and then saw him striding along the footpath in her direction, a shopping bag in his good hand. She tried not to feel anything – she tried very hard.

He was wearing a billowing short-sleeved shirt with one too many buttons undone, stonewashed denim shorts with a drawstring and a pair of flip-flops. He smiled when he saw her, hurrying to catch her and pressing a kiss to her cheek when he did. Jo was well past the age of girlish blushes, but one bloomed up her chest anyway.

'You look like you belong here,' was all he said after taking note of her dress. Damn him, it was a perfect compliment and she hoped it was just the sunshine melting her insides. 'Come on, it's time for fried baby octopus, paella, croquetes and crema catalana for dessert!'

'Is that supposed to be breakfast, lunch *and* dinner today?'

He shrugged – a good sign because it wasn't accompanied by a grimace of pain. 'No, you are sharing with me!'

'Is that why you wanted to meet for lunch?'

'One of the reasons,' he replied, giving her a wink. But he took off before she could bluster an annoyed reply that she wouldn't mean.

When they arrived at the little café on the water, with wicker chairs, a faded sunshade and lush, low trees providing relief from the heavy heat, she forgot everything except the creak of her stomach, the scent of seafood and garlic and the slight tang of olive oil.

The kids would just have to forgive her for enjoying herself.

15

Jo had a tattoo on her left shoulder.

It shouldn't have surprised Adrián, but he hadn't been able to stop staring at it all afternoon, since he'd caught a glimpse of it over lunch in Cadaqués. It was one of those birds with a long beak that flapped its wings very fast. The artwork was nice, but faded enough to suggest she'd had the ink a long time. He wanted to ask her about it – and run his fingertips over it. And his lips, if he was honest.

Carles had been giving him amused looks as the older man's family dribbled into the house with food and drink and the lazy, post-siesta time gradually turned into a fiesta. Adrián had been eating all day, but when in Spain, he could always eat a little more.

Although he noticed Jo texting Liss every few hours, she'd relaxed since their tense arrival yesterday. She smiled a lot, tilting her head as she listened to Carles's relatives tell their life stories in stilted English. Her new dress was soft and flowing, but it wasn't the pretty new clothes that attracted his gaze. It was the way her bare shoulders – with that tattoo – showed her emotions: rising for uncertainty, loosening when she was happy and dropping into laziness occasionally when she sat back sipping sangria.

'You didn't warn her you were coming here yesterday, did you?' Carles asked in a lull in the conversation.

Adrián tore his gaze from Jo and wondered if he could pretend to misunderstand. He gave up and admitted, 'No, I didn't.'

'She seems happy. Were you afraid she would react like Mónica?'

'Mónica always wanted time with her own family,' Adrián said, defending her out of habit. Looking at Jo was a little less comfortable as his skin prickled with uncertainty. Jo *was* happier here than Mónica had been – the one time she'd agreed to visit Carles. Time in Spain had been so limited and his ex-wife had always wanted to rush to Zaragoza. He'd understood how much she missed her family – he missed his parents, too.

He tried not to compare, to encourage the bitter beast inside him that still reared its head occasionally, but his mind latched onto the fact that Jo could have stayed somewhere else and she hadn't.

'That's a very big sigh, gordito,' Carles said, slapping him on the back as he called Adrián the nickname from his teenage years when he'd certainly been 'gordito' – chubby.

'My life is a very big sigh,' he muttered, grabbing another fried cod ball from the basket Carles's cousin had placed between them. 'I'm full of shit and self-pity – I know.'

'You don't deserve a fine woman like that,' Carles added sagely.

'Exactly!' Adrián narrowed his eyes at his old friend, but found Carles's twinkling with humour. 'It doesn't matter, anyway. How would we ever untangle... us... from the mess of our exes? I refuse to make life more difficult for her.'

'Okay,' Carles said, giving him a calming squeeze on the forearm.

'This place is... different without Esther,' Adrián commented carefully.

'Rest her soul,' Carles murmured. 'I'm different without her, too, but we can't choose how long we have. I'm still here – and so are you.'

The old man had known those words would hit him in the gut.

'Joanito!' Carles called out suddenly to his nephew. 'Bring me a guitar!'

A shout of, '¡Olé!' rose from the someone in the family, making Adrián sit up in his chair. The nephew, Joan, came back onto the terrace with an instrument from Carles's sitting room, carrying it in front of him like a sacrifice, which made Adrián smile. Carles had always had a flair for the dramatic.

Setting his cigar into a little tray, his old teacher took the instrument and plucked quietly at the strings. Adrián remembered Carles years ago telling him that tuning a guitar was like talking to it, getting to know it and coaxing it to sing – which only made him think of Jo again.

The first resonating notes filled the hushed courtyard as the whole family held their breath to hear the maestro. Adrián recognised the song immediately as a favourite piece by the Spanish guitar legend Paco de Lucía. Carles had taught him to play it when Adrián had been about eighteen and it had taken months of practice to master the quick tremolo picking.

The fingers of Adrián's right hand twitched as Carles flicked the strings precisely, creating fullness in the silence and anticipation in each note. Goosebumps broke out on Adrián's arms. The world narrowed to a single moment, to the minute changes in the air as the reverberation of the guitar strings disturbed the stillness.

He was still here.

As the opening strains of the song gave way to rhythm and movement, the terrace came alive with shouts and palmas – the handclapping that had lived in Adrián's blood since his earliest music lessons with Carles. He brought his hands together, the rhythm organic inside him.

He wished he'd come back here sooner. It didn't matter if he had fewer and fewer concerts and was barely paid for them. He was part of this music and that meant he would always have family.

Joining in the shouts with, '¡Eso!' at the end of the song, he received Carles's clap on the back with a grin, his left hand clenching and unclenching against his chest.

'Another guitar for my star pupil!' Carles called, giving him a warm look.

As Adrián picked at the Velcro holding his sling together, he felt Jo's alarmed gaze. He gave her a little shake of his head and a reassuring smile, which seemed to be all she needed to sit back in her chair again. When the neck of the guitar fell into the valley between his thumb and forefinger, it felt like waking up.

He'd played since the separation – of course he had. But he hadn't *played*, forgetting the world, forgetting who he was and living through the strings. He'd been fixated on his own failure and forgot how little that failure actually mattered.

A tug of pain in his shoulder made him adjust his stance, but he found a position where he could reach the frets and minimise the ache. He took a deep breath of the sea air, scented with wild thyme and lavender, and he reclaimed who he was with his fingers on the strings.

* * *

Jo had learned an array of new things that night: it was still stifling hot on the terrace at ten in the evening; sangria got tastier the more of it you drank, and the guitar was the sexiest instrument on the planet.

There were four guitars out, now, held in four pairs of hands, playing alternately together and solo. She'd expected Adrián to be *good*. He performed concerts. But she hadn't appreciated what 'good' meant to her body. She couldn't keep still with the rhythms washing over her and she couldn't take her eyes off him.

When someone had first placed a guitar in his hands, the transformation had been instantaneous – not just in his posture, but in his expression. That intensity she'd come to associate with him escaped just his eyes and took over his body. The chaos in him quieted to make way for the expression of the music.

He smiled and frowned, punctuated the songs with shouts. Jo changed her mind about his hair: it wasn't too long. It was the perfect length to fly sharply into his face as he bobbed over the body of the guitar, his right hand moving furiously and the fingers of his left flying over the frets. He must have bought a shaving kit because he'd tidied up his beard and looked like the rakish musketeer from the flight.

Someone had tied a bandana around his forehead an hour ago to keep his hair back and he had a cigar hanging out of his mouth and she should have been laughing at him, the lovechild of Rambo and the Godfather strumming a fierce, soulful song.

But she wasn't laughing; she was captivated, so thankful it was his left arm he'd injured and not his right, feeling privileged to be here witnessing the music – the family, the bond.

She felt uncomfortable – and was more than a little tipsy – to admit she'd understood Mónica's reasons for wanting a divorce, but now she was learning the woman's reasons for marrying him in the first place.

He took another break – he'd regularly rested his shoulder throughout the evening – and Jo celebrated the opportunity to breathe again, until he approached and stretched out in a wicker chair beside her. She felt the way Liss must have when she'd lined up to see Dua Lipa sign autographs; gosh, teenage feelings were ridiculous at her age and she needed to snap out of it.

His smile dimmed as he studied her. 'You okay? They're a bit much if you're not used to it.'

'No! They're wonderful – friendly. I just... got caught up in the music. Is this flamenco?' she asked as one of the older women – Carles's sister-in-law, Jo thought – raised her hands and stamped across the floor to a chorus of, '¡Hassa gitana guapa!' She didn't dance for long before giving a wide grin and returning to her seat, her long skirt in her hands.

Her husband opened his mouth to sing a crooning melody in the minor key and Adrián joined in the rhythmic clapping, which was both intrinsically structured and laced with free expression.

He leaned close to whisper in her ear, 'Yes, this is flamenco – this song is tangos.'

Jo should have been asking him if the music made him think of Mónica and what they'd lost, but sparks scattered down her skin from where his breath feathered her ear and she couldn't concentrate.

'You are allowed to get up and dance,' he said, studying her with a smile.

That was when she realised her shoulders were moving to the beat and her feet were tapping. 'I wouldn't have the first clue how to.'

'That doesn't matter,' he said in that rough voice of his. 'This isn't a stage. It's Carles's courtyard. Or you could sing something. Pick a song and I'll accompany you.' His smile lit up as he suggested it. 'Yes! They'd love that.' She eyed him. '*I* would love that,' he added freely, as though he had no idea his words sent shivers of confused longing through her.

She hadn't sung in front of an audience for... more than twenty years. She wasn't that girl who had looked forward to the music

school's proms night more than anything else all year – or the
university student who had dragged her girlfriends to karaoke
every other weekend. Jo hadn't been that woman since... since
she'd hidden that identity from earnest Ben. Well, *shit.*

'Just let me get another drink,' she murmured, rising to refill
her glass and grab a piece of bread topped with artichoke and a
tomato-based salsa – and another crunchy fish croqueta would
help soak up the alcohol, too.

'Here,' Adrián said, coming up behind her with a glass of water
that she downed thankfully. 'What do you want to sing?'

'What songs will they know?'

'We have English music in Spain too, you know. Whatever you
want.'

That was how she found herself singing an acoustic karaoke
version of 'Alive' by Pearl Jam under the late-night sky with a group
of Spanish strangers gawping at her while Adrián ad-libbed the
iconic riff on a flamenco guitar with a little too much gusto.

She didn't know if they were just being kind when they
whooped and clapped at the end of the song, but more suggestions
of songs from the nineties quickly followed, although Carles rolled
his eyes. Mercedes insisted on Jo joining her to sing 'Hit Me Baby
One More Time' and Jo felt something like bandages falling away
as she laughed and sang and laughed some more, occasionally
getting up to dance, especially when the music changed back to
Spanish guitar.

A group of cousins crooned a catchy old song called 'Bésame
mucho', which she gathered meant 'kiss me a lot'. The middle-aged
men serenaded their wives and the chorus of the gently rhythmic
song was so memorable she found herself singing along, teasing
Adrián with a wink.

Yes, the alcohol contributed, but the courtyard, the eclectic mix
of music, the hospitality were the true catalysts – and the spark in

Adrián's eye. The Costa Brava was her alternate reality, after all, where joy seemed to flow from her own body and it didn't matter that the actual reality was out there somewhere, with Ben and Mónica waiting in it.

When the first guests rose to go with what sounded like profuse apologies – and equally profuse censure and insistence from the visibly tired Carles – Jo began to feel exhaustion knocking at the edges of her mind too and a scratch in her throat from all the singing. But she was too mellow to mind.

'Work tomorrow! What a poor excuse!' Carles muttered to her. 'I'm sorry to end the party so early.'

'It's past midnight!' she pointed out.

'And?'

Adrián came up beside her and she wanted him to drape an arm casually around her and give her a squeeze. Of course he didn't. 'We live British hours these days, profe,' he explained. 'And we have a lot to do tomorrow.'

Jo's smile slipped at the prospect of the following day. Carles's cousin was lending them her second car, which would get them quickly to Peñíscola, but she didn't want to think of anything that came after tonight. She'd start thinking about Ben and he was no fun.

After Carles shuffled off to bed on his side of the house, Jo and Adrián dawdled to their hallway, their arms bumping. It might have been her fault, but she couldn't bring herself to care when she was rewarded with the brush of his skin on hers.

'You can have the bathroom first,' he offered.

Whether Jo was just too tipsy or not in her right mind, even those words, in his rough voice, shivered through her. Brushing her teeth, her skin felt hot and she was restless and her thoughts refused to focus. The words of that song in Spanish played on repeat in her mind, making her think about kissing.

Back in her room, while she pulled on the spaghetti-strap vest top she'd bought as pyjamas, she suddenly realised he might not be able to get his shirt off. She was unexpectedly buoyed by the thought.

Hearing him coming out again, she leaned on her doorway and asked, 'How's your shoulder?'

He had the sling off already. 'Aches a bit,' he admitted, grimacing as he rubbed it gingerly. 'Perhaps I shouldn't have played so much.'

'Want some... help with your shirt?'

'Ehm, I can get this one...'

His Adam's apple bobbed and her gaze fixed on the neat line of his beard under his jaw. His black hair was peppered with a little grey and Jo bit her lip, for once thankful that some men were even more attractive in their forties.

He reached for the buttons of his shirt, popping two as she stared, her mouth going dry. 'See? I can manage this one,' he said, his voice tight. He fumbled the next button and gave her an awkward smile that caught her in the ribs. 'At least, I think I can manage it.'

He didn't protest when she took over, opening the buttons for him. As the soft material of his shirt fell open, her thoughts scattered. She stepped close to help him peel the shirt away, her heart beating an out-of-control rhythm. Then she couldn't seem to draw back again.

Her palms touched down on his chest, feeling rather than hearing his groan. Warm skin, rough hair, shared breaths. Her head spun, so she clung on tighter.

'Adrián?' she whispered, no idea what she meant to say. So she kissed him instead.

16

Adrián needed about a thousand hands and not just the one that was working properly. With Jo plastered to him, her arms curled around his neck and her mouth fastened on his, there were hundreds of ways he wanted to hold her, touch her. He settled for tangling his fingers in her hair as she tilted her head, sending a rush of wanting through him as the kiss caught fire.

His mind was full of her, fixated on the sound of her voice, the way she'd danced with her glass in her hand, how good she felt – brushing her lips down his neck. *Oooh*.

She swayed against him and he dipped his arm to hold her around her waist, catching her eye, expecting to see the same desire-induced light-headedness in her gaze. But she blinked, her movements oddly dull.

'Bésame...' she sang with a clipped giggle, 'bésame mucho,' she continued, lifting her chin.

'Jo?' he prompted with a gentle smile, amused, but also with a sinking heart. 'Are you drunk?'

'Aren't you, too?' She stretched up until her lips found his cheek and then skimmed to his earlobe, making his breath hitch. His back hit the doorframe as her fingers brushed over his beard and shadows played at the edge of his vision.

'It wouldn't make any difference if I was,' he murmured with a sigh. Grasping her forearm gently, he tugged her hand away. 'Jo, we don't do this drunk.'

'There's no way we're ever going to do this sober!' she pointed out with an exaggerated bob of her head.

A laugh rose from deep in his chest. 'Maybe you're right, corazón,' he said, blinking back surprise as the endearment tumbled out unintentionally. 'But I don't want to face you tomorrow if you regret sleeping with me.'

'I won't regret it,' she said, pressing a kiss to his collarbone and curling her arms around him again. His head fell against the wall with a thud as he gathered himself to resist the endorphins flooding his system from her touch. 'Tomorrow can go to hell.'

That made him freeze and she wasn't drunk enough to miss the change. Her forehead dropped to his shoulder.

'Shit,' she whispered. 'It's already tomorrow, isn't it?'

He skimmed his palm up her spine, breathing out heavily when she relaxed, her head still nestled into him. 'Yes,' he said as gently as he could.

'Ben can go to hell, too,' she mumbled, 'for turning my life into this.'

Adrián stared at the ceiling as he tucked her against him with his good arm, unable to resist settling his left hand on her back too, despite a twinge of pain. 'You were beautiful tonight.'

'Shut up,' she responded with a sniff. 'I'm trying to get through the self-pity, if it's already tomorrow and we're not going to have sex and make it all go away.'

Ouch, it had definitely been the right thing to put a stop to the kissing. 'That's okay. Let it out.' He pressed a light kiss to her forehead, lingering there when the scent of closeness, the tickle of her hair on his lips calmed him. 'I could hold you all night,' he said with a sigh that sounded like a purr.

She stilled against him, strength seeping away. 'Then do it,' she said, her voice muffled against his skin. 'Don't leave me alone tonight.'

'I won't,' he promised softly, easing her up. 'But let's get you to bed.'

'Why do you have more muscles than Ben?' she mused, her fingers tracing his chest. He grasped her hand to still it, pressing another light kiss to her knuckles, unsure if she needed an answer. 'You're not that much younger than him, you know – younger than me. But you're *hot*. God, I sound like Liss looking at pictures of Harry Styles.'

He gulped, going in for another attempt to dislodge her.

'It used to annoy me how attractive you are.'

Distracting her by asking, 'And now?' he urged her gently in the direction of the bed with his good arm around her waist.

'You don't annoy me any more,' she said, her expression oddly serious. She allowed him to shepherd her into bed, her head hitting the pillow heavily. 'I mean, you *do* annoy me. You drive me crazy. But... I kind of like it.'

'Let me get you some water,' he said, patting her bare shoulder.

'Don't need water,' she said, settling restlessly on the bed. 'I'm a sober drunk,' she explained with a straight face, her eyes popping open.

His lips twitched. 'Very sober. You nearly fooled me, but not quite. I'll be back in a minute.'

It was a struggle to get her to drink the water, but he suspected she'd thank him for it in the morning – hopefully not the only thing she'd thank him for. She was a stubborn and bitter drunk – and vulnerable. But she'd asked him to stay. If she needed to be weak for a moment, he would shield her from the world.

She dropped into a deep sleep quickly, facing the window. Adrián climbed into bed behind her, propping himself up on his good elbow to study the way her hair curled around her ear and her arms stretched in front of her in exhaustion.

He could see her bird tattoo in the faint moonlight shining through the gauzy curtains. A hummingbird, that's what it was. He brushed a thumb over the ink, frustrated when his shoulder twinged again.

Leaning close, he pressed a quick kiss to her skin, over the tattoo, and then flopped back onto his own side of the bed to try to get some sleep.

* * *

It was the heat that woke him the next day, simmering over his skin. He rolled over, but that only turned the bed into a rotisserie oven – and brought him into contact with another roasting body. Sitting up quickly, he gasped when a shot of pain tore through his shoulder. If the nurse hadn't warned him it would stiffen up, he might have worried it was getting worse and he'd need surgery.

Jo mumbled something and rolled onto her stomach, her face squashed into the pillow. He couldn't resist brushing her hair off her face and pressing a kiss to her forehead before he fumbled for his phone on the nightstand.

What he saw on the screen had him leaping out of bed in alarm and calling, 'Jo!' over his shoulder as he searched for his shirt – and didn't find it. 'Jo, wake up!' She still didn't rouse beyond a mumble, so he came around to her side of the bed and shook her, too rattled to worry about being gentle.

'What?' she grumbled, pushing herself up and slapping a hand over her eyes with a grimace. 'What's wrong with you?'

A shiver of unease ran down his spine. 'It's eleven o'clock!'

'In the morning?' she asked, her voice raspy. 'God, I feel like shit.'

'Yes, in the morning!' he said, rolling his eyes. 'We have to get moving if we're going to collect the guitar and then drive all the way to Peñíscola!'

'Right, okay. Oh, God, I think I need some of your painkillers.'

'Will you be okay to drive?' he asked.

'I'll have to be.'

'Maybe I—'

'You are *not* driving with your arm in a sling. That car is a manual.'

'Mierda, I can't drive a manual anyway.'

It was her turn to stare up at the ceiling and sigh. 'Maybe I'll feel better after a shower,' she said, hauling herself to her feet.

'We don't have time—'

'I'll be quick,' she promised.

When she emerged from the hallway ten minutes later, he'd resigned himself to the delay and had made two coffees to go with the breakfast Mercedes had set out for them before she left for work. 'Here,' he said, gesturing to her coffee.

'You're my hero, thank you,' Jo said with a groan as she lifted the cup to her nose and inhaled deeply. He couldn't quite stifle a smile at her words and she pinned him with a look. 'Don't get used to it.'

'Why not? I'm not regularly your hero?'

'You can't even dress yourself at the moment,' she said, glancing pointedly at his bare chest.

'This is my hero suit.' He very much deserved that eye-roll. 'Actually, I couldn't find my button-down shirt and I can't get any of the others on.'

'You can't find it? Isn't it—' He saw the moment she remembered what had happened in the hallway last night. Her pinched expression made him very glad they hadn't taken things any further. 'On the floor in the hallway?' she said through clenched teeth.

Adrián shook his head. 'I assume Mercedes cleaned it up.'

'I'm sorry if I put you in a difficult position with your mentor and his family,' Jo said.

He shook his head immediately. 'Don't apologise to me, Jo. I wanted everything that happened last night and Carles had already guessed that there was an... attraction between us. None of this is anyone's fault. Let's get down to the wedding and...'

'And...' she agreed grimly.

'I saved you some toast,' he said, waving his hand over the plate, but Jo's eyes zeroed in on the empty bowl next to it.

'For God's sake, Adrián, how much watermelon have you eaten over the past two days?'

He gave a sheepish shrug. 'It takes me back to childhood – the seeds, the sticky, sweet juice on my face. I hope someone is giving Oscar watermelon.'

Her hand landed on his arm. 'We'll see them today.'

He covered her hand with his own, tracing circles on the back with his thumb. She stiffened but didn't draw away. He wondered if she was thinking the same thing he was: they wouldn't be allowed to touch casually like this once they arrived for the wedding.

'I'll just wrap up some toast in a serviette,' she said hurriedly. 'Let's go.'

* * *

Jo's stomach roiled as she turned the little Corsa back in the direction of Figueres and south to Girona. All the hairpin curves made her feel as though her thoughts separated from her body for a moment and she had to blink away the lapse in concentration.

She was never drinking again. Or perhaps she should have drunk more. At least that way she might not have remembered in sparkling detail throwing herself at Adrián and having him act as the voice of reason and then as her verbal punching bag as she lost it over Ben – a usual occurrence when she was tipsy.

The craziest thing was, she still regretted that they hadn't slept together. Yes, it was a little weird that she'd gone on about how much nicer Adrián's chest was than Ben's, but they were already bound by embarrassing moments. They could have gone a round between the sheets, just to see if it worked.

Then she was back to never drinking again, because if she hadn't drunk so much last night, he wouldn't have had a reason to stop. Her brain nearly shut down when she started imagining what might have happened if he hadn't been so scrupulous. It was a miracle that she'd believed it might be good – an even bigger miracle that she still thought so.

Perhaps it wasn't so surprising, given the way she reacted to the tiny gestures of tenderness he handed out, seemingly unintentionally. The brush of his lips over her tattoo had been the most breath-stealing moment of the last decade and she couldn't believe she'd nearly slept through it.

Adrián had kissed that old tattoo that she'd nearly had lasered off at least ten times. Ben had referred to it as the 'mistake of your youth' with what she'd thought was fond tolerance, but it had probably been concealed contempt.

She took a curve a little too fast and gripped the wheel more firmly.

'Are you sure you're okay?' Adrián asked. 'The last thing we need right now is a car accident.'

No, I'm just reliving the feel of your lips on my skin and it's hell on my concentration. 'I'm fine,' she snapped. 'Nobody needs a car accident – at any time.'

She paused at a roundabout, making sure she looked in the opposite direction to her instincts. Pulling onto a wider road, she took a deep breath. She could do this. What was a little hangover and a bit of sexual tension for a capable woman?

The air-conditioning of the little Corsa – such as it was – couldn't make a dent in the midday swelter as they headed inland, skirting Figueres. Adrián fiddled with the ancient radio until he found a station playing pop music and the distraction made the heat slightly more bearable, especially when 'Like a Prayer' came on and all Jo had to do was meet Adrián's eye for them to giggle like a pair of kids, both of them thinking of Madonna and Our Lady of Lourdes.

'I've had this song in my head since the flight landed,' Jo admitted. 'You know that's the name of her daughter: Lourdes.'

'Is that why I've had it in my head too?' Adrián exclaimed, slapping his thigh. 'You've been humming it.'

'Maybe *you've* been humming it and that's why it's in *my* head,' she said defensively.

'Nope, you've been humming,' he said with a smile. 'Like a hummingbird.' He winked at her, sending goosebumps along her skin. 'Does it mean anything? The tattoo?'

'No,' she answered with a smile. 'Not a thing. I just wanted a tattoo and liked the picture in the catalogue. I was only twenty-one.'

'You were brave, when you were twenty-one.'

'Or stupid,' she commented.

'Either way, it's yours now,' Adrián said lightly. 'I like it.'

I know. 'I like it too,' she said, her grin fixed on her face. She glanced at him and then back at the road ahead of her. Her headache had ebbed with the painkillers, she was freshly caffeinated, charged up on their own special variety of banter. 'It's going to be okay, isn't it?' she said softly. 'Today.'

'Yes, it's going to be okay.'

But perhaps Adrián shouldn't have promised something he couldn't deliver.

17

The first signs of trouble were the ones indicating a detour off the motorway as they approached Girona. Adrián's navigation app seemed completely averse to turning around and within ten minutes they were stuck in traffic.

Jo gazed up at the looming cathedral as they inched over a bridge, catching glimpses of the old town in shades of orange, clustered on a hill. There were people everywhere – and cars and motorbikes and bicycles.

'Do you think something is... happening?' she asked, her question sounding inane to her own ears. She swiped sweat off her forehead with the back of her hand.

'Maybe,' Adrián said, sounding as listless as she felt.

By the time they'd inched their way to the airport, it was nearly two o'clock and Adrián was freaking out about whether the office would have siesta hours and leave them waiting until four. Jo pulled into a drop-off area and gestured for him to jump out.

'I hate airports,' she muttered to herself, putting the car back into gear and peering for signs to the short-stay car park. When she parked the car, she realised she was thirsty, but she'd left her plastic bottle at Carles's house and hated the idea of paying €5 for a bottle of airport water.

Calling Adrián, she was at least relieved to hear he'd retrieved the guitar already and was on his way to the car park.

'Is it okay? Not damaged?' she asked anxiously when he returned.

'It's not damaged,' he assured her, handing her the guitar when it was too difficult for him to get it into the boot with one arm. 'I'm surprised you care so much.'

'It wasn't that I didn't care, back in Lourdes. I didn't understand,' she explained – a little snappishly, but she was uncomfortably hot and incredibly thirsty. 'Let's get out of here.'

The roads and roundabouts by the airport were a chaos of confusing signs and twisting motorway ramps and, before Jo realised what was going on, she'd accidentally taken the turn-off to head back into Girona – and then they hit another roadblock.

'What the hell is going on?' she asked, slapping the wheel in a fair imitation of Adrián.

'Here, have some water,' he said, handing her his bottle with the cap off.

'That only solves problems for little kids who need distracting,' she muttered, but she grabbed the bottle and drank half of it in two swigs.

'Have the rest,' he insisted when she tried to give it back.

'You have it,' she said, shaking her head. 'We'll stop on the way and get more. How long is the drive again?'

'Three-and-a-half hours.'

'If we ever get out of Girona,' Jo muttered.

'Dios, now you've done it!' Adrián groaned. 'That invisible force will find us and stop us from getting to the wedding again.'

'An invisible force,' she repeated with a snort. 'You mean a manifestation and amplification of our mutual reluctance.' She executed a feisty three-point-turn and headed the car back in the direction of the airport, fuming.

'You know, I was thinking about that,' Adrián added quietly and Jo's stomach sank.

'I embarrassed myself last night, but that doesn't mean I want to talk about this.'

'No, I was thinking about *me*.'

That took the wind out of her but didn't exactly buoy her spirits. 'Go ahead then.'

He paused, glancing over his shoulder to where the guitar was propped up in the boot, partially obstructing Jo's rear view. 'I don't want to get back together with her, so why couldn't I wish her well and keep walking?'

'Is that a rhetorical question?' she asked.

'Yes,' he said, giving her a sidelong glance. 'Because I think I know the answer.'

'Oh, God, another man with all the answers. Enlighten me.' She swiped a drop of sweat off her top lip, peering up ahead to see cars slowing and backing up. What was wrong with this town today?

'It's grief,' Adrián said, his voice high with wonder. 'I don't want her any more, but I'm still sad about our old life and holding on.'

Jo braked as gently as she could – which was not very gently in her current state of mind. The ache behind her forehead had started up again and seemed to echo in her stomach. 'That was a big lightbulb moment?' she asked with a sigh.

He narrowed his eyes at her. 'I thought it might help you to see things that way too.'

'Adrián, I've been separated for five years. I know I'm grieving. I just don't know what to do about it. At least when someone dies they're actually gone, but Ben hangs over me like a bad smell.'

She waited for him to try to fix her or give her advice, to hint that her feelings weren't constructive – anything to feed her weird mood and unsettled tummy. The wedding must be giving her an ulcer. So much for, 'It's all going to be okay.'

But Adrián just nodded. 'I suppose we have to deal with grief in different ways. It was just something Carles said to me last night that made me realise why I was still hanging onto... her, the family – whatever it is I miss.'

Jo didn't resist asking for long. 'What did he say?'

'He just said "I'm still here". It probably won't mean anything to you. Like I said, we're different. But I'm still here. There's more to life than being Mónica Hernández's ex-husband. Maybe I'll play that guitar at her wedding for myself too, to show who I still am.'

All of Jo's fight drained out of her and her vision blurred with tears. How could he be so peaceful? Mónica had left *him* – and without watching her language, Jo suspected. But this obviously passionate man was calm about the wedding, while everything still turned over inside her when she thought about Ben.

I'm still here.

Jo wasn't. She was a forty-six-year-old woman. Outside of her job and her role as parent, she was invisible. She barely had time to blink in her busy life. It hurt to think she'd been walking around in circles for five years, looking for a way back to the land of the living and failing to find it.

Of course she was fucking grieving. She was grieving thirteen years of her life lost.

'Jo?' Adrián's voice sounded distant, as though the Corsa had suddenly grown to the size of a coach and he was calling from the back seat. 'Are you all right? You look... pale. Jo?' His voice grew agitated. 'Jo, pull over, corazón. You're worr— *Oh shit!*'

With an almighty heave, Jo's body ejected the meagre contents of her stomach onto the dashboard.

* * *

Adrián lunged for the steering wheel with his good arm, hollering, 'Brakes!' as the car lurched to the right. He managed to swerve away from the crash barrier as the vehicle mercifully slowed.

The Corsa was so old it still had a handbrake lever, which he engaged in a panic, then flicked on the hazard lights. Jo slumped on the steering wheel alarmingly, but the horn sounded and she jerked back up, clutching her stomach.

Tipping her head up, he peered into her eyes, noting the sheen of sweat on her forehead. 'Fuck,' she moaned, which he took as a good sign. 'I feel really weird.'

'Just stay with me, okay?' he crooned, stroking her cheek and taking in the mottled rash on her chest.

She nodded weakly. 'I'm sorry—'

'No, shh. I've got you,' he promised her. 'Right, okay,' he muttered to himself, taking far too long to consider the problem. 'We don't have any water.' He pressed a quick kiss to Jo's forehead. 'Stay there. I'm just going to grab something to clean up and see if I can get someone to stop.'

She protested weakly when he took his hand away, but he shushed her gently, grasping the door handle and anticipating some relief from the sauna inside the car – except it turned out the car was in a sauna and not the other way around. The afternoon sun belted down on him and he realised they couldn't stay where they were for long.

Opening the boot and rummaging in his shopping bag, the best thing he found to clean up the sick in the car was a pair of his new boxer briefs from Lourdes, which he snatched up with a sigh. A car roared past and didn't stop, despite his waving.

The next, though, did stop, flicking on their own hazard lights and rolling down the window. It was a family stuffed in like cartoon characters, the car bulging with people and equipment and cuddly toys.

'¡Hola, buenas tardes! mi... novia necesita agua! ¿Puedes ayudarnos?' He barely hesitated over calling Jo his girlfriend.

'Sí, sí, claro,' the father said as the mother rummaged at her feet. Adrián nearly fainted with relief to see the cool box in the footwell. The father explained they were headed all the way south to Málaga – a couple of days early to avoid the high prices of school holidays – and had come prepared.

The woman loaded Adrián up with soft drink cans, all of them blessedly cool. A litre of bottled water followed, as well as a pack of baby wipes, and he thanked them profusely, propping everything up on his sling and waving away offers of help to carry them to the car.

Before the family even drove off, he rushed back to the open passenger door and dumped his bounty on the seat. Frustrated at his lack of mobility, he grasped the Velcro fastening of his sling between his teeth and tugged, loosening it enough to get the thing off. His shoulder twinged, but it was the least of his worries.

Popping open a can of soft drink – he didn't even notice which type – he closed Jo's hand around it and helped her hold it to her lips to drink.

'I can do it,' she insisted weakly. 'Oh, wow, this is the best thing I have ever tasted.'

He pressed another can to her forehead, rolling it over her face while she purred with relief. 'I think you are dehydrated – and suffering in the heat.' Just how badly, he couldn't be sure.

'Are you going to make a menopause joke?' she shot back, but her eyes were closed and her head was propped against the seat.

'You have no idea how happy I am to hear you getting back to normal. You scared me.' He was still a bit scared, especially of the angry rash on her chest. A quick search on his phone located their next stop – away from Girona and not back into that nightmare traffic – and he memorised what he could of the route.

Quickly swiping up the bit of sick caked onto the steering wheel and obscuring the speedometer, he tossed the wipes and his poor boxer briefs in the rear footwell with a grimace and came around to the driver's side, opening the door.

'Out you come,' he said, grasping her around the waist with his good arm. She plopped her legs out and allowed him to shepherd her into the passenger seat, her head heavy on his shoulder. Quickly hanging one of his T-shirts over the window and pulling down the sunshade in front, he clipped her in and raced for the driver's seat.

Settling himself in, he took a deep breath, his hand hovering over the gear stick. 'It can't be so hard,' he whispered to himself. He knew the theory of driving a manual – at least he was old enough for that. He tugged the stick into neutral and turned the key in the ignition.

'Have you finished that can yet?' he asked as he gingerly gripped the wheel with his bad arm, leaning forward when the pain and stiffness in his shoulder protested. She obediently took another slug as he pushed in the clutch, changed into first and the car lurched forward unsteadily.

Once he'd coaxed the little car up into fifth, he raced down the two-lane motorway, pushing the speed limit. He hated that he couldn't drive *and* check on Jo, so he drove in a frenzy, barking at her intermittently to take a drink.

Steadying the wheel with his bad arm, he fumbled for the bottle of water in the centre console and plopped it in her lap, risking a quick press of his palm to her forehead. Still sweaty.

'How big do you think my bladder is?' she asked and he wondered for a moment if her voice sounded stronger, but he could see that rash in his mind's eye and hurried on. The fact that she didn't say anything about his terrible driving was not a good sign.

Fumbling for another can of soft drink while doing his best to steer, he pressed it into her hand. 'Drink!'

'God, you're bossy,' she muttered, but she held the can to her forehead before opening it and taking a swig.

Peering at the road, he exhaled in relief when he saw the turn-off he'd been watching for. After twenty-five minutes of veering around corners, jerky gear changes and two sudden stalls, he pulled up in front of a blocky, concrete building with the words 'Hospital Comarcal de la Selva' set above the entrance in white lettering.

'Do you want to go in by yourself or shall I park first and take you?' he asked, torn between his need to get her seen quickly and his reluctance to leave her alone.

Her head rose suddenly, as though she'd been asleep. 'Where are we?'

'The hospital. Here, I'll park and take you in. That's a better idea.' He started the car again, but it stalled immediately when he tried to take off. With a grunt of frustration and pain from holding the wheel with his bad arm, he tried again.

'What? Adrián, we don't need the hospital,' Jo said.

He turned to her in agitation, but paused to find her studying him, her back straight and her eyes clear. His gaze dropped to her chest. Even the rash looked to be fading. 'Just to be sure,' he insisted. 'You nearly passed out.'

'I didn't,' she contradicted him. 'I don't need a doctor. You said it yourself: I was dehydrated and suffering from heat exhaustion. I'm already feeling much better, so that must have been it.'

'I'd really rather—'

'I'm okay,' she assured him. 'I'm sorry to—'

'No! *I'm* sorry I made you—'

'You didn't *make* me do anything—'

'I can't let anything happen to you!' His chest heaved as he stared at her. The fact that she was arguing back with fervour suggested she was probably right and Accident and Emergency was a step too far. But he'd been so worried.

She watched him silently, her gaze flitting to his shoulder, to the hand resting on the gear stick. 'I'm feeling much better. Here, let me look something up.' A moment later, she'd found a site on her phone and read out, 'Symptoms of heat exhaustion: headache; dizziness; being sick, et cetera. Sounds right, hmm? Here it says to seek medical help if: the person is still unwell after thirty minutes of cooling; has a seizure; is confused; has a fever, fast breathing or a fast heartbeat. How about we just find somewhere to keep cool for half an hour. You can monitor me. If you're still worried, we can come back.'

He frowned at her, knowing she had a point, but not happy about it. 'We're here now.'

'Do you want to spend hours this afternoon in A&E?'

He really didn't. 'You'll let me look after you?' he asked, a warning in his voice.

'Yes.'

He took another quick glance at the maps app on his phone before giving a sigh. 'All right then. Just one second. Stay there!' He reached back with his good arm for the disgusting boxer briefs and the pile of wet wipes, dashing out of the car to pop them into the bin by the hospital entrance.

When he got back into the car and mopped up his hands with one more wipe, he grasped her chin to peer into her face, brushing a thumb over her lips to feel her breath and pressing his fingers lightly under her jaw to find the jump of her pulse. She was sweaty and warm, but not clammy as she'd been earlier.

Perhaps if he looked after her, she'd be okay.

18

Jo wasn't so sure about putting her wellbeing into Adrián's hands ten minutes later, when he hauled her out of the car and marched her down the street, his arm around her. But her legs were still wobbly and she admitted – only to herself – that she needed the support.

He'd shoved his bag and the rest of the rapidly warming drinks into her backpack and slung it over his good shoulder, shepherding her immediately into the shady part of the road where the towering stone pines protected them from the sun.

When they rounded the next corner, Jo's breath caught. Adrián peered at her in alarm, but she smiled, gesturing ahead to the sandy cove of glistening silver-blue water. He made a brusque comment, as though she should have known where they were going, and propelled her forward. She didn't need any further motivation to head for the water.

He sat her down on the edge of the boardwalk to slip the straps of her sandals through their buckles, batting her hand away when she tried to take over. She noticed with alarm that he'd taken the sling off and had a vague memory of him ripping the Velcro open with his teeth.

She should protest, insist she could look after herself, but she didn't. She soaked up the firm touch, the gruff tenderness of his hands – or 'hand', as he still favoured his left. Her thoughts were caught up and when she really should have objected, it seemed suddenly too late and she found herself pushed down into the water, clothing and all.

'Wait, what? What are you—'

That was when she realised the sea felt absolutely heavenly. A gentle wave lapped at her arms – blessedly cool. The lingering cramps in her stomach loosened almost immediately. Water soaked up the bodice of her dress, bringing relief, and she cupped her hands in the clear sea to splash her face with a happy groan.

Water trickled down the back of her neck, then Adrián's cool hand followed. She glanced behind her to see him gathering more water in his hands. His gaze focused, he dribbled the water over her shoulders, brushing his hand over her skin. Jo gulped, assailed by a new weakness that had nothing to do with dehydration. She swayed backwards towards him.

She felt lightheaded again, but not faint as he settled in the water behind her, encouraging her to lean back on him. She shouldn't have, but she did and it was wonderful. Her head lolled against his collarbone and she melted in a much more pleasant way than she had in the stifling Corsa an hour ago.

Breathing slowly in and out, she took in the greenish blue of the water at the edges of the bay, the clear bubbly waves around her and Adrián, the deep blue of the Mediterranean as it stretched out towards France and Italy. Headlands enclosed the protected cove, weathered and pockmarked brown rock, criss-crossed with crevices. Trees and bushes, from dark pines to the apple-green crowns of Mediterranean oaks fanned out on top of the rocks, interspersed with houses on the hills.

She never wanted to move – and not because she was tired. The lethargy had faded, leaving in its place a moment of stillness she hadn't realised she'd craved.

Adrián's arm snaked around her waist, holding her against him. She felt his breath against her forehead as he rested his chin there. His other arm floated in the water next to her, his hand drifting over her thigh but not touching down.

Studying his hand, with the blunt fingers from pressing guitar strings for thirty years and the brush of black hair on the back, she marvelled that it was no longer simply 'not Ben's hand'. It was *Adrián's* hand – familiar. Reaching out, she pressed her palm to the back and slipped her fingers between his. His thumb came up to brush hers in return.

She stared at their joined hands through the rippling water and wondered at all the awful things that had brought her here to this beautiful bay – to this beautiful hand in hers.

'I can't believe... I might not have seen this place if...'

'If you hadn't vomited on the dashboard?'

Jo grinned, glancing back to find him also watching their hands, his thumb now stroking continually along hers. His joke should have shattered the softness between them, but Jo still felt alarmingly mushy. 'If I hadn't drunk too much last night.'

'If the guitar hadn't got on the wrong flight,' he joined in.

'If we'd landed in Zaragoza instead of Lourdes,' she added, her voice trailing off as her thoughts became dangerous. 'If Ben and Mónica hadn't decided to get married,' she added, her heart beating in a warped rhythm.

Adrián turned his face to hers, his lips a breath from her cheek. 'You're still here,' he said quietly – an observation.

'I'm here, in this moment,' she repeated with a laugh. 'With you,' she added daringly. His arm tightened around her. 'We aren't going to get back in that car and head south tonight, are we?'

'I don't think that would be wise,' he agreed, his rasping voice peppering over her skin. 'We could get some food at that beach bar,' he said, pointing behind them. 'We probably shouldn't stay in the sun much longer.'

'Even a beach bar might not appreciate us turning up with our clothes soaked in seawater,' Jo pointed out, settling comfortably against him. 'Let's find a hotel and clean up. I hope we have one presentable outfit each.'

'Shit, I don't think I have any underwear,' he said.

Feeling young and frivolous and full of butterflies and not caring at all, Jo burrowed closer, enjoying the way his hands settled casually on her body. 'I'm sure that won't be a problem.'

His lips twitched. 'I used them all to clean up your vomit,' he pointed out.

She pulled away again with a groan, her hands full of his shirt. 'Are you trying to spoil the moment?'

He shook his head, gazing at her with a light in his eyes she was beginning to recognise. 'No, I'm just proving that *nothing* will spoil this moment.' He stood and held out his hand to pull her up. The strength had returned to her legs and her head was clear. 'Come on, Jo. Let's get you out of the sun.'

* * *

Jo's finger hovered between the icon for the messaging app and the one for making phone calls. Liss and Dec had both written asking when she'd arrive. Ben had sent clipped instructions about parking at the hotel. She was glad to hear they'd survived the trip in the heat-wave at least and she needed to let them know about her own mishap.

But she set her phone down again on the bedside table in the small hotel room and gazed out of the sliding doors instead of sending that message.

She missed her kids. She needed to get to this wedding to support them, to work through any last-minute feelings. But right now she was *here*, staring at the glistening sea and the jagged fingers of rock jutting out into the water, the patches of turquoise, hints of white waves and dark shoals – and listening to Adrián hum inconsistently in the shower, singing a line occasionally of a song she didn't recognise.

She was definitely *here*.

When the door of the bathroom slid open five minutes later to reveal her travelling companion in his jeans and nothing else, there were few places Jo could think of that she'd rather be – despite that silly gold chain.

'Better?' he asked her, peering into her face.

She nodded, lifting her chin for him to grasp with soft fingers as he studied her face. 'Hydrated, cool. Everything's okay now.'

'Good,' he said, his voice deep and raspy and skittering over her skin.

Then kiss me. She wasn't quite brave enough to blurt that out. Instead, she took a deep breath and said, 'And I'm not drunk.'

'Hmm?'

'I know exactly what I'm doing,' she confirmed. 'Completely in my right mind.'

His Adam's apple bobbed as his gaze lifted sharply to hers. 'What— What *are* you doing?'

She'd rather hoped he might get the hint, but she also appreciated the importance of full disclosure and open communication. Standing slowly, she looked him square in the face – no smile, no blush, no uncertainty – and said, 'I'm about to kiss you.'

His eyes drifted closed and his breath whooshed out. 'Good, because I need to kiss you back so badly.'

Jo remembered the frantic touches of the night before – even if her memories were fuzzy around the edges – but this first kiss wasn't frantic. It was slow and emphatic and stubborn. The way he clutched the back of her cotton vest top and swallowed a groan etched itself into her.

'Are we— Can we? Do you want to—' he murmured as his lips skimmed across her cheek to close just below her ear.

She looped her arms around his neck and came nearer. 'Yes,' she said. '*Yes.*'

'I don't have a condom,' he pointed out with an adorably earnest expression.

'It's okay,' she reassured him. 'I have an IUD and...'

His lips twitched. 'It's been a long time for both of us.' His palm ranged up her back and down again, down further. He bit his lip. 'I hope this isn't bad.'

'It might be,' she said, sharing his smile. 'But I'm willing to give it a try.'

His mouth met hers again, this time with a taste of the urgency of the night before. She grasped his face in both of her hands, wallowing in the kiss, in how good it felt – how good she felt.

He groaned her name as she pressed kisses to his face. 'I'm more than willing, Jo,' he rasped, his good hand tight on her body.

It might not have been the airbrushed, tumble-into-twisted-sheets, glimpses-of-taut-bellies, Hollywood film sex. There was some stopping and starting, a few amused smiles and a grimace or two when they forgot about Adrián's shoulder. But they got there – somewhere Jo had never expected to reach right now.

She hadn't realised her body needed it. She would never have guessed how easy it could be to let Adrián enjoy her with his hands and mouth on her skin – how she would blossom under the touch.

He kissed her and clutched her tight and burned her with those dark gazes of his that burrowed under her skin. Getting lost in the stolen moment with him dragged something secret into the light, something she didn't have to hide. As he came apart in her arms, his expression tight and hot, she tumbled with him, tired and whole and languid with relief.

19

Oxygen had only just returned to Adrián's brain in sufficient quantities for coherent thought when Jo's phone rang – of course. She dropped her head to his chest for a quick moment and he fluffed her hair, but then she hauled herself up to locate her phone in her backpack.

Taking a slightly wobbly breath, she pulled herself together to take the call. 'Sweetie? What's up?'

All he could think was: thank God the call hadn't come five minutes earlier – or *she* hadn't come five minutes later, since he'd valiantly – miraculously – held out until she got there. But his stomach still sank as he realised what she had to tell her kids – what he would have to tell Oscar too. She explained in stilted tones that she'd got sick from dehydration, rushing to reassure her daughter – he was fairly certain it was Liss – that she was okay, but that they wouldn't be getting back into the car today, just to be safe.

'I know this keeps happening. I can't believe it myself. Are you... hanging in there? And Dec? How's Oscar?' She perched on the armchair to listen, then seemed to remember she was naked and leaped up again. Adrián forced his gaze away in case she was self-conscious.

'We'll do something on Wednesday, just the three of us,' she promised. 'Oh, Dad wants to do what?' He wasn't sure if Liss would hear the choking noise she tried to smother. 'We'll work it out, Liss. As soon as we can: you, me, Dec and three enormous ice cream sundaes.'

He thought she was trying to wrap up the phone call, but it wasn't working.

'I get it,' she said gently. 'They're not your family and no one can force you to feel like they are. I'm proud of you for keeping it together. It'll be easier when we get there tomorrow – not just me, Oscar's dad. You won't be stuck all together when Adrián and I arrive, okay?'

She paused, grimacing as she rubbed the back of her neck.

'I'm fine,' she replied to something he hadn't heard in a measured tone. 'We get used to people with time, right? Oscar isn't punching you any more and Adrián and I... well, we've needed each other, with everything that's gone wrong.'

Adrián tried not to wince at her lukewarm words, but it wasn't anything he hadn't expected. He picked up his phone and started scrolling so he wasn't so focused on her private conversation. After a few more reassurances, she ended the call. He didn't look up, giving her space to react to the conversation without him watching. She sat heavily on the bed and stared out of the sliding doors at the deep, rippling blue of the Mediterranean, saying nothing.

'There was a cycling event today,' he commented blandly, still looking at his phone. 'That's why the roads were closed and the traffic was shit. There was some kind of road race.'

'Oh,' she murmured in reply. He glanced up to find her studying him. 'Is this the modern equivalent of lighting up a cigarette after sex? Orgasm achieved, let's talk about the news?'

'I thought you'd rather hear that than the poem I just composed to your breasts.'

She lifted a hand to her chest unconsciously before dropping it again with a frown. 'You idiot,' she teased.

'Do you think I'm joking?' he asked, flashing her his phone screen with the Notes app open.

'Show me!' she demanded, holding out her hand, but he held his phone to his chest and shook his head.

'It's embarrassing how much I like your breasts.'

The flush rising up her neck to her earlobes made him wish he truly had written a poem – although perhaps not about just her breasts, as lovely as they were. She rummaged in the bedclothes for her shirt and shorts and tugged them on, making him stifle a sigh of disappointment.

'If you ever want to see them again, show me your phone,' she said boldly.

He couldn't hand over the device quickly enough, enjoying the twitch of a smile on her lips as he did so.

'Huh, it's a shopping list,' she said drily.

'I'm sorry to disappoint. Next time it'll be a poem. I promise.'

'You're naked in bed writing a shopping list,' she repeated.

'The contents of my suitcase is dispersed across the Pyrenees and I don't have any clean underwear to put on. Do you want me to remind you what happened to my last pair of clean boxers?' he asked.

'No!'

He leaned over the bed to her, tilting his head up to capture her mouth in a brief, soft kiss. He grinned up at her when she blinked at him in a daze. 'I'm hungry.'

'Such a romantic,' she muttered.

By the time they made it back down to the beach bar – Jo mercilessly teasing him for going commando in his jeans – the place was already closing. After splitting the stale old toast from breakfast and Jo's last five squashed muesli bars – the fifth carefully broken in equal halves by Adrián – they climbed back into the rather whiffy car and headed for Lloret de Mar with the windows down.

His shoulder ached, but it wasn't the tight stab that told him something was wrong. It was only the pull of ligaments – healing, although in need of rest. Jo grabbed the sling from where he'd tossed it into the footwell earlier and strapped it on in the car park.

'Thanks,' he said, giving her a kiss that shouldn't have felt so normal. 'Come on – this way,' he said, grasping her hand and heading for the beach. She looked longingly at the bar they passed with inviting white umbrellas shading tables looking out over the long stretch of sand, but he tugged her further along the headland.

'Did I neglect to mention that I'm hungry too?' she grumbled.

'Shh,' he responded. 'There's somewhere better just a little further.'

The paved footpath followed the rocks, the sea crashing below them in the afternoon breeze. Adrián felt faintly nervous and more than a little silly to be treating this like some kind of bizarre first date, after they'd spent five days straight in each other's company and had just slept together. But when he'd seen the café on the map, he'd wanted to take her, like a lovesick chump.

As they followed the path up and down stairs along the very edge of the coast, a cluster of tables came into view, right by the rocks, under towering palm trees. The bar was set higher up, a white conservatory with umbrellas, playing mellow tropical music.

'There!' Adrián said, tapping a table. 'Better, no?'

She glanced indulgently at him and then out to sea, taking a deep, cleansing breath. There were people swimming in the clear lagoon protected by the rocks. It was a shady, secluded paradise at this time of day – secluded except for the other patrons of the bar.

But the place was so relaxed, Jo looked as though she could fall asleep when she collapsed into one of the wicker chairs.

'Yes, this is lovely. Have you been here before?'

'No. I found it on the map before and thought you... might like it. I mean, I wanted to come here too. It seemed—' It seemed as though he couldn't keep his mouth shut any more. 'Obviously sex with you has come at the expense of quite a few of my brain cells,' he mumbled.

She snorted a giggle, the sound so unexpected he stared. God, he liked her face. 'Are you suggesting we bonked our brains out?'

Joining her with a spluttered laugh, he said, 'It was worth the sacrifice – definitely worth it. You'll just have to be patient with me while I recover from you.'

'Now you're making me sound like an illness!'

'I did get heart palpitations and shortness of breath.' He drew her to him and kissed her before she could splutter a withering response.

The bar served some of the best paella he'd ever tasted, the prawns tender and fresh, tinged with a kick of spice from the chorizo. They only had one beer each, both pouting that they had to get back to buy clothes before the shops shut. When Jo slipped her hand into his for the more leisurely, full-bellied stroll back around the headland to Lloret, Adrián couldn't speak for a moment as his throat clogged, marvelling that he was the fortunate man who got to walk hand-in-hand with this phenomenal woman, even if it was only for today.

Arriving back at their hotel room an hour later, she wound her arms around his neck and leaned into him, tipping her face up.

'Thank you,' she murmured, 'for everything.' She pressed a kiss to his lips – soft, but insistent.

'I'm the luckiest man alive today.' The words tumbled out of his mouth.

Her answering smile was pleased, but sceptical. 'Then let's hope you take some of your luck into tomorrow.'

His skin prickling with misgiving he needed to banish, he hauled her close and did everything he could to show her he'd meant those words, regardless of what happened tomorrow.

* * *

Jo awoke to Adrián's lips skimming between her shoulder blades, his beard tickling her skin. That feeling from the day before persisted – she was still someone else, someone who had sex in the afternoon with a handsome man and then again in the evening.

'Something will go wrong, won't it? Fate has decreed that we don't have to go to this stupid wedding at all,' she asked quietly, before she'd thought it through. Behind her, she felt the air move as Adrián lifted his head to peer at her. She didn't turn, keeping her gaze focused on the glimpse of the sea between the gauze curtains. She felt too guilty to look at him and own the words.

'I didn't think you believed in fate,' he said smoothly, brushing a kiss over her shoulder.

'A blessed rescue from Our Lady of Lourdes, then,' she said, waiting for him to sigh or groan or tease her for her cynicism.

'Jo, you don't need fate or a rescue. You're one of the strongest people I know.'

'And I thought you knew me a little.'

To her surprise, his lips landed on her ear before he whispered, 'I do know you. I know you're going to show up at the wedding with rare grace.'

She sank into the sensations of his lips on her neck and his hand stroking the skin at her waist, thinking she would probably wish she didn't know how good it felt, when they said goodbye. 'I don't really feel the grace,' she insisted miserably. Rolling onto her back, she forced herself to look at him. 'We can't do this – touch, kiss, *anything* – at the wedding,' she reminded him.

'I know,' he said in his raspy voice, full of gratifying regret. 'That's why I'm touching you now, even though it won't stop me wanting to later.'

'You're impossible,' she murmured, pressing her forehead into his collarbone.

'You mean irresistible?' he quipped, his voice high with hope. She hated how his words could make her stomach tumble all over itself as though she could be his dream woman. What a crock.

He tipped her face up and kissed her, an aching, fragile sort of kiss that made her think of her alternate reality shattering, but even these shards were beautiful. They made love one more time, slowly and gently, as though they both knew something could break.

When they climbed into the car after breakfast and a litre of water, Jo squared her shoulders and reminded herself of everything she'd faced alone over the past five years. She was Liss and Dec's mum and if that came with a side-order of ex-husband's awkward wedding, then it was still worth it.

If a little devil in her mind suggested it might be nice for the car to break down or a sudden storm to block roads or a plague of locusts to force them to turn around, it didn't stop her putting the car into gear and heading for the penis place.

20

The car did not break down as they skirted Barcelona in mild traffic, missing all of the sights of that historic city. There was no freak storm forcing them to take shelter in Tarragona, no accidents to leave them happily stranded as they passed a place called Miami Platja – 'Miami Beach' in Catalan. With only a short stop in a seaside town for coffee and more tomato bread with cheese and anchovies and a plate of fresh mussels, they sailed along the motorway with no hiccoughs, right to the exit for Peñíscola.

Jo even managed to successfully navigate the complicated off-ramp, past a park that appeared to be populated with fake dinosaurs. Nothing at all stopped them from cruising into the town, where everything from hairdressers to supermarkets seemed to be named after dolphins, right to the beachfront hotel.

She couldn't quite believe it when she put the car into park in the short-term zone out front. Everything was completely normal, from the patrons drinking their coffee and cocktails at the café next door, to the gentle rush of the ocean. She'd grown to expect drama.

She peered at Adrián to find him regarding her, his brow thick with uncertainty. Did they go in for one last make-out? She licked her lips, not content with the prospect of *not* kissing him. It was odd, considering the number of years she'd managed to quite happily *not* kiss him.

'Mum!'

Positively leaping from the car with both embarrassment and relief that the decision had been made for her, Jo launched herself at the figure emerging from the hotel reception. His eyes were hidden under a thick sweep of brown hair as usual. His shoulders were hunched and he glanced away as soon as he saw her coming, but she'd heard the joy in his voice when he'd called out to her.

She wrapped her arms around him and squeezed, surprised when his spindly arms came around her in response. 'I missed you, kiddo,' she whispered, thinking of when he was small and had to cuddle into her tummy. Now the top of his head was higher than her nose.

Liss appeared and launched herself at both of them, her fierce hug refilling Jo like a jug of sangria – although it was too soon to be thinking of sangria again. 'Oh, thank God, Mum. We're supposed to go to the hairdresser this afternoon and I just *can't* any more!'

'Papá!' A little boy Jo wouldn't have recognised in a crowd dashed out of the hotel and flung himself at Adrián, who was still getting out of the car.

'Oof,' Adrián managed as the human missile made contact with his stomach. But he bent down and hauled the boy up with his good arm, settling his cheek on his son's forehead and then pressing a kiss there. Oscar had straight, spiky brown hair and Jo guessed he was small for his age. His little arms wrapped around his father's neck and clung.

Adrián crooned something in quiet Spanish and Jo had to tear her eyes away before she spent too long marvelling at the joy in his body language when he held his son and started thinking about how much she'd miss that casual affection.

Liss caught sight of something over Jo's shoulder and she turned slowly, slipping her arms around both of her kids. She knew what – or rather *who* – must be standing there, but it didn't make it any easier to force herself to turn around.

Her gaze settled on her ex-husband with a flash of feeling she didn't want. Words like 'new family' and 'first real marriage' rose up in her throat with a surge of bitterness, along with the urge to shout, '*Why did you make my life so complicated?*'

Instead, she arranged a tight smile on her face and said, 'Ben. I finally made it.'

He approached and she resisted a grimace as she lifted her face for a kiss on the cheek. She hated that even a *greeting* was never right between them, that thirteen years of her life were now a source of cold discomfiture.

'I was starting to believe you never would,' he said, as though they shared an inside joke. Liss bristled at the suggestion and Jo's stomach clenched.

'Jo!' Mónica swept through the doors in a jumpsuit made of fine red crepe and a pair of sparkly high-heeled sandals and Jo, seven years older, make-up-free, in a pair of cheap shorts and a T-shirt with no bra, felt the comparison keenly. But Mónica was a picture of ease and grace as usual, grasping Jo in a perfumed embrace and kissing both of her cheeks as though greeting Ben's sister and not his ex-wife.

Jo caught sight of Adrián over Mónica's shoulder, staring at his ex, and a new anger against this woman rose in her throat. She'd had Adrián's love and commitment and she'd thrown it away because she'd been too immature to work through change. The stirring of anger and jealousy on her part wasn't fair – or reasonable – but she felt it anyway.

'You have eaten lunch? Come and sit down. It's so hot. I'll get you a drink,' Mónica said.

'Thanks, I'm—'

'Where is your suitcase? Oh, silly me, we have it! Come on inside.'

Jo glanced back at Adrián, who only shrugged. Perhaps he hadn't noticed she hadn't greeted him.

'Adrián!' Mónica called, making Jo jump. She said something to him in rapid Spanish while he jostled Oscar on his arm and eventually had to put him down.

'Bueno,' he said, seeming to agree to whatever she'd barked at him. He turned to Oscar, recovering a conspiratorial smile. '¿Estás bien, campeón? ¡Vamos!'

He headed for the street with Oscar's hand in his and Jo belatedly remembered that 'vamos' meant 'let's go'. She gazed after him, her thoughts and feelings such a mess. 'Um!' she called after him before she'd thought it through. She caught sight of the guitar in the Corsa and hoped that was the reason she'd felt he shouldn't leave yet. 'What should I do with the guitar? And your bags.'

He just looked at her for a heartbeat and understanding of several different things passed between them: *This is really awkward; we had a good few days while it lasted; goodbye?* 'I'll find you later to get the keys, if that's okay?' *Yes, that's okay.* 'Oscar wanted to go to the park – *now*.' His smile grew lopsided and wry.

'Ah, okay. I suppose the guitar will be all right in the car for a few hours,' she commented.

'Yes, it's not as though Alberto hid the family's valuable heirloom jewellery in the case or anything. Six ruby necklaces in the lining!'

'You insisted the guitar itself was valuable,' she grumbled at his overdone humour.

'I'll come and find you as soon as I get back. Don't you three have a date at the ice cream parlour?'

'Yes!' Dec said, his voice breaking with more enthusiasm than Jo had seen from him in weeks.

'Looks like we have plans!' she said, tugging him to her and trying her best to leave everything else behind.

* * *

Morning dawned on Wednesday – or wedding-minus-two-days, as Adrián grumpily thought of it – with more unpleasant ex-family business on the agenda after a quiet evening when he'd mercifully been able to grab some dinner with Oscar and retreat to their room.

He'd spent the night with a pair of small feet in his ribs because the hotel had no more twin rooms or trundle beds. Oscar slept in any position except with his head on the pillow and performed sleep-yoga at least three times in the night but that was merely one of many reasons Adrián felt groggy that morning.

Even though he was dreading the breakfast room, he hurried downstairs early with Oscar – partly because his son had been up since the crack of dawn. Once inside the room, he made a beeline for the coffee machine. If Adrián had to finally say hello to his ex-parents-in-law that morning, then at least he was going to do so with caffeine in him.

The contrasting feelings should have been enough to snap him out of the haze of contentment from the past five days, but he felt out of kilter, as though he'd travelled to another dimension and hadn't properly returned yet. Everything he saw, he wanted to talk to Jo about, like the time Oscar had been to see the exhibit of arachnids at the Natural History Museum and then talked spiders for three weeks straight.

The doors of the breakfast room swished open and Jo and her son appeared. She wore a fitted linen dress – something from her own suitcase, in contrast to the cheap T-shirts she'd bought when they were stranded and that one flowery dress that had been dunked in the Mediterranean. He'd liked that dress. He liked this dress too.

She glanced at him and his mouth turned up in a smile before he'd decided how to react. She shared his grin with a quick one of her own and then turned away, making him realise he was probably staring at her with a goofy smile. He forced his attention back to coffee, asking Oscar if he wanted to press the button on the machine.

'Adrián?' he heard behind him and he bit back a groan. So much for that coffee.

Turning slowly, he came face-to-face with the man who had gruffly welcomed him to the family twelve years ago when he and Mónica had announced they were married. 'Buenos días—' He cut himself off with the word 'suegro' for father-in-law on his tongue. What was he supposed to call him now? It would be rude to use the first name of an elder, but the man wasn't related to him any more.

'Alberto,' he choked out when Mónica's father appeared to be waiting for him to finish.

The man's only reaction was a twitch in his cheek which Adrián nonetheless interpreted as outrage. Alberto was as austere and straight-backed and paunchy as always, even though Adrián hadn't seen him in three years. Instead of a greeting, Alberto said, 'I'm looking forward to seeing the old guitar.'

'Mmhmmph,' was all Adrián managed in reply.

'Papá, they don't have any Weetabix.' Thank God for Oscar, although his son's Britishness made more muscles in Alberto's face twitch.

With a tight smile for the older man, Adrián nabbed his coffee from under the machine and steered Oscar in the direction of the buffet. 'No Weetabix, but there's something better – watermelon! It's like being allowed to have sweets for breakfast.'

'I can have sweets for breakfast?' Oscar replied in Spanish, his wide-eyed gaze whipping up to Adrián.

A quick glance around the room revealed many a disapproving scowl. 'No, mijo,' he said, ruffling Oscar's hair. He leaned close to speak so no one would overhear. 'But those churros have just as much sugar. Don't tell the tías.'

He'd forgotten how many aunts Mónica actually had, but it was many – and even more who weren't her real aunts, but the family used the title anyway.

Plates piled with watermelon and churros, he ignored the prickle on the back of his neck that suggested he'd provided the entertainment for the morning in the form of his stilted conversation with Alberto, and located a table for two – coincidentally with a good line of sight to where Jo sat listening to something Declan was saying.

Her hair was down around her shoulders – damp and wavy. Oops, he was staring again. When he glanced away, a middle-aged woman gave him a pointed look and panic spiralled up his throat. If anyone found out he and Jo had... done what they'd done, the disapproving wedding gossip machine would have a field day. Mónica would freak out and Jo – he wasn't quite sure how Jo would react, but he wouldn't chance making the situation worse for her than it already was.

Ignoring everyone except Oscar, he sipped his coffee and discussed the episodes of *Bluey* they'd watched together last night, although his son wasn't very talkative that morning. His phone buzzed and he glanced at it, snatching it up when Jo's name appeared on the screen. She'd sent him two emojis, the guitar one and a grimacing face.

He glanced up, briefly catching her eye and trying not to smile.

She'd just fetched a plate of bread and cold cuts – not that he was watching – when the doors swished open again and she froze mid-step. Not a newspaper moved, no plates clinked. The entire room – which was mostly made up of wedding guests – appeared to be watching the ex-spouse show.

'Jo!' came an exclamation from behind Adrián. He was desperate to turn around and see, but he wouldn't, for her sake.

'Rita, hi. Ford.'

Adrián couldn't stand it. He peered over his shoulder to see Jo stiffly accepting kisses on the cheeks from an older couple.

'Sweetheart, it's been an age!' the woman, Rita, declared, squeezing Jo's arms. *Sweetheart?* All right, maybe *keeping* a term of endearment after the dissolution of a marriage was more awkward than giving one up. 'Where are you sitting? We have so much to catch up on!'

Jo's shoulders sank in slow acceptance of her fate and she gave a limp gesture in the direction of her table before leading them to it. Adrián picked up his phone and sent her a vomiting emoji, inordinately proud when she glanced at it and bit her lip around a smile. He watched her tapping something into her phone and waited for his own to vibrate.

She'd sent him an eye-rolling emoji. Unable to resist, he tapped on the kiss emoji and sent it off. She replied with a finger-to-lips emoji, a clear message that they shouldn't be flirting in any form in the breakfast room at Ben and Mónica's wedding hotel.

21

If this had been the sort of wedding Mónica had always wanted, they could have saved themselves some heartache and never bothered with the one they *had* had, Adrián thought to himself later that morning as he tugged at his loose linen shirt. He didn't know if it was normal for weddings these days to have several events beforehand, but it certainly made their quickie affair at the registry office in Madrid seem inferior – and not only because it hadn't been blessed by God and the Pope.

They were taking photos – *family* photos – at the largest labyrinth in Spain. He was tempted to just get lost.

Mónica's aunts were still giving him the evil eye, which, to be honest, he understood perfectly. Not only was he underdressed – he'd grabbed the collarless linen shirt in a hurry as soon as the shops opened that morning – he was a living reminder of the fact that this was Mónica's second wedding, even though they all agreed the first one didn't count. Everyone probably thought he'd dislocated his shoulder on purpose just to ruin the photos with the ugly blue sling.

That was still better than thinking he'd engineered the delays to spend more time with Jo, which he almost wished was actually the case. Then she might believe him when he told her she was beautiful.

She was holding up well – better than he was, he suspected. He might have assumed she'd enjoyed catching up with her former in-laws over breakfast, but he'd heard her vulnerable words on Tuesday morning and he could tell her smile was false. Her real smiles she saved for Elizabeth and Declan, whose full names he'd learned only yesterday. The three of them were so comfortable together, such a *unit*, it made him look forward to his and Oscar's future relationship with joy.

They were gathered at the entrance to the labyrinth in a loose semi-circle around a young photographer with too much energy. Mónica wore a cream dress that screamed 'bride' without actually being a wedding dress, with a little train to her ankles and sequins and embroidery on the front. Ben looked slightly queasy beside her in a grey chaqueta campera, a Spanish country jacket that was cropped and had buttons up to the collar of his white shirt.

What on earth had happened to the woman who'd met him at the lectern at the registry office wearing a flamenco dress and a smile? Had she changed? Or had he never really known Mónica at all, the way Ben had never understood Jo?

Did it even matter?

He tried to hold onto that peace about his life he'd found at Carles's party, that moment of clarity: *I'm still here*. But it had a very different ring to it when he was standing with Mónica's family, about to participate in a photo shoot that no one wanted him in: *I'm still fucking here*.

'You all play in the maze, be natural, smile and enjoy and I'll take some pictures,' the photographer repeated herself in English. 'And after, we do the staged family photos. Just have fun!'

A little hand slid into his and Adrián's bitter thoughts dimmed immediately. 'Is there anything... *in* the maze, Papá?' Oscar asked in Spanish.

'I think there's a dinosaur in the middle – not a real one,' he assured his son when a flash of alarm lit his eyes.

'Of course it's not a real one,' Oscar said, visibly pulling himself together. 'But I meant in the maze, not in the middle. There aren't... people going to scare us or anything?'

'No, mijo,' he reassured him as best he could. 'But let's stay together, okay?' When he studied the entrance to the maze, he was filled with a sense of misgiving and searched out Jo without thinking. She met his gaze, as she often did. It meant something, in this crazy situation – on occasion, it meant everything.

With tittering and laughter that sounded forced, the wedding party disappeared into the hedges. At first, they ran into someone around every corner, requiring Adrián to smile politely and Oscar to submit to pinched cheeks or hair stroking, which only put him more on edge. But soon enough they'd discovered a lonely corner, where they walked the pathways, Oscar's hand brushing the flat, shiny leaves of the tall hedge, the sky distant overhead.

'Is Liss my sister now?' Oscar asked all of a sudden, without looking at Adrián.

He glanced up at the merciless blue sky in hesitation. 'We say "hermanastra", not "hermana",' he explained the Spanish term for stepsister, wondering what Mónica had told him. 'Not much will change. Ben already lives with you, doesn't he?'

'Yes, but Liss only sometimes and she always stays in her room.'

With a deep breath out, Adrián searched for the right thing to say. 'Whatever you feel about this is okay, Oscar. You can't force yourself to love someone. Mamá will make sure Liss and Dec are kind to you, but whatever you feel – it's okay.' If only that were true for his own feelings – grief, bitterness, resentment. Those were just unhelpful – and that was before he added his infatuation with Ben's ex-wife.

'Like you couldn't force yourself to love Mamá,' Oscar said solemnly and Adrián nearly choked on his own breath. What was he supposed to say to *that*? *Actually, no, kid, it was your mum who didn't love me.*

'I loved your mum, mijo,' he said automatically.

'Then why aren't you trying to stop Ben?'

Adrián wasn't paying any attention to the maze any more and they turned a blind corner so quickly that he collided with someone, shooting a hand out to steady himself and finding the curve of a familiar waist.

'Jo!' he blurted out.

'Liss!' Oscar said, his face brightening. Adrián blinked as his son let go of his hand and ran to Jo's daughter.

'Hey, squirt,' she said tolerantly, giving him a poke that seemed affectionate and sending Adrián floating in uncertainty again. Mere mortals shouldn't have to be parents. 'We found the middle already. Want to see?' Liss asked Oscar, dragging him around a corner.

Adrián glanced at Jo to find her blinking, just as astounded at what they'd just witnessed as he was. They were a few heartbeats too slow and by the time they turned the corner after their kids, there was no one in sight.

'I'm sure it was this way,' Jo said with a frown, leading him off to the right, but they hit a dead end. A few more turns later, they had to admit they'd lost the kids.

'They'll be all right,' Adrián said, more to convince himself. 'If they find their way out, they'll wait for us and...'

'If they're lost, they're at least contained in the maze?' Her lips twitched.

'Since we're lost...' He'd meant to say something like, '*There's nothing more we can do*,' but her expression brightened a touch at his words and suddenly he was thinking of a hundred other things they could do now they were conveniently lost. She glanced at the dead end they'd just emerged from and grasped his hand to tug him in there after her. The hedge rose above their heads on three sides and he could have believed they were alone in the labyrinth.

'How was your ice cream date yesterday?' he asked eagerly.

'Perfect,' she said with a smile. 'No Ben, sea views, ice cream waffles with cream and marshmallows. How was the park?'

'Exhausting. I should have just bought him ice cream and dealt with the consequences later.'

'I earned my right to peaceful ice cream parlour visits with many, many hours at the playground when the kids were younger,' Jo pointed out with a pout that drew Adrián a step closer without him realising it.

'At least Oscar wants me here, unlike the rest of the wedding party,' he muttered.

Her gaze flew to his face. 'I can't believe Mónica's dad said that to you this morning.' She stroked her hand down his good arm.

'¡Ay! it didn't surprise me that he was happier about the arrival of the guitar.'

'Still, he shouldn't have been so rude.'

'What about your in-laws? It's like you never left!'

'Urgh, sometimes I think I'd prefer open hostility to pretending that everything's all right. How's your arm?' Her fingers ventured a little higher up his good arm.

'Okay,' he assured her. 'It doesn't hurt – until it does,' he admitted with a wince. 'What about you? No ill effects of the heat exhaustion? Did you sleep okay?'

'Without you?' she said laughing, biting her lip. 'Yeah, I'm okay. I think my... freak-out helped.'

He brushed a finger under her jaw when she stared down at her toes, bringing her gaze back to his. 'I think my freak-out is just beginning,' he admitted. 'Mónica and I got married in a crummy civil registry office in Madrid. What does all this absurd... hype mean for *us*?'

'Adrián,' she said firmly and just her voice was enough to distract him from his pathetic thoughts. When she grasped his forearms, all of his attention focused on her. 'It's not about us – it's about them.'

'Yes, but—' He sighed heavily. 'You're right. I thought *you* were the bitter one.'

'Ha,' she responded to his teasing with a dry look. 'And I thought you'd had an epiphany on the Costa Brava. Grief isn't linear. There are good days and bad days.'

'Today is a bad day,' he said emphatically.

'Yes,' she agreed with an exaggerated nod. 'In-laws and family photos.'

'Why on earth are we even in these pictures?' he grumbled. 'It's like those awkward shots you have with your ex-boyfriend from secondary school at family gatherings, except it's awkward *now*, when we're taking them, and not just years later when you look at them!'

'How did you know I had awkward photos with my ex-boyfriend?'

He wasn't sure if she was joking or not, but the little smile on her lips made all the difference to his mood. 'I'm curious to see them – to see if you have a type.'

'Of man?' she asked, shuffling closer and lifting her face. His mouth went dry. 'I don't think I want to be judged on my taste in men right now.'

'Good point. Ben's Spanish suit is definitely questionable, although he is quite good-looking.'

'This is a nice shirt,' she said, her palm touching down on his chest. *Yes.* 'I'm a little disappointed you managed to get it on all by yourself.'

'It's loose,' he explained inanely, but his thoughts were tangling the closer she came. 'Have you found something to wear to the wedding, since your dress went on a pilgrimage without you?'

'No, the frock shop pilgrimage awaits me tomorrow morning,' she said, scrunching up her nose. 'Although at least Liss wants to come with me.'

'I like this dress, but it doesn't show your tattoo,' he said, hoping he didn't sound overeager. His hand settled on her shoulder and then drifted to stroke the back of her neck.

'I never show off my tattoo when Ben's family is around,' she explained, but her voice wasn't quite steady as he brushed his fingertips over her skin. *Much better.*

'Jo?' he asked with his last coherent thoughts. 'I thought we weren't supposed to be doing this?'

'We aren't,' she agreed softly, but then she stretched up and brushed her lips over his and nothing else mattered.

'Okay,' he murmured before returning the kiss – trying for light, but too keen to manage it. He cupped her cheek and soaked her in, his thoughts fuzzy as though it were thirty-seven degrees again.

'¡Dios mío! Aren't we at the middle yet? I haven't even seen the photographer.'

Adrián jerked back so quickly he was worried the sound would travel to where one of the aunts was talking in Spanish on the other side of the hedge, their footsteps shuffling.

'Maybe she's got one of those drones and is taking photos from above,' came the response, also in Spanish.

He glanced at the sky in sudden alarm, but they would have to be very unlucky to be caught making out by a photographer's drone – if she even had one. Rustling at the end of the hedge near their dead end made him push Jo back a respectable distance and then the two women came around the corner, catching sight of them. A cartoon scowl crossed one face, the other was lit up with curiosity, which was even worse.

'Adrián? What are you doing hiding in a dead end? Who's that? Jo? The ex-wife?' She knew very well who Jo was and also how to correctly pronounce her name, but she still used a guttural Spanish 'j' that sounded more like 'Ho'.

'Ehm, we're looking for our kids. They seem to have disappeared.'

'You lost the children! That poor boy will be clinging to his mother again!'

Adrián took a breath in through his nose, trying not to think of all the times he'd been chided for being a mother hen when he should be a tough father figure and leave the clinging to Mónica. 'Hmm, is that the photographer?' he said, cocking his head as though listening. 'That way, perhaps?' The two women rushed off as quickly as they could – which wasn't speedy, given one walked with a crutch – and he gave an almighty sigh, his chest heaving enough to hurt his shoulder. 'I hate this maze,' he muttered in English to Jo.

'I liked it up until a minute ago,' she said, squeezing his arm. 'But we should find the kids. That was... a close call.'

He followed her out of their bubble, taking the hint that they should have stuck to the original 'no kissing' plan. 'We're lucky it was María Dolores who found us. María Rosa would have subjected us to the Spanish Inquisition,' he said lightly.

'That's a terrible joke,' Jo replied without looking at him. Her eyes scanned the hedges as though she could see through them. Pausing, she glanced at him and asked, 'Would she really have grilled us?'

'No,' he reassured her. 'I'm not even sure that *was* María Dolores.'

She spluttered an inarticulate response. 'I'm seriously questioning my taste in men right now.'

'Just my luck,' he said, winking at her.

The urge to take her hand was so strong he had to have a firm word with himself to resist, but when they turned a corner and emerged abruptly into an open square, he was relieved he hadn't risked it. An enormous – and rather poorly rendered – brontosaurus stood in the centre, vines growing up its legs. The three kids stood together, pondering the statue.

'It looks like a pantomime dinosaur,' he heard Liss say. 'I keep thinking someone's going to leap out or it will open its mouth and yell, "It's behind you!"' Adrián smiled, thinking about where Liss had inherited her sense of humour from.

'I think he's smiling,' Oscar said solemnly.

'Unless it's a she,' Dec added. 'I don't see a—' Liss whacked him on the arm.

'They're not going to sculpt a penis onto a pantomime brontosaurus in the middle of a maze!'

Oscar clapped a hand over his mouth. 'You said penis!' he mumbled through his fingers.

'There's nothing wrong with that,' she said, her tone peeved. 'It's the anatomical term.'

'All right, kids,' Jo said while Adrián was still feeling rather dumbfounded. 'We've found the middle. Are we ready to get out of here and find the bar?'

'I'm not really sure drinking will help, Mum,' Liss said with half a smile that suggested she might be genuinely worried.

'She meant ice cream,' Adrián defended her.

'Oh, I've found the children!' They all turned to see the photographer sweeping into the middle of the maze. '*Two* little brothers now!' she said with exaggerated sympathy for Liss as she snapped away. It was not the way to make Liss smile, but if Mónica wanted candid shots to immortalise this happy day, this was what she would get.

She turned to Jo and Adrián and he froze in panic, wondering if they were standing too close or she could see in his expression that he'd been making out with Jo in a maze two days before Mónica's wedding while their kids bickered a few metres away.

Then the photographer made everything worse. 'Isn't this cute couple going to smile for the camera?'

22

At just that moment, Jo's former in-laws emerged into the centre of the maze, accompanied by Mónica's parents. Jo squeezed her eyes shut, waiting for Ben and Mónica to appear so they could all break into a musical number about ruining weddings.

Adrián was doing that breath thing again that only poorly concealed his agitation and his arm kept nudging hers.

'Couple?' Rita cried, dashing Jo's hopes that nobody had heard the photographer's faux pas. 'Are you—? With Mónica's—? Is it—?' Rita even sounded hopeful, which grated. *Poor, lonely Jo needs the sympathy of her former in-laws* wasn't a narrative she was interested in.

She glanced in horror at Mónica's parents, who were stiffly expressionless, except Alberto had his jaw screwed shut so tight he'd need a power tool to loosen it for the photos. Despite their frozen faces, disapproval radiated from them.

Much worse, though, was the way Liss's mouth was hanging open, her expression bewildered as she looked between her mother and Adrián. Jo should have put a lot more effort into pretending there was nothing going on.

'Nooohhhh, noooo,' Adrián responded with that familiar, emphatic rumble. 'Dios, look at you all. What did you think? The photographer doesn't know who we are.' He turned to her with an amused smile. 'We're the exes,' he explained with an exaggerated hand gesture.

'Oh, I'm—' The poor photographer turned puce and began to apologise in rapid Spanish until the whole group was laughing rather hysterically to clear the embarrassment.

'Come on, kids,' Jo called. 'Let's find the way out.'

'After the photographer has taken her photo,' Jo heard Mónica's mother Barbara say behind her. 'We need *some* of you both, if we don't have you in the family photos.'

Jo's hairline tingled with embarrassment, relief, amusement, all amplified because she could feel it in the air around Adrián too, in the way he cleared his throat and moved awkwardly on his feet. She caught his eye and struggled not to laugh – it would definitely have been hysterical if she had.

'Shall we pose?' Adrián suggested with a poor attempt at a straight face.

'With the dinosaur, hmm?'

'Oh, just take the photo!' Barbara said with a flap of her hand.

'I just did – I took a couple of shots,' the photographer said with a meaningful smile that made Jo wonder what the photos would show.

They rounded up the kids and headed off into the maze again, precipitating sighs of relief in every corner – except perhaps from Liss. Jo didn't know what to do about her daughter's concerned look, so she ignored it.

'You guys are lucky you don't have to stand up in the stupid photos,' she said emphatically, glancing warily at Adrián. 'You could just go to the bar for an ice cream date.'

Was she testing them? Jo didn't want to lie to her daughter, but there also wasn't a lot she could tell her. She wasn't sure a seventeen-year-old could understand that they'd slept together, but it was probably only in reaction to the stressful situation and their shared turmoil at the prospect of the wedding.

The fact remained that being the two ex-spouses of an engaged couple was not a good foundation for a healthy relationship – if they had the appetite for another relationship at all.

'I'm sure the photos won't take long,' Jo murmured rather helplessly.

They wandered through the maze as the sun rose higher over the parched countryside. Jo began to dream of the sea at Peñíscola that had looked nearly as inviting as their cove near Lloret de Mar. Thoughts of that cove brought her right back to Adrián again and she had to go to some effort to resist asking him if he'd bought any swimming shorts yet.

Oscar seemed to be enjoying himself in the maze – the only one of their grumpy party. She hadn't had time to talk to Adrián about whatever was going on with their kids, whether they'd grown to tolerate each other or not – and damn it, she was thinking about him again. She'd barely known the man a week ago and now he appeared in each one of her thoughts – and feelings.

They'd just reached another dead end, making Liss sigh dramatically and even Dec's shoulders drooped, when the sound of voices made them pause.

'If you're so concerned, go and get a manicure together or something.' It was Ben's voice.

'That's your suggestion?' cried Mónica in response. 'She's Jo's daughter! Jo, who I bet never met a manicure in her entire life!'

It was impossible not to flinch, but the quick squeeze of Adrián's hand and Liss bristling and coming to her side helped her shake off the unintentionally hurtful comment. She found Dec's eyes on her, a long, assessing look that made her spine tingle with misgiving. Then his gaze shifted briefly to Adrián, before bouncing away again as he resumed his usual hunched posture, hands shoved in his pockets.

'This maze was a terrible idea,' Liss said under her breath. Jo was inclined to agree.

'This doesn't have anything to do with Jo!' Ben said from behind the hedge.

'Are you sure? It's like all our plans have been on hold until she got here!'

'Only because she was lost somewhere in France!'

'What would you have done if she hadn't arrived? Called off the wedding?'

'Of course not!' Ben snapped. 'What will *you* do now you are convinced Liss hates you? Call off the wedding?'

Jo's stomach dipped to her ankles and her skin felt cold for the first time in days. Oscar opened his mouth to say something, but Adrián tugged him close and pressed a hand gently over his mouth.

'What do you want me to say? *Yes, let's forget the whole thing?* I haven't seen you smile in days and this is supposed to be the—' At least Mónica seemed to have the circumspection to cut herself off before saying 'the best day of our lives'.

'Perhaps that's because you keep making me jump through hoops. Are we here to get married or to have a holiday with your *entire* family?'

'My family is important to me. I thought you understood that,' Mónica said in a wounded tone.

Jo felt a nudge to her shoulder and was surprised to find Adrián close enough that his arm pressed into her.

'Yes, but we don't need a thousand photos of them! I've done all this before: the engagement party; the welcome party; the rehearsal dinner; the first dance. I don't need to do it again!'

Unable to drop her forehead to Adrián's shoulder as she wanted to, she pressed a hand over her eyes instead. Ben, *you idiot!*

'This is the entire *problem* with us, Benny!' Mónica's tone was rising fast. '*You've* done it all before, but *I* haven't! It's not fair. And even if that wasn't the case, what does it say about how you value our future marriage?'

Jo met Adrián's gaze urgently. Yes, overhearing all this was like a thousand fresh cuts in an old wound, but it was worse for the children. They had to do something. Adrián dropped his hand from Oscar's mouth, pressing a finger to his lips in a final, silent warning to his son. He squeezed Jo's shoulder and then tiptoed away around the corner. Another time, Jo would have laughed at his cartoon-like attempt to walk quietly, his shoulders hunched.

A moment later, from a few rows away, Jo heard him say, 'Ah, María Dolores!' and a string of Spanish in an artificially loud voice. Mónica abruptly – mercifully – stopped speaking and Ben remained silent too. Jo wasn't sure if Mónica's aunt was actually there, but she beckoned urgently for the kids to follow her and sneaked out of their dead end under the cover of Adrián's loud conversation.

She didn't know if she was heading in the right direction for the exit, but the only important thing in that moment was to get away from Ben. A few turns should do it – just another one, two. When she judged them far enough away, she paused to breathe out, long and deep.

That's when Dec said, 'Where's Oscar?'

* * *

Finding a small child in a labyrinth sounded like a very difficult task but the reality was even more difficult than Adrián could have imagined. Any other child might have given up after twenty minutes – or after *two* if the parents were particularly lucky or the child had the attention span of a video-sharing app. But Oscar had disappeared so completely that, instead of a nice family photo, Mónica got a search party with dusty knees.

When a shout finally went up that one of his shoes had been sighted – sticking out from under a hedge as though they were ruby slippers and Oscar was the Wicked Witch – then began the mammoth task of convincing him to come out when he was obviously upset.

Adrián eventually told Mónica to go and wait with the car while he talked their son down. It took nearly forty-five minutes of him ignoring the loud opinions of Mónica's family and waiting and listening and artificial calm. He wouldn't have been surprised if everyone had left and he and Oscar had to get a taxi back to the hotel, but Mónica drove them silently back, looking exhausted, but only a fraction as haggard as he felt.

He returned to the hotel covered in dust, drowning in tension and desperate to make everything bearable for his son. The dust he could quickly dispense with – after washing down Oscar first – but the other two curses were less tractable.

It wasn't difficult to coax Oscar into bed for once. After the excitement – and upheaval – of the day, his son had been like the walking dead during dinner. Adrián was just as tired, but restless enough that he knew he wouldn't sleep yet. He tipped his head back against the sliding door that was open onto the balcony, soaking in the sound of the sea rushing outside and Oscar's even breathing.

With an enormous sigh, he stumbled to the minibar and grabbed the tiny beer from inside, not caring if it cost a hundred euros. He stepped out onto the balcony and slid the door shut behind him so the cool air didn't escape. The temperature outside was still stifling, even though it was nearly ten o'clock.

Perhaps this seaside wedding in a castle had been a stroke of genius after all. The hotel was on the esplanade, meaning he could stare out at the beach as the water changed from turquoise to navy to midnight blue with little white caps. The castle glowed warm orange with atmospheric lighting, where it sat atop a walled promontory at the end of the beach, flanked with whitewashed houses and palm trees. The wisps of cloud were a dull pink as the sun made its final descent behind him, over the land.

He wanted to lean on the railing and look out, but he still couldn't put any pressure on his shoulder so he leaned against the concrete wall separating his balcony from the next one, gazing out to sea and letting his thoughts drift.

The first thing he focused on was the memory of Oscar's face, bewildered and resentful, when Adrián had finally coaxed him out from under the plant where he'd wedged himself. The hour of searching in thirty-degree heat, the frustration of looking for a child hiding in a *maze*, had vanished in a second in the face of the surge of impotence he'd felt.

Mónica had fussed over him, but he'd sensed his ex-wife shared this turmoil. There was no solution to this.

The sound of another sliding door swishing open reached his ears from the other side of the wall, followed by a bottle cap popping off. A pair of hands appeared over the railing, holding a beer – hands he recognised. He tried to keep a lid on it, but his heart leapt.

'Jo?'

The hands jerked and froze and then her head appeared around the wall. 'That's your room?' she asked under her breath.

'No, it's María Dolores's room. I just climbed up to her balcony,' he whispered in reply. Realising one possible unintended implication of his joke, he continued, 'I miscounted. I meant to arrive on that balcony.'

She gave a splutter and said his name with a groan. 'We shouldn't be talking to each other.'

'Are you really afraid of María Rosa grilling us? I was joking.'

She glanced over her shoulder, disappearing again to slide the door shut with a mumbled excuse to Liss and Dec that reminded Adrián that she wasn't alone.

'Oscar might still be clueless, but mine suspect something and I don't know what to say if they do ask.' Her expression was pained and he didn't like it. She glanced warily at him. 'How are you? It looked like Oscar gave you a shock.'

His skin prickled as he churned through the emotions again. 'He does it sometimes – hides, runs away. At school too.'

'Just since the divorce?'

'No,' he said faintly. 'We had the social services on our doorstep when he was three because he worked out how to open the front door and wandered across the street. A stranger found him and called the police.'

'Oh, my God,' Jo said with a choke.

'They don't warn you that parenting can be traumatic – or marriage.'

Her hand appeared on his side of the wall and he grasped it eagerly, rubbing his thumb along her wrist.

'But do you think the conversation we overheard set him off?'

'Most definitely,' Adrián murmured. 'He can't put everything into words like Liss does. It just... boils in him.'

'Dec doesn't express much either,' she pointed out, her voice strained. 'They had time to get used to the living arrangements when Mónica moved in, but there's so much pressure on this couple of days.'

'Maybe Oscar had the right idea,' Adrián quipped. Jo kept a tight grip on his hand, as though she understood he was protecting himself with the joke.

'Do you think they're... overcompensating? Ben and Mónica? I mean, we established that we're far from ready for new relationships and considering how screwed up all of this is, I feel quite vindicated now.'

It was his turn to squeeze her hand and not let go. She held her head high, looking dignified and beautiful as she gazed out to sea with the fading light on her face. But there was sadness in her expression too – so much sadness.

'You think they're having a big wedding to hide the fact that their marriage doesn't have a good foundation?' he clarified.

She closed her eyes as a blush rose up her chest. 'Maybe that's the case. Maybe Ben is repeating history. What happens to our kids if they break up? What kind of message are we sending them?' She swiped at her face and he hated that there was a wall between them.

'Jo, you are a family with your kids no matter what. Every time I see the three of you, it makes me look forward to Oscar growing up. That's the message they'll get – that they're worth your love.'

'God, I hope so,' she said.

'It's the only thing we can do sometimes: hope. For Ben and Mónica too.'

'You really hope they'll build a good marriage? Even though she hurt you?'

'What's the alternative? You want to be right that much?'

She tugged her hand back and her eyes flashed at him. 'No, but if they make it work, then the problem really was with me!'

'It takes two people to make a marriage,' he pointed out gruffly, too tired to soften his frustration with her.

'And only one to break it!' she snapped. 'As you know.'

He stilled, her words washing over him with a dose of remorse. 'Maybe I was taking the easy way out to express it that way. Mónica left me but I gave up too. Like your big wedding, you did everything to work things out with Ben, while I... I just said hurtful things back.'

'So you're the one overcompensating for misplaced guilt,' she commented. 'Are you seriously going to play the guitar for them at the reception? Even though Alberto treats you like shit?'

'I've committed now,' he pointed out. 'I brought the guitar all this way.'

She made a little frustrated noise. 'And you think you weren't committed to Mónica,' she grumbled. 'I suppose it would be a shame if we went to all that trouble for the guitar in vain. Did you tell the airline about the family jewels hidden in the case? I bet they weren't insured.'

'Ha! But you should keep quiet about that. Alberto doesn't know I stole them out of the safe years ago and someone might hear you.' He delivered the joke half-heartedly and then sighed.

'I should get back before the kids work out we're sneaking around.'

'I wish we were sneaking around,' he said, the words slipping out before he could stop them.

'Adrián,' she began, her voice stilted, 'we probably shouldn't have kissed in the maze today. I'm sorry if I gave you the wrong idea.'

'I didn't get any ideas. It's kind of hard to think when you're kissing me.'

'I mean, all we do is talk about Ben and Mónica—'

'And the kids,' he pointed out.

'And the kids,' she allowed. 'I don't regret what happened while we were travelling, but obviously that was different.'

'We're back to PTA adversaries?'

'I'm not on the PTA any more,' she responded drily.

'Not even that? Are we little more than strangers?' He clapped a hand over his chest, hoping this time she wouldn't work out he was covering his distress with jokes.

'I was going to say friends, but if you're—'

'Friends,' he confirmed emphatically before she could finish. 'I don't think I could bear anything less.'

She peered around the wall to eye him one last time. 'Stop being so dramatic.'

As he listened to her footsteps disappear back inside her room, he realised he couldn't do as she asked. Dramatic as they sounded, his words were unfortunately true.

23

'That sounds like so much fun! Can I come along?'

Jo could almost see her daughter's hackles rising. She could only imagine one thing worse than shopping for pretty dresses for a wedding: shopping for pretty dresses with your ex-husband's bride-to-be, while your daughter looked on in mortification.

She should never have mentioned their shopping trip in the breakfast room, where anyone could overhear and try to tag along. Next, she'd have Rita asking to join them. She glanced reflexively at her former mother-in-law, looking away again in alarm to find the woman's eyes on her – in sympathy, as usual.

'Don't you have things to prepare for tomorrow? I wouldn't want to waste your time,' Jo tried diplomatically.

'My facial isn't until one o'clock. I'd love to join you. I know what everyone's wearing, so I can help you!'

Jo gulped, feeling suddenly sorry for Mónica. 'We'd... like some mother-daughter time, actually.'

'But you can do that when Ben and I are on our honeymoon. You don't think I'd sabotage you, do you?' she asked, dropping her voice. 'I'll be happy to see you in something beautiful tomorrow.'

Liss looked ready to vomit now.

'Trust me, the thought never entered my mind until now,' Jo assured Mónica. 'I know you have a much better sense of style and I believe you want me to look nice, but we don't want you to come with us.'

Mónica blinked at her, as though she hadn't been expecting a clear rejection. Jo breathed out slowly, strangely comfortable with the idea of being straight with her.

'I like you, Mónica,' she began, ignoring the sight of the other woman picking her jaw up from the floor. She sensed the fleeting glances of the family and friends in the breakfast room, but she was all done worrying about María Dolores – if she even existed outside of Adrián's bad jokes. 'I mean, I like you within reason. We're never going to be best friends and—' *I'm not sure I can forgive you for being so immature with Adrián.* 'I respect you and I believe you're trying your best.'

Liss was eyeing her as though she thought her mum had a screw loose.

'But this situation is awkward. Your future husband has *my* kids. We're a family built on the remains of two former families.'

Mónica flinched, but she didn't say anything.

'It is what it is. We don't have to pretend to be best friends. I appreciate that there's no open hostility, but we can't be close. You don't have to love Liss and Dec and they don't have to love you.'

That set Mónica off. 'But I'm *marrying* their dad! Of course we have to love each other!'

'You have to love Ben.'

'I *do!*'

Jo tried not to dwell on the fact that Mónica had felt the need to defend her feelings. 'But you can't force love. Oscar is young, but Liss and Dec are almost adults. They have a right to their own feelings – and so do I.'

Wow, it felt good to say that. She wasn't the confused and powerless woman who'd left Ben, unsure of what her life meant.

'You want to marry Ben? You have my heartfelt blessing, even though you don't need it. In fact, you should want to marry him even if I was threatening to scratch your eyes out.'

Mónica's gulp suggested Jo was getting carried away, but now it had all started coming out, she couldn't stop it. The breakfast room was unnaturally silent, but even all those eyes weren't enough for her to backtrack.

'Marrying Ben isn't going to be all rosy – or anywhere near perfect. You have to accept that you can't make my kids play happy families. You might have to meet them where *they* want instead of where you're comfortable. You're going to be a stepmother. This is the reality, even if the priest has found a loophole to call it your first wedding.'

Mónica bristled. 'I do know how that must feel for you—'

'You don't,' Jo said, cutting her off gently. 'But if that's what you want for your wedding, it's your choice. My dress? That's my choice – my feelings too. I'm Ben's *ex-wife*. I won't cause you any trouble, but I'm here – I'm still here.' She just *knew* Adrián could hear her and she wished she knew what he thought of her words. 'Marrying Ben means occasionally dealing with me. I'm prepared to make that relationship amicable – friendly even, over time. But I'm not prepared to pretend that everything is perfect and my first marriage didn't exist.'

She felt Liss's hand slip into hers and her blood rushed in her ears.

'Um, while we're here,' she added. 'I really wanted to help Liss choose a dress myself. I understand she already has one, but if you don't mind, we'll buy another one today.'

'Oh, of—' Mónica looked a little at sea. 'Of course,' she said solemnly.

Ben made his belated entrance at that moment and it would have been impossible to miss the tension in the room. When he noticed Jo and Mónica, he rushed over.

'Everything okay?' The familiar sweep of hair fell over his forehead, as it always did when he was stressed. She knew every inch of his face – his body, his mannerisms. But it was odd how detached she felt when he approached. In fact, she surprised herself by willing him to comfort Mónica, to show her some kind of support during this unavoidable confrontation.

His hand snaked around Mónica's waist. Jo stared for a moment, that tiny gesture making her feelings stumble over each other. She prompted Mónica with an expectant look. She should answer Ben's question.

'Yes,' the other woman said curtly. 'I think so.' She grasped Ben's sleeve. 'Let's get a coffee, mi rey. I haven't woken up yet.'

If Jo hadn't already eaten, she would have had to find a café because there was no way she could stay in the room after that conversation. She floated towards the door, hardly aware of her own footsteps. She could really do with a dumb joke to burst the tension right now, but Adrián was still eating and they'd agreed to stay away from each other – at least she thought they had.

'I'm so glad you're here now, Mum,' Liss said emphatically as soon as the doors closed behind them. 'You're my hero.'

Jo wasn't going to cry – she *wasn't*. 'I hope I said the right thing,' she murmured.

'It was the truth. Someone needed to say it. I'm so tired of pretending – and I'm soooo glad I don't have to wear that hideous dress!' She threw her arms around Jo. 'You saved the wedding.'

Jo choked. Liss was exaggerating but Jo wasn't sure if she truly wanted to give up the protection of her resentment. It had kept her detached – and safe – for too many years. Damn it! She didn't want to cry when she couldn't begin to explain her feelings to her concerned daughter.

Her phone beeped and she gave herself an inward shake as she grasped for the distraction to extricate herself from her confronting thoughts. But she started when she saw it was a message from Adrián.

You were right – honesty is sexy. You're so hot right now.

Stifling a snort, she shepherded Liss in the direction of the stairs before her daughter had a chance to ask what she was laughing about.

Jo was surprised three hours later when Dec's response to her text about lunch informed her he was on the beach. Not the type to sunbathe if there was a darkened room available, Dec didn't explain what had lured him out, so Jo and Liss just exchanged a puzzled look and dawdled in the direction of the waterfront.

The sun beat down on the fortifications looming over the water and the beach stretched as far as Jo could see – apparently as far as the distant blue hills on the northern horizon. The sand was dotted with parasols and people stretched out on towels, but it wasn't crowded.

She was just starting to think about ice cream when she caught sight of Declan and her jaw dropped. His hair was wet and dripping in his face. He was wearing swimming shorts and had obviously been for a cooling dip. And he had an enormous smile on his face as he flicked a neon-yellow frisbee down the beach with a run-up, tumbling into the sand when he threw it too hard.

On the receiving end of the frisbee – or rather, leaping to miss

Dec's wild throws and then stumbling through the sand to retrieve it – was Adrián, also shirtless and wet from the waist down, but with the sling still strapped around his shoulder.

Jo had to stop for a moment to fight the warmth shooting through her at the image they made: Adrián and *her son*. Together. She swallowed the emotion that swelled up in her throat.

Adrián saw her and waved, a grin splitting his face and shivering through her. Dec turned and waved, too, and she noticed Oscar in the shallows, building something with a bright red shovel.

'Just don't let him fall over!' she called out.

'I won't!' called back Adrián.

She laughed. 'I was talking to Dec!' They both turned to her in surprise. 'What?' she said as she and Liss approached on the sand, kicking off their sandals. 'I nursed you back to health. I don't want to have to do that again.' She was aware of Liss's sidelong glance, but ignored it in favour of Adrián's open smile – and his bare chest.

'There are two loungers and a parasol over there if you two want to stay out of the sun,' he said.

'Do they belong to María Dolores and María Rosa?' she asked.

'Something like that,' he said with a laugh.

Hanging their shopping over the back of one of the chairs, she stretched out next to Liss, as contented as a cat in a sunbeam, especially when a glance to her left produced the view of Adrián leaping for the frisbee – and continually missing. He'd tied his hair up in a little ponytail that she would have thought was ugly and annoyingly swashbuckling a week ago.

She was rather partial to swashbuckling today. Perhaps the gold chain was supposed to be piratical.

'Do you have to be so obvious, Mum?' Liss said with a long-suffering sigh.

'Hmm?' She tore her eyes away from Adrián, the hair on her neck standing up at her daughter's queasy look.

'That was painful to witness. If you need pictures of hot guys, I can train the TikTok algorithm for you.'

She nearly asked if TikTok had videos of forty-two-year-old grumpy dads who played the guitar until she realised that would make everything worse. She opened her mouth, wondering if Liss was too old to accept a glib confession that she and Adrián 'liked' each other, but her daughter spoke first.

'Does this mean you're ready to date now? That would be one good thing to come from this wedding.'

'What do you mean?'

'Closure. I always wondered if you'd get back together with Dad because you both seemed so sad.'

'It was a... grief process, Liss,' she said softly.

'Was?'

'Are you so worried about me?'

'No. You don't need a partner to be happy.'

She squeezed Liss's thigh. 'Good answer.'

'But you looked happy just then, ogling Adrián.'

'I wasn't ogling him,' she insisted, but her words trailed off. 'Okay, maybe a bit. But you can be attracted to someone and still not be interested in anything... romantic.'

'Does he know that? It kind of looks like he's sucking up to Dec.'

It did, which was why Jo's stomach was fluttering and doing repeated loop-the-loops.

'He should know.' She bit her lip, deciding Liss deserved at least part of the truth. 'We decided to be friends. Anything... more seems like a bad idea.'

'Mum! Did you kiss him?'

'I don't really want to talk about it. The wedding is tomorrow—'

'You did!'

If Jo wasn't sitting in the shade of the parasol, she would have thought she'd had too much sun. 'It was... intense, when we were trying to get here and everything went wrong. But don't worry. The most important thing is that it doesn't get weird for you kids.'

'The most important thing is taking a chance with a guy you like, Mum. You're old, not dead.'

'Gee, thanks,' she mumbled. 'You'll eat your words when you're my age.'

'I hope I have a hot boyfriend when I'm your age,' Liss said with a sniff.

'Have you forgotten he's Mónica's—'

'Of course I haven't forgotten!' Liss said, sitting up. 'But if it was someone else, I bet you'd use the excuse that you're Dad's ex-wife! I'm a teenager. I know it's hell when you like someone, but if it's hell anyway, why not try it out?'

'I can't believe you're encouraging me,' Jo said, emotion rising up her throat. 'After all the angst about Dad, why would you think it's a good idea for me to start seeing someone?' The 'someone' sat uncomfortably on her tongue, as though it didn't matter who, when the 'someone' was the *only* reason she'd even entertained the idea of dating – *dating!* That awful activity where both parties posture and suffer and pretend they're normal. 'And what about Oscar? I thought you didn't like him!'

'I didn't like how Mónica keeps trying to make us a family – which you fixed for me this morning. If he was just some kid... sometimes he can be sweet. Dad barged over us, sitting us down to "tell" us stuff instead of asking. You're asking and it makes all the difference. I feel like part of things this way – and I'm shipping you two a little as well.'

'I'm asking because I'm uncertain,' she pointed out. 'And don't get too attached to the idea of me finding someone new. *Everything* has gone wrong for Adrián and me so far.'

'I trust you,' Liss said. Simple words, but they acted on Jo like fire on clay. 'If you trust him, then go for it!'

If you trust him... Wasn't that the question?

Jo didn't need any encouragement to turn and look at Adrián, where he was talking to Dec about something, pointing out to sea. He noticed her and gave her a grin big enough to be seen from the yacht out in the deep water. How strange that they'd arrived in Peñíscola, survived another day from hell yesterday, but this little parallel world had travelled with them. Not only that, but their kids had jumped through the portal too.

Could they really take all this back to London with them? Was closure something she could find at this wedding amidst so much embarrassment and hurt?

24

'Adrián, can Oscar come and watch a few episodes of *Bluey* with us before bed?'

Liss's question as they wandered into the lobby of the hotel after an early dinner that night took Adrián by surprise. 'Do you and Dec like it too?' he asked in confusion. The sudden mental image of him snuggling up on the sofa with Jo while their kids sat in front and they all laughed caught him in the guts.

It was miles away from the picture they'd made at the pizza restaurant they'd been dragged to for dinner with the rest of the immediate family. Jo had seemed nervous and withdrawn, which he didn't like at all. The wedding was tomorrow. Of course she was withdrawn.

'We got into it in Zaragoza,' Liss explained with a bright smile – a little too bright. 'You wouldn't have to come. We're just in the room next door.'

'Oh, I love *Bluey*. Oscar probably shouldn't get to bed too late, but a few episodes is a great idea if you're sure you and your mum don't mind us piling into your room.'

Liss was blinking at him, unimpressed. Her eyes were a darker blue than Jo's, but there was a sparkle in them and a tilt to her smile that was so familiar, he struggled to remember that he barely knew her.

'Oh, Mum won't like *Bluey*,' Liss said, dropping her chin and enunciating clearly.

'Why not?' Adrián said in mild offence. 'I know it's a kids' show, but it's really funny, with lots of hidden messages for parents.'

'Adrián,' she said through clenched teeth. 'I've been watching Oscar off and on for a week. You don't have to stay. Mum doesn't have to stay.' She met his gaze and raised her eyebrows.

Understanding dawned slowly. Surely she couldn't mean— He glanced at Jo, who was staring pensively at her sandals as they headed for the stairs. He had fond memories of undoing those sandals.

'Liss, I appreciate the thought, but you don't—'

'You two are hopeless,' she said, cutting him off.

'It's just not the right time,' he said gently.

'Will there be a better time?'

With a shot of panic, he realised they would all leave on Saturday and he might never see Jo again. The prospect was intolerable. Their footsteps echoed in the stairwell as they climbed the two floors to their rooms.

Outside the door of Jo's room, Liss paused and said, 'Mum, Oscar is going to come and watch some *Bluey* with us.'

Jo still seemed distracted, which only sharpened Adrián's panic. 'Oh, what's *Bluey*?'

'It's a TV show for kids,' he explained. 'But it's wonderful – funny and insightful and sometimes it makes you cry.' He trailed off as he felt the amused gazes of the whole family.

'It makes you cry?' Dec repeated teasingly.

'Well, yes, it's very... poignant.' His gaze flitted to Jo to find a hint of a smile on her lips.

'I might have to check it out,' she said.

There was something in the way she watched him intently that tightened everything up inside him until he heard himself saying, 'Do you want to have a drink? On the balcony? The kids should be okay if they're all crying in front of *Bluey*.' He held his breath.

'Sounds good,' she said lightly, but something shifted, as though spending time together was a bigger deal than it should have been, after all they'd been through. She was glancing at her shoes again. Was this... a date? He flushed to his hairline. Were they ready for that?

When they arrived at their doors, Liss opened up and shooed them in the direction of Adrián's room. 'Oscar complains when people talk while he's trying to watch TV,' she explained.

Adrián grinned at her. 'He does. Did I... already apologise for leaving you stuck with him for so long?'

'Sometimes being stuck with someone means you get used to them,' she replied, looking him square in the face.

He opened up his room, which was sweltering even though he'd left the curtains closed. As he tugged off the sling, he cranked up the air-conditioning so he and Oscar would be able to sleep and fetched two more tiny beers from the restocked minibar before leading a quiet Jo out onto the balcony where the evening breeze brought a refreshing hint of the cool night to come. Taking a seat across the table from her, he popped the caps and tapped his bottle against hers without looking at her for too long. He didn't like the hesitation between them, but he also didn't want to risk her leaving.

An ocean view soothed everything, in his opinion. He gazed at the castle as the lights came on, bathing the brick crenellations in an orange glow, and then out to the distant horizon. The air was salty and the sight of the beach, now mostly empty, reminded him of the afternoon he'd spent getting to know a boy who made cutting jokes just like his mum.

'Did my kids set us up?' she asked doubtfully.

'They did,' he said after clearing his throat. 'Liss did. I don't know if Dec had anything to do with it.'

'Were you trying to get on Dec's good side today?' she asked.

'Yes,' he admitted readily, glancing again at the rolling sea. 'I didn't think he'd like a manicure, so—'

Her foot nudged him – hard – under the table. 'You don't need to suck up to my kids.'

'I know,' he said, unable to stop himself continuing, 'but if you're not around, they're the next best thing.'

Her mouth dropped open. After a moment of studying him with something like dismay, she stood slowly. Worried he'd laid it on too thick and she was about to leave, Adrián leaped to his feet as well. But she didn't turn to go. She stepped closer.

Lifting her face, she brushed her lips over his. Why did it seem more fraught every time they kissed? He pulled her close and enjoyed the relief before resting his forehead against hers and waiting a moment to get his breath back.

'Are you sure you want to look Liss in the face after spending our time kissing?'

'Kiss now, work that out later,' she murmured, her lips against his.

Worried about making their situation worse, he scrambled for some order to his racing thoughts. 'I thought we were supposed to just be friends,' he reminded her, hoping she'd say, '*Screw it. There's obviously so much more between us.*'

She hesitated, shrugged and gave an inarticulate noise and then just kissed him again – the only answer she seemed capable of giving. Adrián grasped her cheek and stilled her with a firm kiss.

'Shouldn't we talk about this?'

'I'm so sick of talking,' she said, her voice thick. Their lips met again, hot and sweet this time with the taste of crumbling intentions. He couldn't have held a rational conversation if he'd wanted to with her mouth on his. 'Don't talk, just... show me,' she whispered between unsteady breaths.

He understood her in his instincts – in his blood – feeling the vulnerability, the old hurts she usually wouldn't admit to. And he understood in his heart what she was inviting him to do – the step she was taking, that might be the wrong one, but it didn't matter because it was in his direction.

Gathering her gently with his bad arm, he lifted his other hand to her face, stroking his thumb over her cheekbone, her jaw, her bottom lip. A breathy kiss to her hairline was: *You're an amazing woman.* A nuzzle to her jaw told her: *I'm going to miss you so badly after the wedding.* A slow, gentle kiss to her lips meant: *I'm afraid you'll say no if I ask to see you again when we get home.*

Her eyes were closed and her hands fisted in his linen shirt. Despite the unexpectedness of everything that had happened, she felt more real to him than anything in his life with the exception of Oscar.

She was so beautiful, he needed to show her how he saw her.

Grasping her hand, he pulled her inside, curling an arm around her when she shivered at the change in temperature now the air-conditioning had done its job. Tugging her to the entryway, he turned her gently with his hands on her hips until she jerked in surprise at the sight of herself in the full-length mirror.

She tried to turn away, but he held her in place, holding her gaze in the mirror. Words were on his lips, but he had to say them with his eyes and his hands. Grasping the hem of her T-shirt, he eased it up and over her head, watching the movement of her throat as he nudged her out of her comfort zone.

Pressing kisses to her ear and neck to distract her, he watched her eyes grow dazed as they followed the movement of his hand skimming gently over her body. Catching her gaze briefly, he ducked to press a lingering kiss over her tattoo. Her breath was unsteady. His eyelids drooped at the tenderness gushing inside him.

With a final, firm kiss over the hummingbird, he urged her to turn and tipped her chin up with his fingertips, feeling the flutter of her pulse. He leaned down and when his open mouth met hers, he thought for a fleeting moment it meant: *te quiero.*

'Adrián,' she whispered, her voice tight with emotion that shuddered through him as well. Her arms wound around his neck and the afternoon being together as some kind of family had been perfect and he wanted her and she was here in his arms where she belonged—

There was a knock at the door.

As they were standing right in the entrance, the sharp sound rang out like a crack and they wrenched apart.

'Mierda!' he muttered under his breath, smoothing his hair in frantic alarm.

'It's probably just one of the kids,' Jo whispered in reply.

Adrián was halfway through a nod when the knock came again, followed by a strained, familiar voice saying, 'Adrián? I have to talk to you – now!'

His stomach sank heavily and filthier curses rose on his tongue. He glanced at Jo in panic, struggling to gauge her thoughts – her feelings – from her grim expression. She clearly didn't want to be caught with him.

'I'll try to get rid of her quickly—'

'No!' She stopped him with a hand on his arm. 'She'll see me!'

To buy time, he raised his voice and said, 'Eh, ¡un momento!' He only just remembered to speak in Spanish. Dropping his voice to a whisper again, he said, 'What else are we supposed to do? Hide you behind the curtain?'

She glanced around her in dismay. 'The bathroom. I'll hide in the bathroom.'

'You don't have to do that. She won't stay long, I promise. I'll just see what she wants – and when she sees you, she definitely won't stay long.'

Jo shook her head fiercely. 'She can't see me here.'

'Why not?' She hadn't understood him when he'd kissed her with all of his hopes, or if she had understood, she didn't share them. That realisation was more frustrating even than Mónica's untimely arrival.

'Don't be daft, Adrián. It's their wedding tomorrow. It's awkward enough to be here as the ex-wife of the groom. I'm not going to be the other woman as well!'

'You're not the other woman, for fuck's sake!'

She turned away and he grasped her arm to stop her, but she tugged it back angrily. 'Don't leave her waiting!' A moment later, the bathroom door closed in his face.

25

Adrián wrenched the main door open with too much force, but Mónica didn't seem to notice as she swept into the room with her chin high and a wounded air. He wondered what he'd done wrong and then caught himself. Whatever this was, it wasn't about him any more, no matter what his ex-wife thought. He didn't need to be defensive.

But she stepped up close, grasping his upper arms and tipping her face to his and unease whipped up his throat.

'I'm so confused!' she cried in Spanish. 'I'm supposed to be getting married tomorrow and I don't know if it's the right thing!'

'Supposed to be?' he repeated, his voice high. His dismay at the prospect of the wedding *not* taking place was a new development.

'I don't even remember why we got divorced, Adrián!'

Knowing Jo wouldn't understand the Spanish was only a small comfort as he gulped with misgiving. 'You were unhappy,' he reminded her.

'I'm unhappy now and that's not your fault!'

He gritted his teeth. 'It's not Ben's fault either. Don't you love him?'

'I loved *you*,' she said and the cold tingle on Adrián's skin was another surprise. It was discomfort, repulsion even.

'You weren't sure about that at one time,' he pointed out.

'Love isn't how I thought,' she said with a sniff. 'There's something I need to do. I can't get married without it. Will you help me?'

'Hmm?'

'I need you to kiss me,' she said emphatically.

'No,' he said categorically, panic simmering in his stomach at the thought of Jo hiding on the other side of the flimsy bathroom door, probably remembering Ben cheating on her.

'I need to remember what it was like so I can find some perspective on marrying Ben!'

'No!' he said more firmly. 'I'm not going to kiss the bride the night before the wedding!'

'I'm *asking* you to help me! Why not?'

'I don't want to!' he said, throwing his arms out for emphasis and groaning when the movement jerked his bad shoulder. 'It won't solve anything anyway. I'm your past, Mónica – at least any romantic relationship we had.'

'You used to call me "mi amor",' she said softly.

'What does Ben call you?' he prompted.

'Mónica,' she said with a grimace. 'He doesn't understand that sounds so distant. British people can be so distant.'

'I know what you mean,' he responded. 'But to him, your name means something precious.' The way his name spoken in Jo's voice was his favourite way to hear it.

'How do you know that?'

'He wouldn't be here *marrying you* if he didn't love you.'

'But he had Jo,' she added, her voice cracking.

'And I can guarantee he's not in Jo's room asking to kiss her right now. He's probably in his own room dreaming of seeing you walk down the aisle tomorrow.'

She took a step backwards and plopped onto the bed, her hand rising to her forehead. 'I'm so stupid.'

'You're not,' he said kindly. 'It's an emotional time. Maybe we skipped this part by having a low-key wedding. Maybe you have the right idea now, celebrating the magnitude of the commitment.'

'I don't... what if I don't deserve him? He's so strong and in-control.'

Unlike me, he thought with a wry smile. 'You don't have to deserve him. You only have to love him.'

'And he has to love me,' she added with a pout.

'I'm pretty sure he does, but what do I know? I understand it's tradition not to see the bride the night before the wedding, but you're thirty-nine years old, not a blushing virgin. Go knock on *his* door instead of mine.'

She peered up at him. 'You seem different. More assertive,' she said thoughtfully. 'I like it.'

'That's... nice,' he muttered in reply. 'But you don't have to like me any more.' His gaze flitted to the bathroom of its own will, marvelling at the truth of those words. If only Jo could understand them. 'You don't need to be here tonight, Mónica. Go and get some sleep.'

To his surprise – and relief – she took his advice, rising from the bed with a sigh and trudging to the door. When she paused, Adrián noticed she was looking at Jo's shirt, scrunched up on the floor, and he held his breath.

When Mónica turned back to him, her expression was pensive and perhaps a little wry. 'I'm sorry I disturbed you. Good night, Adrián.' She left with her head as high as when she'd arrived, a tight smile on her lips.

* * *

Jo had never been claustrophobic, but her chest was tight and she couldn't seem to suck enough air into her lungs in the abject darkness of the cramped bathroom. She'd been so concerned with her dramatic departure that she'd forgotten to turn on the light and the switch was on the outside. Her leg bounced with the need to escape – the bathroom, the situation, *her life!*

The voices outside the door grew louder, Adrián's tone sharp, and then the hotel room door opened and closed with a final snick and Adrián sighed so deeply she heard it where she was hyperventilating in the dark. The bathroom door flew open and as desperate as she'd been to get out, she cringed away from the light – away from Adrián.

'Jo?' he asked, his voice raw. 'You didn't turn the light on? Are you okay? Mierda, I'm so sorry she came by.'

She rose to brush past him, but his hand clasped her upper arm. She had to go. She didn't want to do this, couldn't fathom how she'd ended up here, freaking out and upset and just as small as she'd ever felt with Ben.

Swiping her shirt up and refusing to remember the tenderness of his kisses on her skin or think what would have happened if Mónica had recognised her clothing on the floor of Adrián's room, she shoved it over her head and slipped her arms in.

'Jo, talk to me,' he said, an edge to his voice. 'What's wrong?'

'I can't do this,' she muttered.

'This... the kissing? We don't have to do that.'

'None of it! I can't do any of it! I don't know what I was thinking, letting myself get involved with *you* of all people, with Ben mixed up in all this!'

'I told Mónica not to get me involved. I told her – I was quite proud of myself actually – that I'm not her *anything* any more. I even *meant* it!'

Jo swallowed. 'That's nice, but it's not true. You're a co-parent.

You're her ex-husband. She turned up at your room when you were about to get it on with someone new! I'm not— I can't take the ups and downs of this – the fear, the resentment against Mónica. It's such a mess and I was just starting to hope I could be happy as I was.'

He gulped visibly. He liked her – maybe even a lot. She didn't want to see him with his brow knit in consternation, hurt and disappointment on his face. But she'd hated hearing him with his ex and it was safer just to stay away.

But she wasn't prepared for what he said next. 'I've seen you happy, Jo,' he murmured. 'You're stronger than this.'

'It's not about being strong,' she insisted. 'I don't want to do it again. I don't want to feel out of control like this. I have kids who rely on me to keep the family together!'

'I know the timing is bad—'

'When is a *good* time to get involved with the ex-husband of your ex-husband's wife?' Every time she said those words, they sounded worse. 'It's bad enough that I have to be here to watch him, wonder if he's making a huge mistake.'

Adrián was looking at her, but with none of that spark of intensity she'd remarked on when they'd first been stuck with each other in Lourdes. Another coil of grief wrapped itself around her heart. She should never have grown so attached to him. Here was a moment of heartache she should have avoided, but she'd walked right into it.

'Wondering if he made a huge mistake not coming after you five years ago?'

Heat rose in Jo's cheeks. Had she meant that? Did she still have feelings for Ben? Surely she wouldn't be so mixed up about Adrián if she did. She didn't even know how she felt any more, except for afraid and cynical and *angry*.

'Part of me agrees, he's an idiot for letting you go,' Adrián said softly. 'But mostly I wish I had nothing to do with him. Maybe I wish I'd never married Mónica.'

'But you *did*. It's not your fault. I don't blame you for *my* feelings,' she said, squeezing his forearm out of habit and then tears pricked as she realised she shouldn't be touching him. 'I'm the problem. I can't do this again.'

'Do what?' he asked, his voice rising. 'I'm not suggesting we get married tomorrow! I just thought maybe we could... date back in London!'

'Date?' Jo repeated with a bad taste in her mouth. 'After everything that went wrong with Ben, *dating* is my idea of hell.'

'Casual sex on a road trip was okay, though?'

'Don't put it like that,' she scolded. 'It doesn't do either of us justice.'

'But you regret what happened?' he prompted, his tone dark. He reminded her of the man who'd got angry about checking in his guitar and snapped at her when upset. Those recollections didn't help her resolve, though. She'd never believed he was perfect, but he'd been real and that was somehow better – or worse.

'I didn't at the time,' she assured him. 'But now... I just have to get through the wedding.'

'And then? After they get married, do you think you'll be able to leave Ben behind then?'

'I don't know,' she snapped in reply. 'But I know I can't make you any promises!'

'No one can make fucking promises! I know this is complicated, but when I was talking to Mónica, I finally realised her feelings had nothing to do with me. But you? Ben is still there, making you frightened.'

'So walk away!' she dared him. 'From me. You don't deserve this.'

'Neither do *you*!'

'It's my life. You've found your exit. You can walk away from this stupid wedding and start again, so *do it*.'

He drew back and stared at her, his eyes wide and fiery and his brow low and she wished he wasn't quite so handsome. The blasted man had always been inconveniently handsome. 'Will you come with me? Into a new start?'

She shook her head immediately and he stared up at the ceiling with a groan. 'We can't be each other's new start, not when Mónica appears and opens everything up wide again.'

'You didn't understand the conversation in Spanish,' he insisted with a shake of his head. 'It wasn't about me. It was about Ben.'

Jo's shoulders slumped as his words washed over her with the opposite effect from the one he'd intended. She remembered Ben apologising for sleeping with his colleague, panicked and regretful. She recognised Adrián probably didn't realise he was lying, but he was – and that was its own small betrayal.

'There was more to it than that,' she accused, making his gaze snap to hers indignantly. 'I don't speak Spanish,' she agreed smoothly, 'but there is a word I've learned in the past week that she definitely said. "Bésame". She said bésame. She wanted you to kiss her!'

'But I didn't do it!' he insisted.

'I know. I understood "no" in Spanish too. But she wanted to. And I listened to her say it and I—' Damn it, the tears were pricking her eyes again, remembering how she'd tried to hold herself together in the bathroom – and that morning after confronting Mónica, that afternoon while talking to Liss on the beach. 'I don't want to be scared. I don't want to wonder. I just... don't need any of this.'

He studied her, his expression slowly closing in until his brow was pinched and his lips pursed and his long eyelashes bunched over narrowed eyes. 'I know the situation is shit,' he said softly, 'but

I thought it would be worth it – I thought *we* would be worth it. *You* would be worth it to me, Jo.'

She slammed her eyes shut. She had fault lines and weak places where she'd tried to glue herself back together, but they were so close to ripping open again. She should never have believed she could do this.

'We should get back to the kids,' she mumbled, whirling towards the door, needing the perspective of sitting next to her children to remember who she was, that she would make everything okay because it had to be okay for them.

But it didn't help. She slipped back into her hotel room to see a little black-haired boy leaning his head on Liss's arm as he stared, gluey-eyed, at the laptop propped at the end of the bed. Dec was doing something on his phone on the single bed, but Liss was watching avidly as well, with half a smile.

When Liss looked up and that smile abruptly fell from her face, Jo's composure slipped as well. Giving a slight shake of her head, she just climbed onto the bed, Liss and Oscar moving over to make room for her. Adrián followed her into the room and perched silently on the other side, wrapping his arms around Oscar when his son climbed into his lap as the next short episode of the animated series started up with its jaunty song.

As the little family of dogs went about their daily life, with their moments of touching normality and overwhelming love and good-will, Jo blubbered nonstop, worse than the mystic spring at Lourdes. She felt Adrián's alarmed glances and Liss's hand slipping into hers and squeezing, but there was nothing she could do to stop, even if she wanted to.

Liss put her to bed she didn't know how much later, she was so exhausted. She'd been crying inside for so long, it didn't seem strange to have cried on the outside.

26

The first mishap on the day of the wedding was the fault of the bad hotel room coffee and a terrible night's sleep.

Jo sat at the foot of the double bed as the early-morning light slanted through the curtains, careful not to wake Liss, who would sleep for hours yet, the lucky thing – especially now Jo had accepted the inevitable and got out of bed. She'd tossed and turned all night, not quite awake, but not asleep enough to dream properly. Instead, her brain had followed the tracks of all her worries like a miserable rollercoaster, semi-consciously obsessing.

Declan was on the single bed, also still deeply asleep, and if Jo was going to get through today with any semblance of dignity, she needed coffee, and not the crappy stuff in the little sachets that needed to be drowned in condensed milk – also weirdly in sachets – to be palatable.

It was not a morning for instant coffee.

She nearly padded down to the hotel restaurant in her pyjamas, knowing that Mónica's family wouldn't be up for hours yet, but the prospect of running into Rita or Ford or any of the handful of people she knew from London was enough for her to grab the first thing she found in her suitcase.

It was the flowing dress from Cadaqués. It was slightly stiff from salt and smelled a bit of the sea, but she pulled it on, telling herself she was just in a hurry and not trying to re-enter her alternate reality that might get her out of attending the wedding – among other benefits.

Closing the clasp on her sandals, she snatched up her purse and grasped the handle of the door, tempering her movements at the last minute to make sure she didn't wake the kids. But opening the door slowly and silently didn't make it any better that she found Ben on the other side, his fist raised to knock.

If she'd only managed to sleep late, she might have missed his knock and been able to avoid this conversation.

Her insides flipped and twisted as memories from the night before assailed her: the discomfort in the black bathroom, listening to Mónica's desperate tone as Jo had realised Ben and Mónica would always stand between her and Adrián. Jumbled amidst those wretched memories were strange and miserable thoughts about the man who stood at her door, his pale hair askew and his brow low.

'Ben,' she said quietly in greeting. Brushing past him to close the door behind her so the children wouldn't hear, she asked, 'What are you doing here?' with a sigh of resignation.

He rolled his lip between his teeth in thought and Jo wondered if she'd ever seen him so uncertain – perhaps that time he'd admitted his infidelity. She swallowed a sour taste in her mouth.

'I'm... can we go for a walk?'

'It's the morning of your wedding,' she pointed out darkly.

'That's why it's so important. Just a walk. It's so early no one will see us. I hoped you might be up already.'

A thread of misgiving wound around her middle and she should have listened to it. If he was worried about being seen with her, then she shouldn't go with him. Mónica would be upset – a feeling Jo deeply, wretchedly understood. But at the same time, she should be able to go for a simple walk with her ex-husband, the father of her kids, without his new wife getting angry.

'I brought coffee,' Ben added, cocking his head in a way that gave Jo a tingle of nostalgia. His hair flopped over his forehead, even though it was thinner these days. 'Double shot with just a splash of milk,' he added.

She was stupidly touched, before perspective rushed in after her moment of weakness. 'Are you looking for a medal for remembering how your wife of thirteen years drinks her coffee?' Without waiting to ponder the surprise in his expression, she slipped her coffee out of his hand and headed for the stairwell.

'Are you... still angry, after all this time?' he asked as he trailed her to the ground floor.

'There's not an easy answer to that,' she replied. He fell into step beside her. He was taller than Adrián, bulkier too. He'd played cricket at university – an opening batsman. He walked with one hand in the pocket of his jeans and it felt so normal – comforting even – that Jo wanted to panic and maybe throw up. The scent of him teased her nostrils and that too brought back pleasant memories and there truly was something wrong with her.

She expected him to chide her for being angry – as he had when she'd stiltedly tried to explain why she had to leave. But he said, 'I wasn't sure if it was normal to still feel something.'

Jo's hair stood on end. 'I tried to feel nothing for a long time, but as soon as I stopped...' Fresh tears pricked behind her eyes and she couldn't finish the sentence. That was what Adrián had done: he'd made her feel again. And look where it had got her.

'Do you... I don't think we can ever go back, but do you think it was a mistake? The therapy? The separation? Marrying me in the first place?' Ben asked quietly.

She glanced up at him in surprise, coming to a stop where they stood on the beach, a few feet from the rushing waves. Her answer tumbled out before she could stop herself. 'No. Marrying you was not a mistake.'

'Does that mean you think this – my second marriage – is a mistake?' he asked carefully.

'My opinion doesn't matter,' she said softly. 'Or it shouldn't, anyway. I only gave you my opinion on *our* marriage and that's in the past.'

'Is it?' He released a heavy breath. 'Sometimes I'm not so sure it ever will be.'

God, she knew how that felt.

'Jo, I... if you still had feelings for me, why did you leave? Why didn't you talk to me? I was hoping...' He ran an agitated hand through that swish of hair at the front. 'I wanted to hear you were completely fine, that Mónica was welcome to me, that I just needed to shake off this feeling that we're not... done.'

The anguish in his voice was echoed inside her and there was nothing she could do to stop a tear falling – as though she hadn't shed enough last night. She swiped it away, shaking off Ben's hand when he grasped her upper arm in concern.

Closure... That's what he wanted from her. But if she hadn't been able to grant it to herself, how did he expect her to give it to him?

'What do you want me to do?' he asked in a pleading tone. 'I panicked, worrying that part of me still loves you and—'

Jo shook her head, needing to stop him. 'You don't, Ben,' she said gently.

'But I *care* about your feelings.'

'That's not the same as loving someone,' she pointed out. 'If you think you can love someone with *part* of yourself...' Ouch. Was she talking to him or to herself?

'Do you think I never loved you? I *tried*, Jo. I tried everything I could think of!'

'You tried to keep us together,' she agreed, her voice reedy. 'But you didn't try to work out why we were unhappy.'

'We weren't unhappy!' he insisted. 'Do you have any idea how much I missed you when you moved out? Did you think I was congratulating myself on being single again? I found Mónica, but it wasn't easy, if that's what you think.'

She laughed humourlessly. 'I don't imagine it was easy. But we were unhappy.' She studied him soberly, wondering if she would need to remind him.

'Because I made one mistake – that you said you forgave me for, by the way – you reduced our whole marriage to unhappiness?'

'It wasn't the mistake, Ben,' she said gently. 'It was your reasons for it. You knew deep down that we weren't right.'

'*I* knew? *You* left!'

'Someone had to have the guts to do it!' she insisted, her throat scratchy. She imagined with a flash a different kind of alternate reality – one where she and Ben were still married, still going on holidays with Liss and Dec to family resorts with clubs for teenagers and bickering gently.

She'd sign up to do one of the organised activities and Ben would pout about her not wanting to spend time with him and she'd cancel her place, thinking that only retirees actually joined those groups anyway.

Gosh, he'd been so insecure about their relationship. Her first instinct was to wonder what she'd done wrong, but she caught herself. Insecurity stemmed from a lack of trust and she'd never done anything to lose his trust. He was the one who hadn't granted it.

She thought with a jolt that she'd rather have the heartache and hurt pride of the past five years than that sedated marriage back.

'What are we supposed to do now?' Ben asked, his voice agitated. Jo recognised his tone, the passive-aggressive desperation of a man who was used to having all the answers. She didn't have to respond to that tone any more.

'Muddle along, admitting we don't know shit about relationships!' she said with an unexpected laugh.

'Have you lost your mind?'

'No,' she said lightly. 'But maybe I need that on a tattoo: "I don't know shit about relationships",' she mused, tapping her bottom lip with her finger. The out-of-control feelings from the past week rose up inside her like a shot of adrenaline.

'You what?'

'If you want me to tell you to marry Mónica, then I'll have to disappoint you.'

'You think I shouldn't marry her?'

'I didn't say that,' Jo snapped. 'But you shouldn't ask. I've spent more time *avoiding* thinking about the two of you than actively thinking about you over the past year. You have to find your own answer and stop relying on me to do the emotional work!'

He drew himself up. 'But if you think I don't know shit about relationships, surely I shouldn't be getting married today.'

She hesitated, her mouth hanging open. The wind whipped her dress around her legs as logic and emotion tussled inside her. The sun was higher in the sky now, sending out golden patterns over the rippling water.

'I suppose marriage isn't an expression of certainty.'

'What else is it?' Ben said with one of his dismissive snorts. 'Although I suppose our marriage is a testament to the truth of that statement.'

'Maybe an expression of hope,' Jo murmured, undeterred. 'Like lighting a candle or saying a prayer. It's an expression of trust – in many things, but mostly the other person. Trust is so much deeper than certainty.'

The horizon blurred as moisture gathered in her eyes again. Like those tears, more words just kept coming.

'It's like choosing or performing music.' She couldn't help remembering the striking image of Adrián pouring out his passion with a guitar. 'Being brave enough to stand in front of your partner and ask for acceptance. It's about *faith*.'

She'd never had faith in Ben and he hadn't had faith in her – they hadn't trusted each other with their deepest needs.

'Is something wrong? Not about the wedding?' Ben asked. 'I think I could count on one hand the number of times I've seen you cry.'

She blinked at him. 'I cried, didn't I?' At least there had been times when she'd wanted to.

'When Liss was born,' he said. 'But other than that... I can't think of an occasion.'

It was a poor time to have landed on the Water Works square – and she'd obviously played too much Monopoly with Dec when he'd gone through that phase. It seemed all she could do was cry.

'Something's set me off,' she admitted, trying to ignore the little voice telling her exactly what – or who – had set her off. Damn him.

'Are you going to be okay? I really... I know the whole "first wedding" thing must have seemed insulting to you, but I truly didn't intend it that way.'

'It's not to do with the wedding,' she assured him, her nose tingling. 'I mean, in some ways it is, but—'

A sudden thought ripped right through her sentence. *Wasn't* it because of the wedding? Hadn't she said to Adrián that everything was about the wedding right now? Surely she was crying because her ex-husband was getting married that day and everything in her life seemed to be running away from her.

But no. She was frustrated and her pride was pricked, but that wasn't why she was crying. It was Adrián – just him. She wished she could blame hormones, but that wouldn't cut it either. What had he done to her?

With a deep sigh, she looked Ben square in the face. 'Look, if we're finally being honest with each other, I should probably tell you that I slept with Adrián.'

His eyes bulged and he swayed on his feet as he gaped at her, struggling to form words.

'Don't look so shocked,' she said, admitting to herself that she would have been shocked by this news two weeks ago. 'These things happen, right?'

'But not to you. Was it... better than me?'

'Oh, come on, Ben,' she groaned. 'That's your first question? What do you want me to say? He's got a tiny penis and no idea what to do with it?' She struggled to remember if she'd made these irreverent jokes with him during their marriage and wondered how she'd ever stifled them, if she hadn't. 'Ask Mónica if you're so curious.'

He gave an exaggerated grimace. 'Was it... meaningless, then? Casual?'

It was her turn to open her mouth and then hesitate. 'No?' she tried out. 'Definitely not meaningless, but... I don't know what it means.'

She'd thought she was being sensible last night – so sensible – and then she'd turned into this blubbering mess. Now she was talking to Ben like an adult – like a *friend*. Her alternate reality was taking over the real world.

'Did you plan it all with him then? The problem with the flight?'

She shook her head. 'It all happened while we were travelling, not before. I wasn't planning to tell you because I didn't want to add unnecessary drama to the wedding but...'

'Where there is Mónica, there is always unnecessary drama,' Ben said with a twitch of his lips.

Jo paused, staring at him. 'Do you like the drama?'

He winced as he considered his answer. 'I... she ran over me like a freight train when we dated. I didn't think I could handle it, but —' He gulped, staring out to sea. 'I don't know. She woke me up or something and now I won't say it's always easy, but I... *want* the drama. At least when we argue, we feel something.'

There was a twinge of sadness inside Jo at his words, but only a twinge. Mostly, she was fascinated by his bewildered expression, by the idea of him rolled under the freight train that was Mónica's passion. It was... amusing. Whatever Jo's emotional wobble had been, it wasn't vindication or revenge. It was honesty: messy and difficult and occasionally beautiful.

'I'm happy for you, Ben. I mean it.' She said the last part for her own benefit. 'You have all the answers you're going to get from me. Maybe you should go and find Mónica? You might not be the only one with last-minute doubts.'

'She wanted to do this big wedding thing right. She said we shouldn't see each other beforehand.'

'There is no "right",' Jo said gently.

'What about you? And Adrián?'

'I don't know,' was all she could say. 'I don't want to scandalise Mónica's aunts, so it'll have to wait until after the wedding.' When hopefully she would have more courage than she'd shown up until now.

'I think Mónica's aunts like being scandalised,' he said, a full smile stretching on his lips. They must have had lots of good times over the years as well as the bad ones, because that smile was intimately familiar.

Jo shared his laugh. 'In that case, I should definitely get back before they make up some drama about us.'

When they reached the rainbow dragon playground across from the hotel, he grasped her elbow and squeezed. 'Thank you,' he said earnestly, 'for being here. For not slapping me in the face a hundred times. You're a strong woman, Jo, and it was an honour to... make some gorgeous kids with you.' He snorted a laugh at the way that sentence had ended.

'Did you speak too soon about the slap in the face?' she quipped with mock censure. 'But they are gorgeous kids, despite who their dad is.'

His grin widened and he pulled her into a hug. Jo's arms came around him, a body so familiar and yet... the moment was new. She could bear the touch, enjoy it even. She'd worked something out of her system.

She didn't know what to do about Adrián – if she was ready for anything. But today was about Ben and Mónica and surviving the wedding. Adrián still had to play his guitar with an injured arm and a whole lot of angst. Thinking about a date when they returned to London felt banal and somehow petty on the day of a grand wedding.

But once there were no more mishaps, would there be anything left between her and Adrián?

She and Ben strode companionably back to the hotel, Jo marvelling at the unexpected twists and turns of the past few days – a labyrinth of emotions. They shared a smile, both not quite believing it had been so easy to talk openly about the past and the present and their tangled lives. Reaching the sliding doors to the hotel foyer, Jo suspected they shared the fresh perspective and a new sense of peace.

And that was when they noticed that all hell had broken loose in the breakfast room.

27

Oscar had woken early as usual and only so many games of Uno could keep him from dying of starvation, so Adrián dressed reluctantly in a pair of slightly misshapen linen shorts he'd bought the day before and one of the billowing shirts that were easy to put on, stuck his feet into his flip-flops and trailed his bouncing son down the stairs to the breakfast room, dragging his feet.

He didn't want to see any of the people on the other side of the door – he didn't want to see people. Oscar was a pleasant enough distraction, but the wedding was starting to feel like a room with shrinking walls and spikes.

He didn't want to see Jo – well, his pride didn't. The rest of him had been difficult to convince. He really didn't want to see Mónica in case he bit her head off in frustration. He didn't want to see Alberto and Barbara, or the aunts and cousins who all knew he'd inherited Alberto's guitar.

At this rate, he'd sit down to play at the reception and something dark and angry would come out. They'd all think he wasn't over Mónica and shroud their schadenfreude with overblown sympathy and he'd drown his sorrows with too much anisette, making Jo grateful for her narrow escape.

As it turned out, he didn't even need to enter the breakfast room for trouble to come to him.

'¡Ahí viene! ¡Los vi juntos en el balcón – abrazándose!'

The aunt using crutches hobbled through the doors, giving her pointed finger a morning workout. Adrián stilled, grinding his teeth as his mind raced to find the least-bad response – or *any* response to the aunt's shrill testimony that she'd seen him 'hugging' someone on the balcony. He didn't have to guess who she meant. Mierda.

Mónica appeared in the doorway of the breakfast room. 'Calmate, tía María Dolores.' Adrián swallowed an untimely laugh with some effort. It *was* María Dolores who had hurt her foot – and she did exist. 'I'm sure there's an explanation for whatever you saw.' Mónica's gaze snapped to his as though saying, 'There had better be an explanation.'

If what María Dolores had seen was him with his hands all over Jo and their mouths quite busy, his explanation wasn't going to be satisfactory.

'And Anamaría heard them smooching in the labyrinth!' María Dolores added with a humph. Damn, that was it. Not María Rosa. That other gossipy aunt was called Anamaría.

'We were not *smooching* in the labyrinth,' he muttered.

'But you *were* being amorous on the balcony!' she said triumphantly.

Adrián opened his mouth and took a deep breath, but he still couldn't decide if he could conceivably deny it. If he hadn't been so raw from last night, he might have declared that it was true, that he and Jo were a thing now.

But as it was, what was the point in opening this can of worms in front of Mónica's family if the 'thing' between him and Jo hadn't meant much?

Another aunt – María Busybody was probably her name, which rhymed in Spanish and he felt quite clever for thinking that one up – rushed into the fray. '*I* saw them holding hands! They were leaning over the balcony like Romeo and Juliet and he kissed her hand!'

Adrián was fairly certain he hadn't kissed Jo's hand, but he rather regretted the oversight now. 'It was not like Romeo and Juliet. Juliet was up on a balcony and Romeo below, calling up to her. My room is next to Jo's and the balconies are connected. It wasn't like bloody Shakespeare at all!'

'But you were? Kissing Jo?' Mónica asked quietly – too quietly.

'Not with a balcony wall between us!'

She unfortunately wasn't put off by that. 'In the labyrinth? On your way to Peñíscola? Last night? Did you seriously start something with Ben's *ex-wife* on the way to my *wedding*?' Her voice grew quieter and higher-pitched and Adrián's hair stood on end.

'I knew he was a rotten egg, Mónica,' the other aunt hurled into the conversation. 'Let him go and marry Ben's wife in a registry office and divorce her there too!'

He tried not to flinch, but it was difficult.

'He's just trying to upset you!' María Dolores insisted.

'I am *not*!' he insisted. 'Yes, something happened with Jo, but it didn't have anything to do with this wedding – at least not how you're thinking.' He wasn't sure if Jo believed that, but he did. 'We didn't say anything because I knew how your family would react and I didn't want to make a scene.'

'Oh, you didn't want to make a scene, but you got it on with my fiancé's ex!'

'Trust me, that fact nearly stopped us in the first place – and will probably stop anything else happening.'

'Anything else?' she asked, her voice nearly a shriek. 'Are you two going to get married in some bizarre wife swap?'

María Dolores crossed herself.

'We don't have to do this now—'

'Mamá! *Mamá!*'

The argument was cut short by the arrival of Oscar, sweeping in through the automatic doors at the front of the foyer. Adrián hadn't even realised the boy had run off and his stomach swooped with guilt. Today of all days, he needed to be there for Oscar and try to put Jo out of his thoughts.

Oscar ran to Mónica, burying his face in her tummy. 'He visto— ¡He-he visto!'

Adrián dropped to his haunches and peered into his son's face. 'What did you see, cariño? Whatever it is, we can sort it out.'

The boy hiccoughed through a sniffy nod and opened his mouth, his breath choppy. 'At the rainbow dragon, I saw Jo and Ben!'

Adrián's mouth snapped shut and he felt Mónica's frantic gaze, but didn't meet it.

'They were *hugging*, abrazando, like he and Mamá do – like you and Mamá used to. Y tambien se besaban. Kissing too!' he blurted out, mixing his languages.

'¡Santísima Madre de Dios y espiritu santo!' María Dolores was muttering.

'I'm sure there's a reasonable—'

Rita and Ford Watters chose that moment to emerge from the breakfast room, Ford with a restraining hand on his wife's forearm. 'Well, *I* saw Mónica coming out of Adrián's room last night! The night before her own wedding!'

Adrián shot to his feet. 'Nothing happened!' he was quick to insist. 'If you'd kept watching a little longer, you would have seen Jo come out afterward!'

'Jo was right there in your room last night?' Mónica squealed. 'When I was trying to get you to kiss me!'

'I *knew* something had happened!' Rita said, her voice low and quaking with outrage.

'Well, *Ben* is out there "hugging" his ex right now!' Mónica hurled back.

'I never liked you. I don't know what Ben even sees in an immature, melodramatic—'

Adrián clapped his hands over Oscar's ears. 'There's no need to be rude to the bride!' he snapped. '*You* don't have to like her.'

'Well, thanks,' Mónica said.

'If she's even a bride any more!' Rita said, causing a collective gasp from the family members who could understand English; María Dolores stood by in barely contained suspense as though she could will the words to become Spanish. 'And *you*—' Rita pointed at Adrián. 'It will be all your fault! Keeping something going with both of them, ruining Ben's happiness twice over!'

He knew her words stemmed from prejudice and her own affront and bore no resemblance to the truth, but they still hurt. He'd never been enough for anyone. He'd tried to make Mónica happy and it had had the opposite effect. He was only at this wedding for Oscar and he kept losing track of his son. And Dios, he'd been angry and unfiltered with Jo and it was a miracle she was even talking to him any more, let alone that something had developed between them – something that he still couldn't shake off.

'No one's ruining anyone's happiness,' he responded evenly. 'Mónica only wanted to talk last night – as Ben obviously needed to do with Jo.' Unless they really were kissing, which the panic centre of his brain insisted they might be doing. 'Yes, something happened between me and Jo while we were stuck together trying to get to this wedding.' He hoped they couldn't hear the 'fucking' he'd left out before 'wedding' with a superhuman dose of self-discipline.

'But it didn't mean anything – to anyone. It just happened in the moment, the pressures of an unexpected road trip, heatwave madness – something like that. It doesn't have any impact on Mónica and Ben's enduring love!'

His declaration was met by silence and it felt as though he should have had a drink in his hand to round out the moment with a toast. But he slowly realised that the gathered wedding guests were staring over his shoulder and he felt a distinct breeze at his back.

With a sinking sense of doom, he turned slowly to see exactly the person he most wanted and didn't want to see right then – as well as Ben, with his hand at her back. He needed to kick something – preferably himself.

'Um, good morning?' Ben tried. 'You're all up early.'

28

Busy. Jo had to keep busy, which was difficult when the wedding party was in uproar. Ben was talking down his parents in one corner of the breakfast room, while Mónica's animated conversation with one of her aunts got slightly out of hand in the opposite corner. Adrián appeared to be attempting to corral the rest of the guests into the other corner, away from the carnage. She wouldn't have been surprised if he pulled out some balls and started juggling.

She hadn't realised she'd been so happily single for five years, when the alternative was this: upset and embarrassed, with a whole extended family of strangers looking at her and judging, both for things she'd done and things she *hadn't* done.

What she most wanted was to disappear out of this mess. She caught Oscar's eye where the boy stood frozen by the orange juice press and she realised he was thinking the same.

She approached him and asked, 'You want a juice?'

He nodded dumbly, staring up at her as she placed a few oranges onto the wire feeder.

'Can you press the button?'

Nodding again, he gulped and studied the machine before pressing the button and watching solemnly as the mechanism started turning. Jo stood back with him as the first orange dropped into the apparatus and was explosively destroyed, shattered and pulped.

'I know you're feeling a lot of things right now, Oscar,' she said softly, 'but I was hugging Ben only as a friend. I understand why you got worried and I'm sorry for making you feel that, but Ben loves your mum, not me.' When had that statement become a relief?

'Do you love my dad?' he asked, his voice strained, and all the strength faded from Jo's body until she felt like those pulped oranges.

Her throat was thick and that blubbering mess feeling closed around her again. No, of course she didn't love Adrián. They barely knew each other. But then why had it hurt so much to hear him describe their relationship as meaningless?

Oh, no, was this why she felt so shit? Because she'd fallen too hard for a man who made bad jokes, wore a thick gold chain and unbuttoned his shirts too far? None of her thoughts helped her produce an answer for a seven-year-old. No wonder falling in love was usually the purview of the young; it was impossible when you understood the full spectrum of grey in relationships.

She noticed Oscar didn't seem to be waiting for an answer, but was staring past Jo, to where his mother had managed to shake off her aunt and was now furiously whispering with Ben. He tried to slip an arm around her and she pushed him away.

'You're nicer to *her* than me!' Mónica accused.

'Nonsense, but she was able to hold a sensible conversation about this!'

'If you want sensible, you should marry someone else!'

'I know!' Ben responded in a tone Jo wasn't sure she'd ever

heard from him before. 'If I wanted sensible, I would *not* be here today ready to marry you.'

'Are you? Ready?'

At least nobody in the room was looking at Jo any more. Ben leaned down and spoke gruffly to Mónica, ushering her to the door of the breakfast room and out. Something about the tilt of Mónica's head made Jo think she was enjoying herself.

Perhaps there would be a wedding today after all?

'That cup is overflowing.'

Jo turned to Dec in distraction, at first wondering when he had arrived and only afterwards computing exactly what he'd said. 'Shit!' she hissed, leaping for the button on the machine. 'You didn't hear that, kid,' she said to Oscar over her shoulder.

'What's going on in here?' Dec asked out of the side of his mouth, leaning close. 'Did Dad screw up the wedding?' He rubbed his hands together.

She gave him a whack on the arm. 'Don't look so happy at the prospect. There are a lot of feelings involved.' She glanced meaningfully at Oscar, who was staring at the door his mum had just disappeared through.

'Yeah, like my aversion to wearing that stupid outfit standing at the front of the church with Dad. I'm not a flower boy. I don't mind Mónica, but Adrián had a better plan.'

She trailed him absently as he strode to the buffet and began filling a bowl with strange chocolate cereal that would probably give him cavities, topping it with churros and fudge sauce. Noticing Oscar standing helplessly with his enormous cup of juice, she beckoned for the boy to come with her.

'What plan?' she whispered to Dec. 'Did he say something to you when you were playing frisbee on the beach?'

He shrugged as though he couldn't quite remember and a fog of frustration and confusion whirled around Jo. 'He just said he liked you – ew – but he wanted me to know he would back off and let us get used to the idea slowly.'

Jo didn't often feel old, but with all the blood rushing through her arteries today and the rollercoaster of the past twelve hours, she felt each of her forty-six years as though it were a century.

'He... likes me,' she repeated slowly. Her eyes searched out Adrián without conscious thought, angling her head to appreciate the fine lines of his broad shoulders, the glint of that necklace that she didn't hate so much any more. He was handsome and funny and real and... talking to his former father-in-law, who had a grim expression on his face.

As she watched, Alberto's gaze moved slowly over Adrián's shoulder and caught Jo's with a zap. His expression hardened further and she swallowed.

'Maybe I should just get out of here,' she mumbled with a hand on Dec's arm.

'Hmm?' Her son was oblivious as usual.

'Mum!'

Jo whirled at the sound of Liss's urgent tone, making poor Oscar spill his juice. She steadied the glass with one hand, smoothing Oscar's hair unconsciously as she waited for Liss to approach. 'What is it?'

'I think you should come and see,' she said with dismay. 'And Adrián too!'

He was already there, hunched in front of Oscar, mopping his shirt in that caring way he had with his son that made Jo feel weak-kneed. 'What?' he asked, looking up.

'It's your room,' Liss explained to him. 'Go and look. I'll help Oscar get breakfast. He should probably stay here,' she added quietly.

Jo met Adrián's gaze in alarm and they hurried off together. 'I don't know what this is about,' he said as they took the stairs two at a time, 'but I am so glad to be out of there.'

'Tell me about it. And you aren't even the "other woman",' she said through gritted teeth.

'Oh, but your former in-laws accused me of ruining everything and everyone in that fucking room.'

'Well, *your* former in-laws are spies with big mouths!'

'You think I'm going to argue with that?' he snapped.

'By the way, I thought you said María Dolores was a figment of your imagination,' she accused.

'I thought she was, but she exists,' he said, his voice high. 'I've invented the instrument of my own torture.'

'Did I already point out how much you exaggerate?'

'I think you'll find we're both taking out our frustration on each other – again,' he said, his tone still sharp.

Her mouth dropped open and she studied him as they took the last few steps to their floor. It didn't sound very healthy and yet... she felt better already. When he fumbled for her hand and gave it a squeeze, all without looking at her, she could almost believe the world had righted itself again after the loop-the-loop of the past few days.

Adrián went ahead, but stopped short when the doors to their rooms came into sight. '¡Maldito infierno!' he bit out. She suspected it wasn't the first time he'd said something along those lines that day.

Rushing to catch up, she gasped when she saw what had stopped him. His hotel room had been broken into – the bolt was dented and warped and the door splintered.

'What the hell?' he muttered. 'The only thing of value I have is — Joder!' He shot frantically into the room and she hurried after him, hearing his desperate tone echoing in her mind. 'It's gone. It's *gone*!' he cried, throwing up his hands and then groaning as the action wrenched his shoulder. 'God *damn* it! They're not only gossips and spies, one of Mónica's family is a fucking *felon!*'

Jo had the fleeting thought that if Ben had lost his temper like this, she would have cowered and panicked and probably fled, but with Adrián, she stepped closer, reaching out one hand and waiting for his haze to clear so he noticed her.

His chest heaved with agitation and he squeezed his eyes shut for a long moment. When he opened his eyes again, he fixed his gaze on her, grasping her outstretched hand gruffly.

'It's my fault, isn't it?'

'How is it your fault that your room got broken into?'

He met her gaze solemnly. 'The jewels. That stupid joke. Someone must have heard us.'

'What?'

'Either that or it really was an inside job, but we can't throw suspicion on Mónica's family today of all days. It has to have been that. I'm an idiot.'

'You couldn't have known—'

'Shit,' he said breathily, as though he'd been doing exercise. 'We have to call the police.'

That much was definitely true. 'Want to use my phone?' She produced her mobile and handed it over after tapping the passcode.

He paced as he held a rapid conversation with the police in Spanish and then hung up. 'They're sending someone soon to log the crime scene. I offered to go to the police station in Benicarló to give a full description of the guitar and file the report because I doubt Mónica will want an officer sniffing around the wedding. But I have to go today – now, if I have any hope of getting back here in time.'

'I'll go with you,' she offered automatically.

He glanced up in surprise.

'How did you think you'd get back when you can't drive a manual? And getting out of this madhouse will be an added bonus. I'd better go and see what the kids are up to. Come find me when it's time to go?'

* * *

Adrián looked up eagerly five minutes later at a noise from the door, imagining Jo had forgotten something – or just come back to wait with him because the kids were fine. He was still giddy from the moments spent alone with her, their strange version of normal that had quickly become his favourite version.

But it wasn't the woman consuming his thoughts who appeared in the doorway as the broken panel creaked open. It was his former father-in-law with his usual stony expression – actually, it was probably a touch stonier.

He approached with slow steps, his handmade leather shoes squeaking on the cool tiles. His red linen shirt was unbuttoned halfway down his chest, allowing his grey hair to overflow through the gap. He held a hand to his chest as though he was about to challenge Adrián to a duel – in flamenco dancing.

He braced himself as Alberto approached – a little too close as usual. Adrián was from Madrid and then London. Zaragoza personal space was a few generations back in his family. Alberto raised his hand and Adrián grimaced as it moved towards him in slow motion.

But the slap never came. Alberto just clapped him on the shoulder – hard – and that was nearly as bad for his poor ligaments. Adrián swallowed his cry of pain and grasped his shoulder gingerly. He should put the sling back on, at least as protection from the violent displays of emotion from members of Mónica's family.

How odd to think that a week ago he'd been on a motorbike cruising through the Pyrenees, about to have his head in Jo's lap while he was mindless with pain.

'Alberto,' he said roughly.

'Adrián,' he replied, peering at him. Adrián peered back, still struggling to work out what this conversation was supposed to be about. 'Jo told me what happened to the guitar.' He pronounced her name 'Ho', like the rest of Mónica's family. Adrián was pretty sure the old man knew how he was supposed to pronounce it.

'It's... unfortunate,' was the only safe thing Adrián could think of to say. 'The thieves must have known how valuable the guitar was – but not understood how valuable it was to this family,' he added, staring at his feet.

'This family,' Alberto repeated with a humph. 'This great family with an ex-husband and an ex-wife and two stepchildren.'

'Do you... shall I apologise? I am sorry about the guitar. I did my best to look after it – I always did my best.'

Alberto's expression changed – only a fraction, but enough for Adrián to suspect there were some deep feelings under there. 'I understand, Adrián,' he declared, clearing his throat. 'I believe you loved Mónica. But you have to understand she's my only daughter. I'm not rational when it comes to her. I'm all feelings,' he said solemnly.

Adrián arranged an equally solemn expression on his face. 'Children have that effect.'

'That's why, when I heard the guitar had been stolen, I realised I owe you an apology.'

'Nohhhh,' he denied immediately. 'Perhaps I owe *you* an apology for not giving you the opportunity to celebrate Mónica's first marriage – for not giving *her* the opportunity.'

Alberto shook his head sharply. 'I invited you to come—'

'"Invited" doesn't quite indicate—'

'Yes, I insisted you come to the wedding with questionable motives – revenge, if I'm being entirely honest.'

Adrián had absolutely nothing to say in reply to that. Fortunately Alberto was more interested in saying his piece than waiting for replies.

'Yes, revenge. I didn't want to admit it to myself at first, but it's true. I wanted to rub your face in this celebration – and give your pride a swift kick in case you hadn't realised yet just how much you'd lost.'

Adrián gulped. 'I realised,' he said softly. 'Every day I'm reminded that we aren't a family in the same way any more. I *grieved*.'

Alberto regarded him closely. 'I did too. And perhaps refusing to allow you to return the guitar was an act of grief.'

'You have no idea how well I understand that,' Adrián said with a bitter smile. 'Perhaps *wanting* to return the guitar was also part of my grieving.'

'A part I denied you,' Alberto said, his voice wavering. 'It was not fair. It wasn't fair to make you come here and play for me – for Mónica at her next wedding. I wanted it to hurt for you too, because it hurts me to think she will carry a broken marriage with her for the rest of her life.'

'I understand it hurts,' Adrián began, 'but lots of things hurt. Mónica is happy with Ben. Your pride is difficult to heal, but pride is more trouble than it's worth in my experience.'

'And you are happy? Without Mónica?'

'I've... adapted,' he explained. 'I have regrets. I don't know if you ever stop asking yourself what might have been, but I'm looking forward, not back – or I will once this wedding is behind us.'

'You don't have to play the guitar. When I realised my true reasons for insisting, I felt guilty and unfortunately became even more stubborn, but now the guitar has been stolen...'

'It feels like a kind of circle,' Adrián offered. 'You gave me the guitar to bind me to you because I didn't take the time to build a true relationship with you. I insulted you by marrying Mónica without inviting you and you needed insurance. I shouldn't have taken away her chance for a big wedding – your chance to celebrate your only daughter.'

'It was a long time ago, Adrián. And we both know Mónica. If she'd wanted a big wedding back then, she would have had her big wedding. People change – especially my daughter,' he added with a meaningful look. 'You aren't the only one to carry the blame and now I release you. You don't have a guitar to play anyway.'

Adrián waited for the burden to fall from his shoulders, for the feelings of failure and guilt, the regret and grief to uncouple themselves and fly off. It didn't happen – not because the feelings were still choking him, but because the feelings... weren't even there any more.

Yes, he'd complained and rolled his eyes about being the subject of gossip and ridicule among Mónica's family, but that was just his pride. His feelings about his marriage, about Mónica? He'd drawn a line under them somehow – perhaps with a stick in the sand at Lloret de Mar. Or perhaps it was an answer to his prayers from Lourdes.

'Pity I still need to go to Benicarló to report the guitar missing,' Adrián grumbled, although he paused in thought, realising he was looking forward to the sweaty trip to Benicarló in the Corsa more than he was looking forward to the fancy dinner after the wedding. It was a disaster, a misadventure – exactly what he and Jo excelled at.

'Alberto!' his brother Gustavo called, rushing into the room and mopping his forehead as he caught his breath. 'I heard what happened! I hope the bastardo takes good care of it and knows the value of a luthier guitar!'

'I'm pretty sure that's the entire reason he stole it,' Adrián mumbled.

'What are we going to do? We can't have a wedding without "Entre dos Aguas" and "Un Beso Mas".'

Adrián felt a withering smile grow on his lips as he contemplated a night playing flamenco and Spanish guitar favourites and... he probably would have enjoyed it, actually.

Gustavo snapped his fingers. Appearing to have the same thought at the same instant, Alberto grasped his brother's shoulders and shook him.

'José Pascal!' they said in unison.

'He doesn't go anywhere without his Alhambra.'

'Talks about it all the time.'

'But will he let the boy play it?'

Adrián stifled a snort at being called 'the boy' but listened avidly to the conversation flitting past him.

'He'd better. Today is my daughter's wedding day! Once I've given that Englishman a kick up the arse.'

Adrián did not envy Ben in the slightest. 'Ahem, I thought I was released from my blame?' he spoke up.

'Your heart is released from your blame – yes,' Alberto said. 'But your hands are required! We're going to have a party!'

29

'Can you get your shoulder out of my face, fartface?'

'Can you get *your* elbow out of *my* ribs, poohead?'

'I've got the bed wetter's car seat in my face! I can barely move without fracturing my skull.'

'Well, I can barely listen to anything you say without fracturing your skull!'

'I *don't* wet the bed!'

If Jo hadn't been driving at fifty kilometres per hour, she would have thumped her head against the steering wheel in exasperation at least three times.

'Is this the truth about having multiple children that no one tells you?' Adrián asked weakly. 'How have you survived this for fourteen years?'

'It's the three of them,' she said through gritted teeth. 'Mine aren't usually like this. Adding a third has tipped them over into insanity.'

'Insanity is right. Why did we bring them again?'

Jo didn't bother to answer. He'd been standing there when Liss and Dec had run after them through the foyer, dragging Oscar behind them, demanding their own freedom from wedding hell. They hadn't exactly been able to say no.

'How long do you think this is going to take?' she asked. It was eleven o'clock and the wedding was in three hours. She imagined there wasn't a lot Adrián could say about a stolen guitar, but she also didn't want to make any assumptions about the efficiency of the police in this tourist area. She'd been shocked to discover the guitar actually was worth several thousand pounds and was insured, so he needed to go home tomorrow with a police report at least.

'It probably won't take long enough for us to miss the wedding,' he quipped.

She eyed him. 'I only hope someone will text us at least if they decide not to go through with it,' Jo mumbled.

'Shh! Do you want Oscar to run away again?'

'Ehm, I need to pee!' Oscar called out. 'But I *don't* wet the bed.'

'Hang on, sweetie,' Jo called back. 'We'll be there in five minutes.'

Adrián's gaze snapped to her and she could feel the unasked question: *Did you just call my son 'sweetie'?*

'Okay, I'll... try,' Oscar said, his voice high.

'Uh, Mum?' Liss said warily. 'He drank *a lot* of juice this morning. Like, another whole glass after the one that spilled.'

Jo swerved onto the hard shoulder and slammed on the brakes.

Oscar gasped. 'A little bit came out!'

'Out of the car!' she bellowed, but Adrián was already there, hauling open the door as Dec undid the distracted Oscar's seatbelt.

He almost made it. When father and son turned back to the car, leaving a wet mark on the concrete barrier at the side of the road, they both looked mortified. Adrián helped Oscar step out of his soiled underwear and they studied his shorts critically.

'They'll have to do,' Adrián said. 'You tried, mijo,' he said, roughing up the boy's hair and propping his arm on his knee to peer into his son's face. 'You did really well to hang on as long as you did.'

He pressed a kiss to the top of Oscar's head and Jo couldn't help staring. Had she always found it so sexy to watch a man being tender with his kid? And despite Adrián's prodigious temper, he wasn't using it on the boy.

'The seat's a bit damp,' he said quietly, appearing at the passenger door. 'Do you have tissues? We don't have any towels or anything.'

After he'd settled Oscar on a wad of tissues, taken his own seat and pulled the door closed, Adrián sat back with a sigh. Jo couldn't help reaching out and giving his arm a squeeze and his hand covered hers immediately. They both looked straight ahead and not at each other and Jo wondered if he too was asking himself how big this thing between them was and what it meant that this madcap car journey felt more right than their doomed attempts to stay away from each other.

Speaking of doom, the clock was ticking. Jo switched the car back on and shoved it into gear. 'I can look around for a pair of shorts for him while you're at the police station if you like.'

Adrián paused before answering. 'He'd probably appreciate it,' he finally said, clearing his throat.

After reaching the sun-baked, sand-coloured town of endless beach apartments and striped awnings, they got caught briefly in a series of one-way streets and Adrián's questionable ability to give directions.

'Turn here – no, not there! Here!'

'Where is "here"?' Jo snapped, navigating a traffic island with a sprawling olive tree on it. She turned into a long avenue lined with palms, a view of the beach at the end. After a few more turns, they found the police station and Jo managed to park around the corner, tucking the Corsa in between two other small cars. Oscar hopped out like a shot and Adrián rushed after him.

Once Liss and Dec had unfolded themselves from their cramped seats, they looked expectantly at Jo. 'Okay, kids,' she began, 'first shorts, then ice cream.'

Dec grinned, bumping his shoulder against Jo's – what counted as affection for her fourteen-year-old and she treasured it. 'I was hoping you'd say that.'

She turned to Adrián. 'You'll give me a call when you're finished?'

He nodded. 'I'll text you if I get an idea of how long it will take. I think *Two Hospitals, a Police Station and a Wedding* is the name of our film,' he added with a sigh.

'It doesn't have a great ring to it,' she said wryly, but she was wondering if it sounded like a romcom with a happy ending.

He approached, grasping her arm and leaning close, before he froze and dropped his hand, blinking. He shouldn't press a kiss to her temple in front of the kids but she wished he had. Instead, he tugged Oscar over, placing his son's hand carefully into hers and looking between them meaningfully. She gave him a small nod and gripped the little hand tight.

Half an hour later, they were sitting at a chiringuito – a beach bar, and it was Jo's new favourite word in Spanish – around a white plastic table, with three enormous ice cream sundaes. Jo had been powerless against Oscar's big dark eyes that had lit up when he'd seen the picture of the one drenched in Smarties and chocolate sauce, with the result that her kids had demanded something equally ostentatious.

In truth, she felt sorry for Oscar, in his weird blue shorts with a crab on the bum, looking a little lost. She'd only ordered a coffee for herself, wondering if Adrián would be finished soon enough to join them. She thought of the other chiringuitos they'd visited together: in Cadaqués and Lloret de Mar. She rather wished Adrián were sitting opposite her right now, framed by the view of the marina with boats bobbing and the golden sand stretching away, the boardwalk dotted with palm trees.

Ice creams devoured, Oscar and Dec headed for the playground – one overflowing with enthusiasm and the other out of sheer boredom. Jo fiddled with her fingernails, remembering the conversation about the manicure. Her nails weren't nicely shaped – they weren't even clean that day. So much for wowing the guests at her ex's wedding.

Not that it mattered. She'd allowed Ben a hold on her pride for too long – or perhaps she'd held onto a false sense of pride for too long. So she was an ex-wife? That designation sometimes came with complications, but *life* came with complications. In the chaos of the big day, what mattered were these little moments – spent as a family.

* * *

Adrián rushed out of the police station with his phone to his ear. Making his statement had of course taken forever, requiring a million signatures and ten thousand copies of his passport and a hundred explanations of why his Spanish identity card had expired.

'Hello?' came the answer after Jo's phone had rung for a long time.

'Liss? It's Adrián. I'm finished. Shall I meet you all at the car?'

'Um, you should probably come down here. Oscar got stuck on the climbing frame and...'

Oh, fuck. 'Right, okay. I'll be right there. Can you send me a location pin?'

'I don't know Mum's code. But we're right on the beach, just down the street from where you were.'

The sight that greeted him when he reached the boardwalk took the wind out of him. At the top of the rope climbing frame hunched Oscar, buffeted by the breeze that had swelled since they'd first arrived in Benicarló. And below, squeezing through the rope honeycomb ten feet off the ground, was *Jo...*

His breath rushed out and his skin tingled. He'd been smitten before, but this... God, *this woman.* His insides flipped and churned, devastated by the prospect of a final goodbye tomorrow and stricken with hope that the instant return to their normal that morning meant he might still be able to change her mind about seeing each other when they got back to London.

But no, she was a woman, not a girl whose head could be turned by a bunch of flowers and a love song. Besides, he didn't have a lot to offer her: bad jokes and a whole lot of baggage. Just *himself.* As he watched her navigate the climbing frame to reach his kid, he loved the idea of entrusting himself to her.

She could entrust herself to him, too. He knew without doubt that he could treasure her, the woman with the beautiful voice and the meaningless tattoo, the mother, the cynic, the *ex-wife.*

I see you, Jo.

Oscar cowered in a particularly violent gust of wind and Adrián rushed forward, his copy of the police report whipping out from under his arm. But that would have to wait. Oscar and Jo were up a climbing frame in a dangerous wind and—

'Get your hands off the climbing frame, Juan Adrián Rivera Morales!' Jo bellowed before he'd even closed his fingers around the ropes. 'I don't want to make it *three* hospitals!'

Shading his eyes, he looked up at her. 'Are you okay?'

'I'm fine!' she insisted. 'Oscar is fine. Nobody is afraid of heights.'

He glanced to Liss and Dec, their wide-eyed grimaces suggesting Jo wasn't quite telling the truth. He gritted his teeth and tensed, ready to jump into action if anything happened.

'Dec tried to get him down, but he wouldn't come. He's been up there for half an hour now,' Liss explained, coming to stand next to him. He glanced at his watch: one o'clock. They were only fifteen minutes from Peñíscola, but he couldn't show up at the wedding in his flip-flops and Oscar couldn't be a page boy in—

'Is that a crab on his bum?'

'We tried to talk him out of it,' Liss said, stifling a smile. 'But he's named the butt-crab and everything.'

Adrián choked on something between a groan and a hysterical laugh. 'What did he call it? Pinchy?'

'Actually, it's Crabface.'

'Well, we need to get Oscar down before he falls on his crabface.'

Liss snorted a laugh. 'Mum will get him down.'

'I know she will,' he said softly.

But it was a painstaking process. She had to help him over the first gap with an arm around his waist because his legs were too short. After a few feet of climbing, he nearly fell because his fingers were stiff and raw from clinging to the ropes. She had to hold him and reassure him and coax him down the next few rungs.

A metre from the bottom, Oscar's confidence suddenly returned and he scrambled down like a monkey, diving into Adrián's arms. He crouched to squeeze his son tight with his good arm and then hauled him up, the boy's arms wrapping around his neck.

'Oye, that was brave, mijito. You scared Papá for a minute.'

'Going up was okay, but I didn't know how to get down,' he sniffed, burying his face in Adrián's neck.

'It happens,' he reassured his son gently. 'Let's just check that Jo is all right too.' Putting Oscar down as smoothly as he could with one arm, he reached up to where Jo was about to make the last jump down, wrapping his arm around her waist to help her.

He could feel the weakness in her, the slight tremor, and he didn't let go even when her feet hit the sand. His chin against her forehead, he held her as she got her breath back, grateful – so grateful – that she was okay, that he could hold her like this.

'Thank you,' he whispered. She tried to shake her head, but he pressed a smacking kiss there, which stopped her quite effectively. '*Thank you*,' he repeated. Could she tell he meant something different, something *more*? He wanted to blurt everything out, all his feelings about seeing her at the top of the net: how afraid he'd been, how touched, how it felt like too much, too soon, but there wasn't anything he could do to stop it. Instead he said, 'And now,' drawing back reluctantly because if he started talking, they'd never make it to the wedding, 'we have to find Mamá and Ben and the church. We might just make it if we hurry.'

Oscar dragged his feet, his brow furrowed, and Adrián was worried for a moment he was going to stubbornly refuse to attend his mother's wedding. But he took Adrián's hand and asked, 'Is Jo going to the wedding? Liss and Dec?'

'The abuelos too. Everyone will be at the wedding,' he assured his son.

Oscar nodded gravely. 'Okay then,' he said in English. 'But I'm only going if Crabface can come too.' Liss and Dec snickered.

'No one else will be wearing crabfaces,' Adrián said solemnly.

'I don't care. I like these shorts.'

He sighed, stepping up onto the boardwalk as quickly as Oscar could manage. 'If you have to, mijo.'

'Right,' Jo said, tapping her sandals on the edge of the boardwalk to clear the sand. 'Did you get a copy of the police report for the insurance?' When he said nothing, she groaned, her fingers rising to her temples and rubbing. 'You didn't?'

With a sinking feeling, he remembered the sheets of paper blowing away as he rushed onto the beach in a panic. 'Shit,' he muttered.

30

'Found it! I've got it!'

Liss came running over from the concrete retaining wall separating the beach from the marina, flapping the papers over her head. Adrián rushed to meet her, relief coursing through him. Compared to the kids missing the wedding, the insurance money wasn't significant, but it would have been one of the stupidest mistakes of his life.

'Oh my God, thank you, Liss,' he said as he took the papers, keeping them in his hand this time and not tucking them under his arm.

'Do I get a cut of the payout?'

He eyed her from under his brow, which was the only response she would get to that joke.

She shrugged and continued, 'I don't need a thank you hug, though. You can save them for Mum.'

He glanced at his watch and headed for the boardwalk, Liss falling into step beside him.

'Whatever you did wrong last night—'

'Why do you assume it was me who did something wrong?' he snapped.

It was Liss's turn to give him a dubious look. 'I know adults always say both parties were at fault.'

Her implication made him queasy. 'Your mum wasn't at fault,' he defended immediately. 'It's just complicated, although I'm sure there was more I could have done to make things better.' Like swallowing his pride and telling her how deep his feelings ran.

'I was going to say I'm pretty sure Mum will forgive you. She just spoiled Oscar rotten.'

A grin made its way across his lips. 'Did she?'

'But this information doesn't mean you have my support,' she said gravely.

His smile faded. 'I don't?'

Pointing her finger at him, she said, 'You're on probation.'

'Really not a word I wanted to hear on my way back from a police station, niña.' He closed his mouth, wondering how the mild endearment had slipped out.

'What did you call me?'

He cleared his throat. 'It's just a habit in Spain. To use the name of a person you like can be insulting, create distance. I just called you "little girl", but I hope you don't take it as an insult. I know you're not a little girl.'

She nodded slowly, digesting his words. 'What do you call Mum?'

The hair on the back of his neck stood on end and heat prickled over his face. '"Corazón",' he answered, his voice not much louder than a whisper. 'Also, I didn't intend it. It just came out. It means "heart".' He pressed the backs of his fingers to his cheeks.

'What did you call Mónica?'

He met her gaze ruefully. '"Mi amor",' he answered her straight. 'But now it's back to Mónica.' She didn't reply for a long moment. 'I won't call you niña if you don't want,' he said softly when they were nearly back at the boardwalk.

'I suppose it depends on whether Mum lets you call her "corazón",' she said. 'But even though you're on probation... I like you too, Adrián. I like how you are with Mum.'

His throat clogged. 'Me too,' he mumbled. 'I like how I am with your mum too.'

* * *

Adrián was in an infuriatingly good mood. He fiddled with the radio in the car as Jo navigated them out of Benicarló, connecting it to Liss's phone, and they drove back to Peñíscola singing along to the most upbeat pop music in her daughter's library.

'You know this song, don't you?' Adrián prompted her when 'Watermelon Sugar' came on.

'I wouldn't want to interrupt you two and your karaoke,' she responded, checking her blind spot before merging onto a roundabout.

'Ohhh, come on,' he wheedled in that rumbly tone that she felt in her toes.

'We're rushing to the wedding!' she insisted.

'Singing and driving isn't the same as texting and driving,' he pointed out in mock earnestness.

'Why are you so happy? Your guitar has been stolen and we're going to be late to the wedding!'

'We'll make it!' he disagreed cheerfully, pausing to sing some of the words and smile at Liss.

'Oh, for Christ's sake,' she muttered. 'So many roundabouts!'

Liss leaned forward and sang the little bridge section of the song, which Jo definitely did know – very well, in fact, given how many times Liss had turned it on at home.

With a final twitch of her pursed lips, she opened her mouth and sang along. By the time they rattled into the underground car park at the hotel, she was tapping her fingers on the steering wheel and even Dec had joined in with the next song, mumbling the occasional chorus.

She switched the engine off with a laugh. 'Right,' she said, turning to the children. 'Chop chop. We've got ten minutes to get ready – if that.'

Adrián glanced at his watch. 'Eh, five minutes?'

'Shit,' Jo said under her breath. 'Can you call Mónica?'

'I don't think they have pockets in wedding dresses. Maybe you can call Ben.'

'Maybe they've called the whole thing off.'

'I know, I'll call Alberto,' Adrián said suddenly, scrolling on his phone screen as they all got out of the car. His conversation with his former father-in-law was surprisingly chatty. 'All done. They can't wait long, but if we hurry, we'll make it.'

'Was that really Alberto? I thought he hated... everyone.'

'Not me,' he said, giving her a wink. 'I'll tell you later.'

They rushed upstairs, Adrián pressing his hand to her back, making her jump and eye him. He was acting as though he'd forgotten their conversation the night before, which admittedly she wished she could. Except for one thing: he hadn't kissed her. That was another oversight she would rather like him to correct, if they had a moment alone, which they wouldn't have until... maybe ever.

Rushing into the corridor, they came to a sudden stop outside their hotel room doors, piling into Jo. She had to grab Oscar to stop him toppling over.

Adrián and Oscar's door was no longer dented and broken, but it wasn't there at all.

'Well, that's... an efficient repair job, I suppose,' Adrián muttered. 'I hope no one's stolen my suit.'

'I'm happy no one could steal Crabface,' Oscar said cheerfully.

'Come and get changed in our room,' Jo offered, her throat closing too late to stuff that stupid idea back down. He appeared in the doorway of her room a moment later with a suit bag and an awkward smile.

'I'm going to use their bathroom!' Liss announced, brushing past Adrián.

'I'll use the bathroom here,' Dec squeaked, dashing to claim that door.

Adrián's awkward smile tightened. 'Come on, mijo. Let's at least put a nice shirt on,' he said, ushering Oscar to the far side of the room. He fussed over Oscar, turning away pointedly.

Jo grimaced to remember she was still in her salty dress and hadn't showered that day. Grabbing a handful of wet wipes with silent thanks to that family from the motorway, she mopped what she could and retrieved her dress from its hook with a deep breath.

Crunch time for Joanna Watters. She bit her lip, trying not to imagine Ben's family's reaction to her wearing this dress. Instead, she was looking forward to Adrián swallowing his tongue when he saw her. The floral fabric reminded her of the day before, when everything had seemed possible.

She watched him help Oscar with his little tie and warm softness crept through her body. It wasn't a question of all the problems she'd have to overcome to be with Adrián, it was whether she could imagine *not* being with him and increasingly, the answer was: no.

He straightened, his hands dropping to his waistband, and Jo averted her gaze in panic. Yes, she'd seen it all before, but in a situation that had been entirely inappropriate for little eyes. She brushed her own spaghetti straps down her arms and shimmied out of the dress, a little devil in her mind wondering whether Adrián was peeking.

The dress she'd bought for the wedding was similarly easy to slip into. She didn't have the right bra for the neckline, but she'd got used to the feeling of not wearing one. With the blue crepe of the bust light on her skin and the rough embroidered skirt flaring in its fairy-trim glory, she felt cheeky and pretty and entirely *herself*.

On her way to the mirror near the door, she caught sight of Adrián gawking at her, the waistband of his suit still undone and his linen shirt halfway down one shoulder. There was no way she could stifle it. Jo burst into laughter.

He shook himself out of it enough to notice his current state of dress and turned an appealing shade of Spanish tomato red. But Jo was distracted now too, glancing from her own reflection in the mirror to the view of Adrián shrugging all the way out of his shirt – or at least attempting to.

Satisfied that she still believed she could pull off the low-backed hippie dress, she approached Adrián hesitantly. 'Do you need some help?'

His gaze dropped to where her hand gripped the smooth, patchwork-and-lace skirt. 'That dress is... f-fantastic on you,' he stuttered. When he zeroed in on her shoulder, she knew he was imagining her tattoo and possibly remembering his mouth there – that's certainly what she was thinking about.

'Here,' she said, lifting her hands to help him out of the linen shirt. She tugged his dress shirt up over his shoulders, coming around to his front to work on his buttons.

'I can... do that part myself,' he murmured.

'Shh, I'm having fun,' she replied, the backs of her fingers brushing his sternum and enjoying his gasp of breath.

'Oh, cut it out, Mum!'

She snatched her hands back at Dec's grumbling, but she couldn't quite dim her smile. Adrián nabbed a silver tie from his suit bag and strung it around his neck as he shuffled his feet into his black leather shoes. He couldn't quite reach to tighten it, so she finished the job for him, smoothing the material down his chest.

After taking a minute to brush and fluff her hair and slop on a touch of tinted moisturiser, mascara and a swipe of lipstick, she stuffed her feet into the low, strappy heels she'd brought with her and looked around for the others.

Dec wore his striped, collared shirt and a pair of jeans (she hadn't been able to talk him into anything more formal), his hair brushed out of his face. Liss emerged from the other bathroom with a harried expression, her winged eyeliner and mascara making her big blue eyes pop. Her new frock was a patterned turquoise silk maxi-dress with ties at the shoulders.

Adrián stepped out of the room, his fitted jacket in place with the sling strapped over it and his hair not quite neat. His beard was a touch scruffy, but Jo grinned to see him polished up, shoulders back, his head tilted with that earnest intensity that was all his own.

And in front of Adrián stood the little boy that was so much a part of him, in his own black jacket and tie and... his new swimming shorts with a crab on the bum.

God, I love this family, rose the sudden, intense thought.

'That was twenty minutes!' Liss said, breathing hard.

'Okay, we'll have to run!' Jo said with a grimace as they headed for the stairs.

They made a strange group, jogging in their finery along the esplanade, Jo taking up Oscar's other hand when the boy wanted to stop to argue about going to the playground. Jo felt as though she should wave at the staring beachgoers and tourists in the cafés.

They headed for the pale crenellated fortifications with the profusion of irregular white apartment blocks rising inside. Jo started to puff and lose steam as they stormed the ramp up to the first level of the citadel.

The walls were built directly onto the blanched stone and the cars parked at angles looked entirely out of place at the foot of the fairytale castle with its little round towers. Jo's legs ached and she had to slow to a walk when they reached a brick staircase flanked with palm trees that brought them to a road lined with restaurants overlooking the vast bay.

They climbed and climbed, past white terraces with wrought-iron balconies and decorative tile detailing. Adrián set the pace, leading them up a cobbled lane where the bell tower of the church popped into view.

'Thank God,' Jo wheezed, completely charmed by the narrow streets and crumbling whitewash, but desperate to arrive at the church and end the mad dash. Up one more ramp and they came out into a square, where the castle rose out of the rocks and a humble stone church stood to the side.

Adrián let go of Oscar to grab Jo's hand, hauling her up the steps to the portal of the church.

'Gosh, it's a... pretty nice place to get married, actually,' she said, panting, and Adrián wrapped his fingers more tightly around hers.

He heaved one of the church doors open and they spilled into the back, which felt suddenly dim after the bright sunshine reflected off white stone outside.

Just as they entered, Jo heard the priest repeating himself in English, saying, 'If anyone knows of any reason why this couple should not be joined in holy matrimony, speak now or forever hold your—'

Adrián's shoes made a loud clack on the flagstones and the priest gaped at their ragged arrival, the two exes and the children, a little windswept and a lot late. The ripple of heads swivelling in the pews eventually reached the front until every guest was blinking at them in varying degrees of disapproval.

'Eh, welcome?' the priest said, recovering.

'Forever hold your welcome?' Liss repeated with a doubtful expression. All eyes were still turned expectantly in their direction.

'Ehm, no objections!' Adrián said waving his hand for emphasis as he repeated himself in Spanish. 'Many congratulations to the bride and groom and sorry we're late. I had an appointment with the police.'

Jo whacked him lightly on the arm as a ripple of unease worked its way through the gathered family and friends.

'I mean—'

'We're here now,' Jo said, ushering Adrián forward with a false smile for the guests.

Ben beckoned for the children to come to the front, where one of the tías took charge of Oscar, taking him into the sacristy to prepare the cushion for the rings, his little crab-butt glaringly obvious to the entire congregation.

Jo was left clutching Adrián and glancing around for a spare pew. Someone finally moved over, allowing them to squeeze in. 'I'm so sorry we were late!' Jo reiterated as silence still shrouded the church. 'Go ahead and... marry them – with our blessing!'

She plonked into the pew next to Adrián, wishing she could disappear into the floor. The next best thing was letting her forehead drop to his shoulder and shaking with laughter when the guests turned their attention back to the bride and groom so the service could continue.

How many scrapes had she got herself into with Adrián? She couldn't count them all. But as he nudged her hand with his, Jo suspected that even if she could, she wouldn't change a thing about the past ten days.

But the next ten days? And the ten after that? She had to decide if she was brave enough to try it all again with Adrián – she had to decide before he walked out of her life tomorrow.

Adrián's stomach was so empty it wasn't even rumbling, it was creaking and sighing in despair. As soon as the adrenaline of the morning wore off, he realised he hadn't had time to eat breakfast – or lunch.

He fidgeted through the bilingual marriage liturgy, drawing scowls from María Dolores next to them. She was living up to her name that morning, making him miserable.

Of course Mónica had chosen the wedding ceremony with holy communion and he swallowed a groan as the priest ritually placed the wafers on Mónica and Ben's tongues. The lucky bastards were allowed to drink wine already, whereas Adrián would have to wait for the reception later.

A gurgling sound emerged from his middle during the silence after communion and he dropped his head in mortification. A choked snort to his right made him glance at Jo – to find her struggling to stifle a smile.

'Is this funny?' he asked her between clenched teeth, ignoring María Dolores's sharp, wandering elbow.

'I am sorry really,' she whispered. 'I know how you are about food. This has got to be the worst day of your life.'

'Coming close,' he choked, grasping his stomach as something seemed to spike him from inside. Was getting sick from hunger a thing? 'Please let it be over soon.'

'Where are the rings?' the priest intoned grandly.

Adrián straightened, peering over the heads of the congregation to catch a glimpse of Oscar's – and Crabface's – big moment. But his son stood frozen to the left of the wedding party, his eyes enormous. The poor kid. He'd been through a lot that day.

Liss hopped up from the first pew and approached him, ducking to peer into his face. They exchanged a few whispered words and then Liss took the cushion and they headed for the sacristy.

Adrián stood suddenly, knocking Jo's knees as he swept out of the pew and hurried down the side aisle and to the heavy wooden door that Liss and Oscar had disappeared through.

He met Mónica's anxious gaze with a quick nod and went to see what had gone wrong. Liss looked up in panic when he came through the door.

'He's hidden the rings!'

'What? Why?'

Oscar burst into tears.

Pinching the bridge of his nose, Adrián dropped to his haunches and tugged Oscar to him in a loose hug. 'It's all right, cariño. It'll be all right, but we need to take the rings to Mamá.'

'I'm s-s-sorry,' Oscar hiccoughed.

'It's okay,' Adrián crooned, tucking Oscar's head into his shoulder. 'I know you have a lot of feelings right now.' He caught Liss's eye and jerked his head in the direction of the door. 'Tell them to sing a song and I'll find the rings as soon as I can.'

Brushing Oscar's hair back from his face, he stroked his thumb down his son's cheek and gave him a weak smile.

'You missed your chance to object to the wedding, mijo,' he joked. 'Are you that upset that Mamá and Ben are getting married?'

'What?' Oscar asked, scrunching up his nose. 'I don't mind Ben. He lets me watch TV all the time.'

'Ah... great,' Adrián said with a grimace. 'What's the matter with the rings then?'

'I thought it was a treasure hunt,' he said, his eyes widening. 'I saw the gold things in here and I thought everyone was supposed to go looking for the rings.'

Adrián sank his head and laughed – loudly, because the organ was playing outside, drowning out the mumbled hymn. 'That makes perfect sense. I love it. If I ever have a wedding—' Those words produced a sudden strangling sensation in his throat as he immediately pictured Jo waiting for him at the altar. It would be on the beach somewhere, with casually dressed guests sipping cocktails and Carles playing the guitar.

Wow, that was getting a bit ahead of himself.

Clearing his throat, he said, 'If I have a wedding, we'll have a treasure hunt. It sounds like the best idea. But for now, can you tell me where you hid them?'

Oscar pointed out a row of gold cups tucked on a shelf at the back of the room and then ducked his head in renewed shame.

'It's okay, mijo. Really. Here,' Adrián said, straightening and opening the door just wide enough for his son to squeeze through. 'Go back and sit with Liss. I'll put the rings onto the cushion and bring it out to you.'

Oscar scampered off towards the front pew and Adrián let the door swing heavily shut – with a sharp clang he hadn't expected. Turning with a frown, he saw the ancient brass doorhandle lying innocently on the floor.

The statue of Mary up on the wall did not approve of his language. All he wanted was this wedding over so he could—

Say goodbye to Jo for good because she didn't want to date when they got back to London? God, maybe he should be wishing the infernal wedding never came to an end. But if he was stuck in this little room, he'd miss out on his last few hours with her.

Of course he wouldn't be stuck, he reasoned with himself. There was a perfectly functional handle on the other side. He'd just have to knock.

With a grimace, he rushed to the back of the room for the rings, feeling like Indiana Jones as he searched in the various golden chalices for Oscar's hiding place. Of course they were in the one tucked into the corner that was less ostentatious than the others, which showed Oscar's keen sense of a good hiding place – or perhaps Ben had let him watch *Indiana Jones*, he thought with a frown.

He was contemplating with chagrin the necessity of disturbing the wedding once more by hollering to be let out, when the door swung open with a blessed screech and Jo stood there, a puzzled frown on her face as she studied the other side of the door handle which she now held up in front of her.

With a shrug, she stepped over the threshold to join him in the room. 'What's taking so—'

He lunged past her, fumbling for the door and finding no purchase on the wood panelling before it banged heavily shut. Overbalancing, he went tumbling into the door with a thump. He finally steadied himself with his good arm and took a few panting breaths, dropping his forehead to the wood.

'Fuck,' he muttered.

'Aren't you worried about swearing in front of Mary?' Jo asked with an amused smile.

'She's used to it,' he snapped. 'Why did you let the door shut?'

He gestured sharply to the other door handle, lying on the floor. 'Now we can't get out from inside and they can't get us out from outside!'

'Shit!' she said, without even a guilty glance at Mary.

'I have the rings!'

'Oh, God,' she muttered, rushing for the door and pushing ineffectually at it, studying the sides and finally giving it a sharp rap with her fist. 'We're stuck in here!' she called out.

'Someone help!' he joined in, repeating himself in Spanish and banging on the door with her.

When the organ music finally died down, they heard scratching at the door and then Alberto called out in Spanish, 'We can't open the door. If you have a credit card, you could try to push the latch. It won't work from our side.'

Adrián rummaged in his pockets for his wallet, frowning when his hands came back empty. 'My wallet is in my other shorts,' he groaned.

'I left my handbag in the pew!'

He flashed her an alarmed look. 'Why did you do that?'

'I didn't think María Dolores would steal it!' she snapped.

'Dios, we're going to be in here for hours, aren't we? I'm going to have to eat all the communion wafers.'

'And I'll drink all the wine,' Jo mumbled. She turned to him suddenly, grasping his sleeve. 'You don't think not having the rings could stop the wedding, do you?'

His heart leaped into his throat. 'I hope not! Maybe we can slip them under the door.' He dropped to his knees, placing the rings on the floor and peering at the tiny gap between the door and the tiles.

'Wow, this thing is chunky,' Jo said, lifting Ben's ring and weighing it in her hand. 'Must be solid platinum.' She snorted. 'He lost his wedding ring during our second year of marriage because he kept taking it off, saying it wasn't comfortable.'

'I never understand that!' Adrián grumbled. 'Why do wedding rings seem more comfortable to women? You get used to it!' He met her gaze with determination. 'We *have* to get these out so the wedding can go on.'

Glancing around the dim sacristy, Adrián was disappointed to find there wasn't even a window – not that anyone would have been able to reach it from the other side and they certainly couldn't have climbed out.

'Where's that light coming from?' Jo asked, looking at the top of the small spiral staircase at the back of the room. Climbing the steps two at a time, she reached the top and called down to him, 'There's a little balcony up here! Quick, bring the rings. I'm right above the altar. We can lower them down somehow.'

'"What light through yonder window breaks?"' he quoted through his teeth, the line from Romeo's soliloquy making him think of his disastrous conversation with Mónica and her aunts that morning.

'What?' she asked, peering down from the top of the steps. 'Was that Shakespeare?'

He hauled himself up the stairs after her. 'I played for a run of performances of *Romeo and Juliet* five years ago,' he explained. 'The guitar arrangement of the theme from the Zeffirelli film is nice. Maybe I'll play it tonight.'

She gave him a questioning look – possibly questioning his sanity.

'This is a Juliet balcony,' he explained with a grin, peering over the railing. 'Wherefore art thou, Alberto?' Leaning further out, he waved his good arm and called, '¡Aquí arriba!'

More swivelling eyes landed on them. Mónica looked one breath away from a complete swoon. Ben had his head in his hand

and at least four aunts were scowling deeply as though they'd overheard all the bad language in the sacristy a moment ago.

'I have the rings!' he announced, passing them into his good hand and holding them up in a triumphant fist.

'Don't drop them!' Jo cried in alarm, grasping his hand and tugging it back down.

The priest appeared beneath them, craning his neck. 'I can catch them?' he called up.

Jo peered down at the potted plants, the vases of flowers, the ornate marble altarpiece and the chairs lining the sanctuary. 'We can't let them get lost.'

Adrián met her gaze, wondering if her reasons for needing this wedding to happen were the same as his: because it was time to move on. God, he hoped so. 'We can knot them in my tie and lower them down,' he suggested.

A smile lit up her face. 'Great idea.' Then her hands went to work on his neck, the backs of her fingers brushing his throat and he was both entirely overwhelmed by everything he felt and blissfully content at the casual touch.

She glanced up to find his eyes on her, goodness knows what in his expression. He was a mess. He wanted the whole crazy chaos with her. He just had to find a way to tell her that would make her believe it could work.

32

Jo wondered how on earth she'd ended up standing at a balcony above the altar, removing Adrián's tie in front of all the wedding guests. To make matters worse, he was staring at her with that vigorous intensity that made her hair stand on end and her knees wobble.

After she'd tried to give up on them last night – on *this*, the intimacy that had wrapped itself around them over the past ten days – she was now relieved to see that fire in his eyes burning again. She probably should have stamped it out, but she didn't have the heart for that.

Instead, she focused on the bob of his Adam's apple as she undid his tie, the line of his beard, where he occasionally shaved at the edge. She barely remembered a time when these little details of him weren't familiar to her.

Was she just as familiar to him?

Slipping his tie from his collar with a twitch of a smile, she took one ring from his hand and knotted it firmly into the end, repeating the process for the heavy platinum ring. The symbolism in those rings made her giddy.

'Here!' She held the tie through the spindles and the priest grasped it to a collective sigh from all the guests.

Adrián sighed too. They stood at the balcony together, their shoulders touching, as the priest blessed the rings and Mónica and Ben faced each other for the vows.

Ben stuttered through his, clearing his throat several times and staring at Mónica. She repeated the same words, in both English and Spanish, shooting out a hand to clutch his sleeve as her voice quavered. They weren't young lovers awaiting a future of wedded bliss. They were two people with a lot of life experience who knew there were no guarantees, but were going through with this madness anyway.

Then the priest raised his arms to declare them husband and wife and the church erupted in cheers – possibly of relief – before he'd even finished his sentence in Spanish, let alone in English. Liss was clapping and laughing. Dec sat in the opposite pew with Rita and Ford, glancing between his parents with a pained smile, as though the experience had been one of the most embarrassing moments of his life. Oscar had found a cosy fold in Mónica's skirt and settled in.

The kids were okay. The exes were married. And Jo was stuck in the sacristy with the acerbic, passionate, tender grump she suspected she'd fallen in love with.

Adrián's chin dropped to his chest and he sagged against the railing as though he'd used up the last of his strength to ensure the wedding took place. Or perhaps he was just expiring from hunger, but that sagging sensation was what Jo felt. She sank to the floor, leaning on the wall, and allowed the relief to flow through her.

The priest called up to them in Spanish and Adrián acknowledged his words with a nod and a clipped sentence in response. He collapsed next to her, his head falling back against the wall.

'He's going to get the church caretaker to open the door for us. Shouldn't be long.'

He rolled his head to the side, catching her gaze. She pressed her shoulder to his and turned her head until her temple was at his chin.

'They did it,' she said. 'They got married.'

'How did it feel for you?' he prompted gently.

A laugh rose up in her chest. 'Like a door closing – a door to a stressful place that I finally found my way out of.'

'The exit of a labyrinth?' he asked, smiling against her forehead.

She nodded, enjoying the brush of his beard over her skin. 'What about you?'

'I feel strangely like the father of the bride,' he said wryly. 'She's not my responsibility any more. I know I shouldn't have felt any responsibility for her after the divorce, but now... it's all gone.'

'You don't even have to play guitar for her,' Jo realised suddenly, raising her head to peer at him.

'Actually, I do have to play – if we get out of here before I die of starvation. I'll borrow another guitar. But I've already worked through that. Alberto apologised for his motives in asking me and now I can—' He paused to consider his words. 'I'll play for me – I mean obviously *for* the guests, but also for me, my pride.' As he said 'pride', he gave a self-deprecating smile, but also straightened unconsciously.

Jo lifted a hand, hesitating a second before opening it on his chest. He stared at that hand, rising and falling with his breaths, and the movement became less regular. 'I like your pride,' she said softly. 'Especially when it's injured.'

'Injuries seem to follow us when we're together,' he murmured. 'We've seen each other at our worst.'

He spoke casually, but the words echoed in Jo's thoughts. They'd sniped and bickered, taken out their own problems on each other, occasionally held back the truth and not held back on the raw emotions. They'd done everything *wrong* for the start of a new relationship. And yet...

'I have been at my worst these past ten days,' she admitted, 'but somehow also my best.' She took a deep breath and spoke the words that should have been impossible for her to say, but had become too difficult to ignore. 'I can... go forward from here. I've realised that now. I don't need to keep holding onto mistakes. But —' She paused to gather strength from the pressure of his shoulder against hers. 'I don't know where to go, or how. I don't want to say goodbye to you, to *us*. But I don't know how things will look when we get back and that scares me. I don't know what we do next. I can't face starting all over again in London, fitting in a dinner here and a coffee there, wondering what we'll talk about, whether there will be anything between us when we're not sharing these experiences any more. We haven't known each other long and I don't know if I'm ready for... us... but nothing else makes sense.'

His brow furrowed and he looked almost comically earnest. 'I'm sure we'll think of something. We've got plenty of time.'

She snorted. 'That's your solution?'

'Did you want a solution? Because I had some ideas,' he admitted. 'I hoped my flight would be cancelled and we'd have to come in the car with you three to Barcelona. Then I thought we'd just keep going. Explore the world.'

'I suppose that is one solution,' she said drily.

'Oh, I have more. There's the one where I convince Liss and Dec that they want to learn to play guitar and I turn up at your house as their teacher.'

'Haha, my kids would probably be on board with that until they learn they have to practise and I'm the one who has to make them do it.'

'Well, I expanded on it too, imagining I was such an amazing teacher that you decided you wanted lessons as well. There was a lot of sexual tension in that scenario. I also thought about writing that poem about your breasts, but it didn't seem fair to the rest of you, so it became a whole pamphlet of poems.'

'A pamphlet?' she repeated in disbelief. 'Are you even trying to be serious?' she asked, genuinely curious.

His response was to press a kiss to the top of her head. 'If I was serious, you'd run so fast we'd end up on different pages of our book.'

'Adrián, we're stuck in the sacristy. I'm not running anywhere.'

He grinned down at her. 'This is a good point.' Moving away from her side suddenly, he sat cross-legged in front of her and grasped one of her hands. 'I don't want to mess up what might be my only chance. I already made you cry and I don't want to put you through that again.'

She shook her head, partly to refute what he'd said and partly because her eyes were stinging again. 'It was good, the crying. Maybe I'd forgotten how to feel something and you made me feel...'

'Incredibly frustrated with me,' he completed for her with a solemn nod.

'That too,' she quipped, but her dry tone didn't quite come out right because her voice was wobbly.

'Jo,' he said, his voice soft and rumbly, 'no matter how things look in London, I want to be looking at them with you.' Her eyes drifted closed as he spoke, his words reaching her in the place where she felt the same. 'I want to stay in your life any way you'll let me. You need a yoga buddy?' He pointed to himself. 'Someone to go join the local choir with? Again, me.'

He spoke clearly and earnestly and she marvelled at the way he could be serious and make her feelings bearable with levity at the same time. She had no doubt he would really come to yoga if she asked him. But that wasn't necessarily his point. A future for them felt fraught and treacherous, but he was trying to tell her it could simply be yoga mats and vigorous gospel music, shared jokes and—

She had a sudden idea. 'You know I never heard you actually play that special guitar,' she said thoughtfully.

It took him a moment to process her change of direction. 'It had a unique sound,' he told her. 'But not the best sound. I prefer my concert guitar, actually.'

Nodding eagerly, she hopped up onto her knees and looked into his face. 'That's it, Adrián. That's what we do next. I want you to play guitar – for me. In London, when we get back home.'

He stared at her for a moment, turning his head a little as though he thought he'd misheard. 'Play for you?' he repeated, a slow smile stretching over his face. 'It's a dream of mine,' he purred. 'I can do that. And after I've played for you, we can all watch *Bluey* together.'

'That's a good plan,' she agreed, the words muffled by her thick throat. She could do that.

'Then one time, when we've watched lots of *Bluey*, we might be able to move on to *Ted Lasso* and cuddling,' Adrián said slowly. 'Then you'll put on a Korean historical drama and I'll get invested, but I'll wait until we can watch all the episodes together. One day, I'll watch the Tour de France all weekend and you'll get angry at me for it and then I'll kiss you and miss a final sprint and it will all be okay.'

She peered at him, trying to process what he was saying when the word 'kiss' was the one in flashing neon in her mind. 'What's a Korean historical drama?'

'Oh, have you got a treat ahead of you. What's something you watch then?'

She considered for a moment. 'Nineties romcoms?'

'Replace "Korean historical drama" with "nineties romcom" then.'

She blinked, certain there was supposed to be meaning in all of this. 'You'd get invested in a nineties romcom – for me?'

'Yes,' he said firmly, 'if I'm watching it with you. Or if I really hate it, you can watch it with headphones in and I'll fall asleep on your shoulder. I just thought we'd start with *Ted Lasso* because everyone likes that, then we gradually work up to watching stuff the other person hates.'

'There is a lot of detail in your plan,' she commented, slowly realising what he meant. He'd already seen her drunk and angry and emotional and he'd never been anything but accepting – and maybe a little amused.

'I have thought *a lot* about this,' he mumbled. 'I haven't stopped thinking about you since the Grotto of Apparitions, when I started to get to know you.'

That had been the magic of the past ten days: they'd got to know one another. He'd listened to her uncharitable thoughts about Ben. He'd put her gently to bed when she was drunk. He'd cleaned up her vomit.

That he was here with her now, coaxing her into plans for a future where she wasn't aggrieved and regretful and lonely, was nothing short of a miracle.

She might not be ready, but she couldn't refuse such a gift, especially when he'd packaged it up so carefully in tiny moments so she wouldn't be afraid.

As soon as she allowed that future of tiny moments to come to life in her imagination, a host of other images flooded her mind: picking him up from work at an aged care facility she hadn't seen yet; fighting over the last chocolate in the box; singing Oscar a lullaby in harmony or shouting for Adrián to go rehearse somewhere else because she was on a call for work.

She could picture it all. A way forward for her – for her family. It didn't have to be so complicated.

'When's the Tour de France?' she asked suddenly.

'It starts in two weeks. Why?' he asked warily.

'I was just wondering if I have to wait until then for that kiss,' she murmured.

'Ah, I did have another idea about that,' he said, peering at her from under his lashes. 'I thought Oscar could get confused about the rings and hide them and then I'd accidentally get locked in the room with all the cups.'

'Mmmhmm,' Jo prompted coming closer.

'When you came to save me, you'd accidentally get locked in too and just before we died of starvation, I'd tell you I love you and beg for a kiss.'

It didn't feel as strange as she would have expected to hear those words, possibly because he'd thrown them in with his signature dry humour, giving her space to adjust to the idea. *I love you.* When she was younger, those words had felt a little desperate, like holding on, because she hadn't understood.

This time, the words sounded like letting go. There was the same thrill of excitement, but a tempered foundation, like a soft landing on a gymnastics mat.

'I think I like that idea,' she said, her chest light.

'You do?' he said, his voice high. 'The last bit... I was worried it was too soon.'

'It's definitely too soon to die of starvation,' she said, biting her lip against a smile. 'And the kiss is about eight hours overdue.'

'And the other part?' he asked lightly, his chest rising and falling in a stuttering rhythm. His brow was knit and he stared at her as though her answer was more important than food.

'Will you have to wait until you're almost dead from starvation before you say it?'

He gulped. 'I wanted to say it last night, but I thought you wouldn't believe me.'

Regret shivered through her, but she released it again. She'd been scared last night, but she wasn't scared any more. 'Maybe I wouldn't have believed you last night. But now we're in a church. Mary's down there listening to every word we say.'

There was a hint of a smile on his lips. 'You shouldn't lie in a church. Wait a minute.' He set to work on the Velcro holding his sling in place, tearing it off, and then both of his hands rose to her face, smoothing her cheeks and bathing her in that tenderness she admired in him. 'You don't have to say it back. I'll keep playing you the guitar. We'll watch TV together, see what happens.'

'Just say it, Adrián.'

Settling his forehead on hers, his thumb brushing the three studs in her ear, he grinned and whispered, 'I love you, Jo.'

She'd thought she was ready, but apparently not. 'Holy shit,' she whispered and burst into tears.

33

'¡Ay! sometimes I worry about the effect I have on you,' Adrián muttered, shifting and drawing her head to his shoulder. 'I know this is hard, the change, trusting me. But all you have to do is let me treasure you.'

'Shut up,' she whined, tears falling in earnest now. 'You don't have to convince me of anything. I already shocked myself this morning by thinking how much I love you.'

His throat closed, his brain struggling to recalibrate. He'd hoped he might convince her to take baby steps together. He'd been prepared to be sensible, even though his feelings weren't. 'Oh, thank God,' he muttered, glancing guiltily at the altar.

She stifled a smile that made him want to kiss her more enthusiastically than was appropriate in a church. 'Were you about to cross yourself then?'

'Blame Grandma,' he said. 'Will you wait until I play guitar for you before you say it?' he prompted, dipping his head to look her in the eye.

Wide-eyed and a little wary, she took a deep breath and then whispered, 'I love you,' with an enormous gulp.

'There,' he said gently, his thumb at her chin to keep her head up when she would have dropped it. 'We did it.'

'Are we crazy?'

'Definitely,' he said with a smile.

'Are you finally going to kiss me?'

'I *am* almost dying of starvation,' he quipped.

'You're lucky I love you,' she said drily, giving him that withering look he adored.

'I'm inclined to agree,' he said, ducking his head until his face was an inch from hers. He was giddy with the closeness of her, with the bursting happiness of returned feelings against all odds. 'But you could kiss me, you know. Any time you like.'

'Fine!' she said in exasperation, clutching the lapels of his coat. Without the slightest hesitation, she brought her lips to his and everything fell back into place. She lingered and he softened his mouth, drawing her in for more. It was a simple gesture, and yet the pressure of her lips communicated such ease – such trust and delight.

'It was so hard not to kiss you when we arrived in this penis town,' he broke off to murmur, coming straight back for more.

'Don't stop now,' she whispered in reply, her arms winding around his neck.

'Never,' he said, smiling against her lips before he kissed her again, stifling a groan when she opened her mouth on his. 'I missed this.'

'Me too,' she said softly, rising onto her knees to kiss him more thoroughly, her arms tight around him.

He forgot about Mary on the wall downstairs, forgot about the altar a few feet below them, that they were in the sanctuary of a church.

Until someone cleared their throat just below the balcony. They jerked apart, Adrián trying to ignore the fact that he'd messed up her hair and probably had her pale lipstick all over his own mouth.

'Uh, I brought Adrián a bocadillo.'

Adrián pressed his face to the railings. 'Dec! Good man!' It didn't matter that the boy had pronounced 'bocadillo' atrociously. He would correct him later, after he'd wolfed down the Spanish baguette stuffed with cured ham. 'Give it here!' He thrust his arm through the spindles and clicked his fingers.

Dec climbed on a chair and was just tall enough for Adrián to grasp the end of the bread stick. Frantically unwrapping it, he shoved the end in his mouth and ripped off an enormous hunk.

'Thank God,' he moaned around the mouthful. 'I love your kids, Jo.' He hadn't intended to be quite so effusive so soon, but Jo just laughed at him. At least he'd learned that the way to her heart was through her sense of humour. Perhaps Dec had known that the way to Adrián's heart was the usual one – through his stomach. It was probably his own wishful thinking that the boy liked Adrián as much as Adrián liked him. He was content to hope.

'They're up on the castle ramparts taking photos,' Dec told them.

'Do you need to get back?' Jo called down. Her tone was concerned, but Adrián told himself it was because she wanted to get back to the kissing. He could get used to being locked in the church with her.

'Dad told me to come and get you two for a photo.'

'Oh, well, unfortunately we're locked in,' Adrián said and perhaps he overdid the false regret because Jo eyed him.

'The caretaker came ten minutes ago,' Dec said, rolling his eyes. 'It's unlocked down here.'

'Really? We didn't—' Jo choked on her words.

'I suppose we should emerge into the sunshine, then. With

food, I could happily have been stuck here a few days,' he said with a pout.

'Me too,' she said with a wink, making him want to kiss her again.

But instead, he stood with a sigh, tugging her up with him. The door in the room below not only had both handles reattached, it was propped wide open with a doorstop.

Jo hesitated at the threshold Ben and Mónica had crossed an hour ago as newlyweds. He snatched her hand and held it tight, striding cheerfully outside as he tugged her along with him. After heartache and healing, a host of mishaps and the miracle of family, the world was blindingly beautiful to Adrián.

'There you are!' called Liss, appearing in the courtyard and thrusting Jo's abandoned handbag at her. 'Come on!' She rushed ahead of them, leading them up the steps to the castle walls where they joined the wedding party again – no hiding, no shame, only pride. He was proud of Mónica, of Oscar, enormously proud of Jo – and proud to be the one to stand next to her in family photos.

They joined in at the edge of one of the group shots, Adrián's arm tight around her, and then the photographer asked with a meaningful smile if they wanted a few photos together. He found Mónica smiling at him and gave her a nod in return, before drawing Jo with him to the highest ramparts, overlooking the bell-tower and the tiled dome of the church, in shades of orange.

'You didn't fool me on Wednesday,' the photographer said drily. 'Here, look.' After pressing a few buttons and scrolling, she held up the camera to show them the photo she'd taken in the middle of the labyrinth. In the picture, they were looking at each other, sharing half-smiles, and so at ease Adrián wondered why it had taken so long to work out this was love.

'We don't have anyone left to fool,' he said softly as he drew Jo against him to pose for the photo. 'Not even ourselves.'

Wrapping his arms around her waist, he pressed a kiss to her cheek. The photographer snapped away as they recorded the amused smiles and little kisses of their first day as... who cares what they were called, anyway?

Oscar rushed to them, as well as Liss and Dec, and they ended up with a series of candid photos of Jo's kids rolling their eyes and Oscar spilling his water down his papá's shirt.

'If there's one thing I've learned this trip,' Jo began earnestly, mopping Adrián's chest with a tissue more thoroughly than was probably necessary in those temperatures.

'Mmmm?'

'It's that we should always have spare clothes.' She chuckled at him. 'Don't look so disappointed. I also learned that I hate labyrinths and I like Spanish guitar and I *love*... paella.' His pout must have been a touch overdone because she laughed harder. 'And you. I love *you*.'

'Good,' he said gruffly. '*I* have learned that you shouldn't deprive people of breakfast or accept lifts from bikers unless you want to meet God.' He paused. 'And also that sometimes disasters can turn into the greatest blessings.'

* * *

Later that evening, after a four-course meal full of mussels and shrimp, as well as steak and salad, and flan for dessert, Adrián fiddled with the borrowed guitar on one side of the room as Alberto's friends set up a cajón. Jo sat back in her chair and watched the fuss, Liss beside her.

'Are you going to dance?' her daughter asked.

'Definitely,' Jo said. 'You?'

Liss made a face but didn't answer either way. 'I've never seen Dad dance. I suppose Mónica will make him do it.'

That brought a grin to Jo's lips. 'I'm looking forward to seeing that.'

With a couple of strident chords, Adrián seemed finally satisfied that the guitar was tuned and he shuffled to the edge of the chair, adjusting the stool someone had found to act as a footrest. Shaking his hair out of his face, his posture transformed him into a classical guitarist. Jo was pleased to notice he seemed to be in less pain now, a week after the accident.

He looked up to where Mónica sat on Ben's lap – a display of affection Ben had seemed uncomfortable with at first but was getting used to, if the proprietary hand on her hip was anything to go by. And Adrián began to play, a slow, touching song that Jo recognised from a film – an old film, she suspected.

His left hand quivering to produce vibrato on the strings, he plucked a warm, sentimental sound from the instrument, harmonies emerging and disappearing again, bass and treble melting into each other as the fingers of his left hand slid over the frets.

'He's really good,' Liss commented under her breath.

'He's a professional guitarist,' Jo explained. *And a care worker.* She loved both of those things about him, but she especially loved that proud tilt to his shoulders.

No one seemed to mind if it wasn't the old luthier guitar. From the sweet love song, he glanced at the man sitting on the cajón and they launched into a lively tune in the minor key, to clapping and cheering from every corner. Alberto was the first on the dance floor, raising his arms and shuffling his feet and punctuating his movements with claps and shouts of, '¡Olé!'

Rita and Ford sat in open-mouthed silence as Mónica dragged a red-faced Ben onto the dance floor and proceeded to completely overwhelm him with the passion of her steps. She coaxed him into stamping and clapping and the whole room cheered when he attempted a slow turn, keeping his eyes on Mónica.

Jo watched Adrián come alive, fiercely strumming and plucking the vivacious songs and drawing out the aching emotion of the slower ones. Alberto and his friends sang in crooning Spanish and Mónica's father even shared a grin with his former son-in-law and clapped him on the shoulder – his left shoulder, which made him cry out in pain, but Jo suspected Alberto hadn't done it on purpose.

After she'd enjoyed the show for a few songs, Jo headed for the dance floor, swaying with her own moves and occasionally copying the other guests, even though she knew she wouldn't get the steps right. Mónica applauded her with an enthusiasm that felt entirely genuine.

She knew Adrián was watching, but she didn't look at him at first – until she recognised the tinkle of the strings at the beginning of the next song.

Alberto whooped and gathered with his friends near the musicians as Adrián began to play 'Bésame mucho'. He gave her a wink when she glanced at him, but he turned towards Alberto as he played and they began to sing.

When Jo joined in with the singing, Alberto beckoned her over, grasped a schnapps glass from the table and thrust it into her hands. After the next chorus, she clinked her glass with his and they both sipped, Jo spluttering and clearing her throat while Alberto sang the verse.

Shuffling around the dance floor with her little glass of liquor, joining in with all the bésame muchos and feeling Adrián's warm eyes on her, she marvelled that this was the most fun she'd ever had at a wedding – including her own.

When he finished the song, she approached with a smile, coming in for a kiss, only to have him snatch her glass and down most of the contents with a cough.

'I could bring you your own if you like,' she asked in amusement.

'I'm good now.'

'Did you... play that for me?' she asked.

'Of course not!' he said curtly. 'Have you forgotten I'm not playing for you until we get home?'

She leaned back on her heels and eyed him, but he glanced up at her with a hint of a smile.

'Maybe you'll have to sing – for me. But tonight is about my pride, remember?'

'I haven't forgotten your pride.'

'Good, then give me a kiss and dance some more.'

She began a mock grumble, but he leaned up and gave her a quick, soft kiss that reminded her of the future they'd imagined together that afternoon. Only a few seconds later did Jo notice that the room had gone quiet and all eyes seemed to be on the two exes.

Jo straightened awkwardly, waiting for whatever censure was coming their way. But Aunt María Dolores just stood in her seat and called something out, clapping her hands for emphasis.

Adrián grinned. 'She wants me to play flamenco,' he explained, calling out to Mónica's aunt in the affirmative and strumming the guitar.

But before he could start up the next song, his phone rang. Retrieving it from the pocket of his jacket with a frown, Jo caught sight of a Spanish phone number before he connected the call. 'Sí,' he answered brusquely. A moment later, his eyebrows flew up and he met her curious gaze as he listened.

After confirming something quickly in Spanish, he hung up and released a full-throated laugh, leaning his head on her heavily. 'It's the guitar,' he said between chuckles. 'The police found it in a field not far from here. It was our fault. The lining of the case had been ripped open – to look for jewels that only existed in my warped sense of humour.'

'That's the last time I'm picking up one of your running jokes,' she said with a groan. 'But is the guitar all right?'

He nodded brightly. 'Not a scratch on it apparently – although I'll believe that when I see it.'

'What's that?' Alberto called out. 'The guitar has been found? Another reason to celebrate!'

'I'm glad it's not damaged,' Adrián said earnestly to his former father-in-law.

'Yo también – me too. Oscar will need a guitar one day soon, no? He can take lessons from the best: maestro Alberto Hernández Ortega!'

Adrián just rolled his eyes and stowed his phone, picking up the guitar again.

Jo leaned on his shoulder and dropped her mouth to his ear. '*I* think Oscar is already learning from the best.'

His lips twitched. 'Oh, so you found out Dec taught him how to play *Mario Kart*?'

'Whaaat?'

With another chuckle, he brought her head down to press a kiss to her mouth. 'Now shh. I have to play flamenco before María Dolores poisons my drink.'

The party grew lively after that and continued well into the night, with Adrián playing on and off, refusing to put the guitar away for good, even though Jo knew his shoulder was aching. When they finally started to wilt at two in the morning – well before the rest of the family was ready to retire – he handed the guitar back to José Pascal and they rounded up the children to head to their hotel rooms – after searching for Oscar for ten minutes because he'd fallen asleep under the linens of his grandparents' table.

Adrián hefted him up with some difficulty, holding his weight with his right arm as the boy dropped his head to his father's shoulder and went back to sleep. When they reached their floor, they were too tired to react to the continued absence of Adrián and Oscar's door with anything beyond a brief groan, and Jo tugged him into their triple room, where he hurriedly dumped Oscar onto one of the single beds.

Exhausted, they collapsed wherever they could, stuffed into the small room.

When Jo opened her heavy eyelids the following morning, it was to see Adrián across from her and she smiled. He was snuggled into Oscar and both of them were blissfully, sweetly asleep on the single bed next to hers. Dec was on a pile of blankets on the floor, out cold, and Liss had turned away and tucked herself into the blankets on the other side of the double.

Her family was chaotic, imperfect, overwhelming – and she loved them so much. Wherever they went next, they would go there together, and that was all that mattered.

EPILOGUE

The Christmas Fayre at the Dowlands Primary School was in full swing when Jo wandered through the gates with Oscar's hand firmly in hers. Dec looked eagerly around his old school, stifling a nostalgic smile.

'Do you think Miss Chukwuka is still here?' Liss asked. 'Or Mr Denham? He used to dress up as Stick Man for the Christmas Fayre.'

'I bet he would have played Santa if there hadn't been such a danger of the kids recognising him,' Jo said with a chuckle.

Outside the main school block, a brick Victorian building with 'Girls' and 'Boys' written over the identical entrances, three rows of kids were lined up on the steps, singing 'Born on Christmas Day' with enormous smiles and some gospel moves. A music teacher Jo didn't recognise stood in front of them, encouraging them with expansive arm movements and exaggerated facial expressions.

'Wow, the choir wasn't that good when we were at school,' Liss commented. Jo snorted a guilty laugh, but she just shook her head when Liss peered curiously at her. Perhaps that money had gone to a good cause after all.

Passing the choir, Jo gave a few self-conscious waves to familiar faces from her PTA years as she bought cups of mulled wine and punch and some misshapen homemade biscuits and then ushered Oscar ahead of her into the portakabin that had been converted into learning support space and a student library.

Inside was a Christmas wonderland of soft fairy lights and handmade decorations in crepe paper, tinsel and velvet – with a soundtrack of tinkling Spanish guitar. Oscar rushed to the corner where an armchair had been draped in red velvet with a stack of wrapped presents to one side.

'Papá!' he called, throwing his arms around the figure in the chair, who was dressed in red and white, with a synthetic beard and curly black hair emerging from under the wonky hat.

'Oscar,' he replied in a low, rumbly voice, 'I'm Father Christmas, remember?'

'I didn't know Father Christmas had an accent,' said a tall girl who was standing to one side, holding her present.

'You weren't so sceptical a moment ago when I said, "Ho ho ho," and gave you that colouring book,' he replied.

'It's a colouring book?' the girl repeated with a grimace and walked off, leaving Adrián grumbling under his breath.

'Can't you at least play something festive?' Jo asked as she approached with a wry smile.

'Do you have any idea how many times I've played "Jingle Bells" already today?' he asked, his voice gravelly. Instead of a festive favourite, he absently plucked an ancient Renaissance piece that had become part of the soundtrack of her life over the past six months.

Ever since he'd turned up on her doorstep with his performance guitar the Sunday after the wedding, sat her down on her own sofa and played her a very corny – but absolutely wonderful – acoustic version of 'Always' by Bon Jovi that had made her laugh and cry all at once, she'd heard him play nearly every day and she missed the tinkles of music in the house when he wasn't there.

He paused his playing and said, 'You could at least give Father Christmas a kiss.'

Jo obliged with a smile, pressing a light kiss to his lips.

'"I saw Mummy kissing Santa Claus..."',' Liss sang in a mumble, catching Adrián's eye to share the joke.

'How much longer do I have to do this? I've been trying to look at the clock on my phone, but then a kid appears and asks if that mobile is their Christmas present. Kids these days.'

'My, my, Santa *is* grumpy, today. Perhaps he's just been hanging out for his milk and biscuits,' she teased, holding the plate out to him.

'Mrs Claus knows her husband well,' he quipped, before choking on the implication of his words. He spluttered around a few shortbread crumbs. 'I mean... Ms Whitecap, Santa's girlfriend.'

'Don't you mean Santa's significant other? His better half?'

'His domestic partner,' he said pointedly, reminding Jo of the rather emotional day three weeks ago when Adrián and Oscar had officially moved out of his apartment and into her house.

'Wow, Santa is a very modern person!' exclaimed a voice from the door. Mrs Begum, Oscar's teacher – and Dec's a few years ago – strode into the room. 'Thank you so much for helping this year, Mr Rivera. We always have such trouble with volunteers. So few children have grandparents nearby in London.'

'Happy to help,' he said earnestly, with only the slightest hint of side-eye at Jo's scowl.

'It's good to see you too, Declan,' Mrs Begum continued. 'It's nice when siblings come along to support their—'

'Stepsiblings,' Liss finished for her with a smile, grasping Oscar's shoulders and giving him a quick hug.

'Indeed,' Mrs Begum said with an amused smile. 'How interesting the way these things turn out.' She glanced between Jo and Adrián and Jo wondered if she was a second away from saying, 'A match made in the PTA.' But instead, she turned to Adrián with a frown. 'But I think we need some more "Jingle Bells". We'll see you soon in the gym for the concert!'

As the teacher disappeared, Adrián took up his guitar with an affected groan and played a few bars in a mournful key. Another student appeared in the doorway, tugging an obviously reluctant younger sibling along and Adrián transformed in an instant.

Strumming a lively rhythm, he gave Jo a prompting look and she sighed, but played along, singing the words to the first verse of 'Jingle Bells'. Liss joined in and the children approached with bright eyes. Slowing at the finish, Adrián put the guitar to one side and hunched to greet the children.

'Ho ho ho! Welcome to my grotto! I've been so busy making presents for children like you. Want to come and tell me your wishes for Christmas Day?'

Jo gave him a quick wave and mouthed that they'd see him later at the concert. Grasping Oscar's hand, she headed for the door, looking back for one more glance at Father Christmas in action, his expression full of mystery and drama.

Just before the concert started, Adrián joined them in the gym, his hair askew and smelling slightly of mothballs. 'Thanks for delivering our angel to the nativity,' he murmured, pressing a kiss to Jo's cheek.

There had been countless moments like this over the past six months: small, tender gestures; silent communication and tired comfort. In contrast to the beginning of their relationship, everything seemed to be going right for them.

He grasped her hand and tangled their fingers as the lights on the stage came up and the principal appeared, a tight smile on her face. 'Uh, before we start, could the parents of Oscar Rivera Hernández please come backstage? There's... just been a small incident with his wings.'

ACKNOWLEDGEMENTS

This was one of those magical books that seemed to write itself which means actually that special thanks goes to my family for letting me bash it out as quickly and urgently as I felt it needed to be written. Little experiences from family life also definitely ended up in the story, including from my own seven-year-old and the pre-teen hints of the future from my eldest. They are a constant source of humour!

As always a giant merci and gracias to Tatiana for everything but especially for helping with the Spanish language and culture in this book (lucky for me you are so multi-lingual and generally wonderful).

Special thanks also to my Lucys, Lucy Morris and Lucy Keeling, for cheerleading and feedback and for being there through the ups and downs of writing and publishing.

I'm so grateful for the entire team at Boldwood Books, especially the guiding hand (or red tracked changes marks!) of my editor Sarah, as well as the copy editor and proofreader – champions as always – and the marketing and production teams who absolutely punch above their weight. I'm so lucky to be on the team!

Extra special mention this time of my husband Sam, without whom this book definitely would never have been written. Eighteen years has taught me an awful lot about marriage (and life and love) and I can't wait for the next eighteen spent on an adventure with my best travel buddy.

ABOUT THE AUTHOR

Leonie Mack is a bestselling romantic novelist. Having lived in London for many years her home is now in Germany with her husband and three children. Leonie loves train travel, medieval towns, hiking and happy endings!

Sign up to Leonie Mack's mailing list here for news, competitions and updates on future books.

Visit Leonie's website: https://leoniemack.com/

Follow Leonie on social media:

x.com/LeonieMAuthor
instagram.com/leoniejmack
facebook.com/LeonieJMack

ALSO BY LEONIE MACK

My Christmas Number One

Italy Ever After

A Match Made in Venice

We'll Always Have Venice

Twenty-One Nights in Paris

A Taste of Italian Sunshine

Snow Days With You

A Wedding in the Sun

WHERE ALL YOUR ROMANCE
DREAMS COME TRUE!

THE HOME OF BESTSELLING
ROMANCE AND WOMEN'S
FICTION

 WARNING:
MAY CONTAIN SPICE

SIGN UP TO OUR
NEWSLETTER

https://bit.ly/Lovenotesnews

Boldwood

Boldwood Books is an award-winning fiction publishing company seeking out the best stories from around the world.

Find out more at www.boldwoodbooks.com

Join our reader community for brilliant books, competitions and offers!

Follow us

@BoldwoodBooks

@TheBoldBookClub

Sign up to our weekly
deals newsletter

https://bit.ly/BoldwoodBNewsletter

Printed in Great Britain
by Amazon